MW01504253

"This is what Americans do"

"…Thoroughly engrossing, rich in detail, and highly inspirational."

"…A small-town donation jar…not only receives contributions, but gives back magic in return. …But who is really behind its magic?"

"Captures kindness in a divided world."

"Libraries will find that…*The Pot of Gold at the Rainbow Café* affords many riches to patrons who absorb its magic and vivid insights on how people perceive and tap into the needs of those around them."

"Dan Chabot's compelling story gives readers food for thought over the motivations for altruism, the impact of searching out secrets, and the real magic within a jar of wealth that embraces an entire town."

--Diane Donovan, Sr. Reviewer
Midwest Book Review

THE POT OF

GOLD

AT THE

RAINBOW CAFÉ

A novel by Dan Chabot

©2025 by Dan Chabot

THE POT OF GOLD

AT THE

RAINBOW CAFE

Copyright © 2025 by Dan Chabot
All rights reserved

ISBN: 9798312550955 print

No part of this book may be reproduced, stored in a retrieval system or transmitted by any means without the written permission of the author.

It is a work of fiction. References to real people, events, establishments, organizations or locales are intended only to provide a sense of authenticity, and are used fictitiously. All other names, characters, places, dialog, events and incidents either are the product of the author's imagination or are used fictitiously. Any resemblance to actual persons, living or dead, is entirely coincidental.

Published in the USA

Cover design by Lynn Andreozzi

Also by Dan Chabot, available at Amazon in print and e-versions:

Godspeed: A Love Story
The Last Homecoming
Emma's Army

Author's note: This book and all its contents have not received any input or influence of any kind from any form of Artificial Intelligence (AI) or similar system of content generation. Nor has the author engaged any AI system for research, assessment, or interpretation. This book is entirely the product of its author, the sole source of its content. In other words, I wrote it myself.

The Pot of Gold at the Rainbow Cafe

For Mary Ellen, as always

PROLOG

Amid all the dire headlines about wars and revolutions, violence and victims, depression and despair, divisions and arguments, natural calamities and international rivalries, remember:

Somewhere a teenager is giving up his subway seat to a lame old man with a cane.

A mom is comforting a lost little boy in a big-box store until his own mom can find him.

A neighbor is retrieving your newspaper so it doesn't get soaked in the rain.

A driver in a long line is letting another one merge.

Somebody is leaving the kids at the lemonade stand a $20 tip.

A stranger in a parking lot is scraping the ice from your windshield, too.

A neighbor is cutting an elderly widow's lawn and putting her trash cans away.

A passenger is giving up his airline seat so a couple can sit together.

An entire town is out looking for a toddler who strayed from his yard.

A homeowner is bringing water to sweating
    workers digging a new utility trench.
A cop is delivering a baby in the back seat of a
    squad car.
A man is paying the bill for the people behind him
    in the fast-food line
A confused, sightless walker is being redirected to
    his bus stop.
Someone is delivering a complimentary coffee to
    the office "coffee girl."
And yes, somewhere a Boy Scout is helping a little
    old lady cross the street.
"It's what Americans do"
Let's not dwell on the 24-hour cycle of bad news.
There's a lot more of the other kind going on around
    us every day.

Chapter 1

THE GRAVEDIGGER

"You look particularly glum this morning, even for a gravedigger," Therese said.

She skimmed a mug of coffee down the polished Rainbow Café counter so expertly that it stopped directly in front of Ezra Prufong without spilling a drop. "Surely things cannot be that bad."

She had concluded from his demeanor that this was probably not the time to greet him in her usual playful manner – "Good Mourn-ing."

"I've been laid off," Ezra said. "No, fired is more like it." He picked up a newspaper from the counter and turned to the want ads.

Ezra, who held doctorate degrees in history and anthropology and had taught at one of America's premier universities, was just one of Therese's eccentric Rainbow Café regulars, or maybe irregulars was a better term. He certainly was the best-educated.

He was wearing his usual shabby gravedigger garb, a far cry from the three-piece suits of his Ivy League classrooms and lecture halls. On getting a whiff of his manual-labor aroma, two other customers quietly moved a few stools farther away.

Ezra was 73, widowed and in failing health, retired from his university post for eight years. He had gladly abandoned academia, no longer willing to abide what he saw as bloated bureaucracy, unjustified tuition hikes, endless politics, the publish-or-perish atmosphere, and especially some of the new "me-generation" students -- pampered, entitled, indulged, clueless and ungrateful.

He had drifted for a couple of years, looking for something to keep him engaged, something meaningful after Edna died, a change of pace. He tried golf, then tennis, pickleball, charity work, even spent two days as a greeter at a big-box store, but nothing really appealed to him until he saw the want ad in the St. Sebastian church bulletin looking for a gravedigger at the parish cemetery.

That certainly qualified as a change of pace for someone who had written several textbooks, authored papers for professional publications, and was considered one of the world's foremost authorities on the lost Great Library at Alexandria and the Ptolemaic Dynasty of ancient Egypt.

The previous gravedigger-custodian had recently joined his former clientele at their permanent new underground address, so there was an opening. Ezra jumped into his new digs, so to speak, with both feet and adapted well to his new calling. Until now.

Therese refilled Ezra's mug, which he already had drained in exasperation. He was drawing circles around want ads that vaguely interested him. For most of them he was colossally overqualified or too old.

"You've been laid off? What happened?"

"Father Dunne said I had become too much of a distraction at the graveside services. I was just trying to help, to share in their sorrow, in my own small way."

Ezra wiped away a tear and blew his nose into a huge red-and-white checkered handkerchief.

Therese knew from other parishioners that some mourners, already beset with grief, became even more distressed to hear the sobs coming from somewhere behind them.

It was Ezra, a gentle, tender soul, caught up in the emotion of the moment and the grim surroundings, overcome with sorrow for families struggling to cope with their loss and the concept of eternal rest. That most of them were total strangers did not seem to concern him.

"I feel so bad for them," he said. "I've been there. This is such a difficult time for families. I just think it helps for them to know that others share their grief."

This was a problem for Father Dunne, because even though few families complained, were quite pleased, actually, to have a stranger share in their mourning, however loudly, his sobs sometimes were enough to disrupt the proceedings and distract from the carefully chosen words of the cleric.

Father Dunne's initial solution was to have Ezra stand a respectable distance apart, nine or ten tombstones away, during the service.

From there Ezra could both share in the grieving and oversee and admire his painstaking work. He carefully measured and excavated each new gravesite to conform with burial regulations, was fastidious in maintaining the cemetery's equipment, even down to the backhoe, a labor-saving concession he agreed to reluctantly, and was obsessed with keeping the cemetery and its graves a model gateway to the Hereafter.

Indeed, St. Sebastian Cemetery was known throughout the region as the gold standard in cemetery maintenance and upkeep. Clerics and cemetery custodians from other towns and even states were frequent visitors, clucking in admiration at the manicured lawns, the polished marble tombstones, the explosion of flowers everywhere, even on ancient graves.

"Why do you want to do this?" Therese once asked him playfully. "You could be playing bridge, or dominating your peers on the shuffleboard or pickleball courts, or even sitting on a park bench feeding the pigeons and squirrels."

"I feel a great generational pull, a tug on my genes, to return to the earth, to my roots," he said grandly. "I am following in the footsteps of ancestors who have gone before."

As a historian, Ezra was well aware and proud that in his new profession he became another in an impressive line of family experts in the mortal arts. Therese learned that it was a long list.

Ezra was descended from an impressive line of graveyard gurus – chopping block executioners, guillotine specialists, gallows hangmen, morticians – the kind of people whose skills made them especially indispensable during revolutions, plagues, natural disasters and wars.

The family came to wealth and prominence during the Great Plague of the Middle Ages. Great-ancestor Godfrey, stepping over bodies in the London streets, saw an opportunity and petitioned the crown for permission to dispose of them. A commercial empire was born, along with permission to use the coveted designation, "Provisioner to the King."

Another ancestor, Francois – Ezra liked to call him the head executioner – presided over the guillotine during the French Revolution.

"Family tradition says Marie Antoinette asked for him personally because it was said that he had a gentle, deft touch when it came to separating people from their heads," Ezra claimed.

Robespierre, who subsequently lost his own head the same way, was a close personal friend of Francois, at least until their relationship was abruptly severed.

The family reluctantly acknowledged that Francoise's own grandfather, Pierre, conceived the infamous practice of displaying the severed heads of defeated enemies on stakes as trophies. As the despised "king's executioner" in those days, his own head later was paraded along the streets on a pike.

History books do not always record such details, but the gruesome reputation of another of Ezra's ancestors, Guillaume, was so great that he was summoned by Henry VIII to be the one who made Ann Boleyn pay for her "crimes."

"Your family seemed to do a lot of business on both sides of the English Channel," Therese observed.

"Yes, we apparently went wherever our particular skills were most in demand," Ezra said.

Family lore held that yet another ancestor lit the fires that consumed Joan of Arc. It was even said, although the family vigorously denied it and struggled to suppress the story, that a Roman Legion forebear had helped fashion the cross for the Crucifixion.

"Vicious lies, spread by our competitors," claimed Mordecai Prufong, an uncle who was chairman of the board of a chain of 34 franchised mortuaries.

In other eras, some of Ezra's ancestors were involved in the sudden demise of the Salem witches, necktie parties for a clutch of cattle rustlers in the Old West, and in modern days even included an uncle, Ignatius Tuck, the electric chair facilitator at a federal prison. He was affectionately known there as Fryer Tuck.

Ezra's own grandfather, Elmer, was one of the millions of casualties of the 1918-1919 influenza epidemic. A mortician in New York, he contracted the fatal disease himself from transporting so many infected bodies from the city morgue.

Ezra wore this cloak of family funereal accomplishments proudly, although as a simple gravedigger he was at the far end of the death industry spectrum.

He fought unsuccessfully against the stigma attached to his second "profession," was quite proud that his father also had been a gravedigger, and was comfortable with his decision to follow in family footsteps, even if they did lead to the graveyard. The transformation was complete; he traded the groomed look and robes of an academician for long, unkempt hair and a scroungy beard, and swapped his suit for shoulder-strap overalls.

Ezra was outspoken in his opposition to such practices as cremation, burial at sea, and especially ostentatious mausoleums such as Lenin's Tomb at Red Square in Moscow and the Taj Mahal.

"It's an employment issue, maybe even a labor union issue. All that does is put some poor gravedigger out of a job," he lamented to Therese. "I'm going to take this up with the union. We should take a stand on this issue."

"I think I would have enjoyed hanging out with your family," she kidded, well aware that Ezra was a connoisseur of morbid gallows humor. Their constant exchange of cadaverous and macabre quips kept her customers laughing.

"And undertakers, well, of course they are so underappreciated," she added. "They are always the last people to ever let you down."

Ezra nodded, with a sly smile.

"I've read they have even started to accept cryptocurrency."

"Yes, it was all over the noosepapers."

Ezra collected examples of dark graveyard humor. He loved to entertain Therese and café customers with droll quips about musicians who were decomposing, distillers and their spirits, or some of the epitaphs he saw chiseled into tombstones over the years:

"I Was Hoping for a Pyramid"

"I Knew This Would Happen"

"Now I Know Something You Don't"

It was common knowledge that Ezra, out of his own pocket, often provided flowers or flags for neglected graves. As the caretaker, he had access to all of the cemetery's records, and as a special touch, sometimes put flowers on graves at birthdays.

This sometime had unfortunate repercussions.

"How dare you?" a woman once shouted at him, throwing a bunch of Ezra's mangled flowers at his feet. "He was a scheming, conniving bastard who made my life miserable, cheated on me, spent all of my inheritance, alienated all of my friends, and tried to destroy my second marriage! Let him lie in oblivion."

Henceforth, Ezra was more judicious in choosing his birthday honorees.

Therese recalled a day when Ezra came into the café carrying a beautiful spray of roses.

"As much as I'd like to think so, I'm sure those aren't for me," she said. "Who are they for?"

Ezra smiled wanly.

"Sorry, no, but you remember my friend Jack?"

She did, because they often came into the café together. She remembered that Jack placed roses on his wife's grave every year for 17 years, on the anniversary of her birthday.

"He died last year, and it's her birthday today, so I'm keeping up the tradition."

Therese could not stop the tear that leaked down her cheek. She came around the counter and hugged him.

As a historian, Ezra looked upon cemeteries as maybe not quite living history, but certainly as dead history. As an academician, he once wandered the world examining ruins in such places as Rome and Greece and Mexico, or exploring monuments like the pyramids in Egypt or Angkor Wat in Cambodia. Now, he often wandered the grounds of the cemetery, even at night, always pausing at his own Edna's grave, jotting down notes about some of the people buried there and looking up their stories.

"This is a history laboratory," he told Therese. "Every tombstone is a story, just waiting to be told. The past is right here, at our feet."

Ezra had done a lot of research into the town and its pioneers, discovering that its origins went back to well before the Civil War.

For a time, he wrote a column for the Horizons Heights *Herald*, describing some of his finds.

The graves of two long-forgotten Revolutionary War veterans were found under an overgrown patch of brambles and weeds, their slate markers barely legible. Ezra looked them up in cemetery and national records and learned that both had been with George Washington at Valley Forge, later moving westward with the expanding nation. He even located several descendants, who were astounded and ecstatic at the news.

Two local veterans' organizations joined to honor their memory at a military rededication ceremony attended by the descendants, city and state officials, hundreds of citizens and representatives from the Veterans Administration. An officer from the Daughters of the American Revolution gave a speech.

Ezra wrote about scandals. Two illicit lovers had been killed by an irate wife. The lovers were buried side by side; on each tombstone an engraved arm and hand reached out toward the other.

He wrote about riddles. One 1852 marker bore a rhyme:
On my death, be well aware
I have buried my treasure under a stair
To find it, there is a way
But more than that I will not say

Over the years, this set off legions of folks bearing shovels, metal detectors and GPS devices, wandering the town in search of stairs and instant riches. Townsfolk became quite leery of strangers carrying shovels eying their back yards. Chain-link fences became common all over town.

Ezra's column about the episode concluded:

That riddle about the stair
Seems to be just a lot of hot air
Wherever it is, it's still hidden
So maybe he was just kiddin'

Ezra wrote about mysteries. Many graves bore markers whose inscriptions had been erased by weather and time. A few had no markers at all, nor was there any record of them in the cemetery registry. Once, when a coffin was exhumed, another was found beneath it.

"It's probably Jimmy Hoffa," wrote a reader.

"We can finally stop looking for Anastasia Romanov," said another.

"Any sign of Amelia Earhart's plane down there?" asked a third.

Ezra was happy to publish their quips. In his trade, a sense of humor was a necessity.

He admired an eclectic mix of gravestone heroes: Shakespeare ("Blessed be the man that spares these stones, and cursed be he that moves my bones"); Woody Allen ("I am not afraid of dying; I just don't want to be there when it happens.")

But there is no humor this day for Ezra Prufong. Besides the outbursts at solemn funerals, Father Dunne has noticed that Ezra now often seemed distracted, sometimes making the graves too shallow, or too wide or too narrow.

He dug one in the wrong family plot, and even placed Mrs. Ballantine's expensive new tombstone on the nearby grave of Mr. Harrison, another new resident.

Mr. Ballantine, who was near the top of the list in the church's registry of contributors, was not pleased. Neither was the widow Harrison.

Ezra was literally crying in his coffee by now.

"I don't know what's going to happen" he lamented to Therese. "All those graves. All those people. All those families and tombstones. What's to become of them?"

It was not long afterward when Ezra himself died, some said of a broken heart, and took up his own residence in his favorite of all places.

At his funeral, Therese was annoyed when nobody rose to offer even a brief eulogy for this caring, tender, generous man.

So she did.

She reminded the mourners of Ezra's illustrious academic career, his altruistic dedication to the cemetery and his second profession, how he shared in the sorrow of total strangers, made the St. Sebastian Cemetery an example to be emulated. She implored others to step up.

"He made a difference, in his own humble way. This is it, the last chance to say something significant about a decent, honest man. Do it now, while memories and stories are fresh. As in all of your relationships, have no regrets later that 'I should have said something.'"

She reminded them of a quote by Harriet Beecher Stowe:

"The bitterest tears shed over graves are for words left unsaid and deeds left undone."

Inspired, several of Ezra's friends followed Therese to the podium. One recalled that on his first day on the job, Ezra was startled to find his own name on an old tombstone – a distant ancestor he had not been aware of.

"He took exceptional, fastidious care of that particular grave, since it was the next best thing to his own. Or maybe the next worst thing."

Another remembered a newspaper column Ezra wrote about a man who instructed that his funeral procession stop at a favorite tavern on the way to the cemetery. He left money with his friend the bartender to give everybody a beer.

One of them, somewhat inebriated, raised his glass and toasted Ezra: "To your health!"

Many laughed aloud again when another friend recalled how Ezra liked to terrorize teenagers who used the cemetery for their midnight beer parties. He told how teens would flee the cemetery in horror when they heard chains rattling, faint screams and moans, and saw ghostly apparitions flitting among the trees.

Several recalled Ezra's penchant for graveyard humor, his quips about being mired in a dead-end job, about all the people dying to get in. And one remembered how Ezra laughed when the cemetery erected a road sign reading, "One way-traffic."

A neighbor, George Smith, left them smiling with a story Ezra told about a court-ordered exhumation of a magician and master of disguises who had bilked lonely widows out of millions of dollars. Authorities discovered that someone else's body was in the grave.

"Ezra's comment was, 'I leave you to draw your own conclusions,'" George said.

Back at the café later, Therese was pleased at the way things had turned out.

"Nobody should leave life's stage without a stirring curtain call, a rousing sendoff," she told some of her regulars. "Especially somebody like him, who lived such a colorful, significant life. Rest in peace, Ezra."

Two days after Ezra's funeral, Therese taped a new sign to the counter jar at the Rainbow Café, replacing one for the library expansion drive. It said, "Cemetery Preservation Fund, in memory of Ezra Prufong."

Contributions trickled in over the next several days, a hundred dollars or so from Ezra's many friends, parishioners and café regulars. Then, on the fifth day, on emptying the jar, Therese found a note.

"A perpetual care fund in memory of Ezra Prufong has been established at St. Sebastian Cemetery," is all it said.

"What a grand gesture. But who's doing this?" she wondered, after confirming with Father Dunne that there was indeed a significant sum in the fund.

It was not the first time a note in the jar had produced what Therese liked to call a "miracle."

Chapter 2

THERESE

Therese herself had been the beneficiary of the first. When she went to work that momentous morning, Therese Martin was a waitress at the Rainbow Café. When she came home that night, she owned the place.

Legend and myth say there's a pot of gold at the end of the rainbow. There's no doubt something strange was going on with that jar at the end of the counter at the Rainbow Café.

It was just a plain old glass jar, an unlikely source and sponsor of miracles. The kind of donation jar you see on counters everywhere, with a couple of crumpled bills and some coins at the bottom, and a little sign soliciting contributions for the Little League, or the Senior Class Trip, for every disease imaginable, or even to help Harriet Harterton replace her expensive hearing aid.

Harriet, who ran the cake and cupcake shop nearby, lost hers when it fell into the cake batter in the electric mixer. She got it back the next day when Caleb Charnley returned it, complaining that he had not ordered a birthday cake for wife Myrtle with a hearing aid embedded in it.

"It doesn't work anymore," Harriet told Therese, explaining her need for a new one. "You might say it got a little 'battered.'"

This particular jar originally stored peaches, and then became a flower vase. Now it dispensed magic and miracles.

Therese went through a lot of peaches. Her famous peach cobblers and peach pies were a menu staple at the cafe, a popular hangout down at the end of main street, close to the river. Other neighbors, and frequent customers, included a bank, a newspaper office and an ice cream shop.

"I should write a book," she often said, reflecting on her daily interaction with the cornucopia of humanity she dealt with across the counter every day. The life of her town, on the edge of the big city, with all of its joys and sorrows, highs and lows, played out every day in the café.

Therese presided over a colorful, eclectic retinue of eccentrics, loners, misfits, oddballs, cranks, nonconformists and other characters. Ezra Prufong was only one of them.

"Just think what you could write," she told herself. "All of them are chapters in themselves. A priest with a standup comic routine. An erudite trash collector with a gorgeous voice. An editor who prints fictitious newspapers..."

And then there were the miracles, or whatever they might be called. As with Ezra, sometimes when Therese taped a new sign on the Rainbow jar, strange things started to happen.

Therese was first exposed to expert cooking and baking skills as a little girl in her Grandmother Martin's Irish kitchen, and then perfected her own later in a variety of restaurant and waitress jobs. Some of her favorite recipes, and subsequently those of her customers at the Rainbow Café, came from those early days with her grandmother, especially her peach desserts.

"There is nothing more flavorful than a just-ripe, big juicy peach," her grandmother liked to say, and little Therese would grin and nod enthusiastically, peach juice dripping from her chin.

The family's original name was Kilmartin, which her grandfather shortened after arriving in the U.S. Therese also exposed her customers to some of her grandmother's other Irish favorites, like corned beef and cabbage, soda bread and potato pancakes.

Therese was 35 now, athletic, still girlishly pretty and petit in the classic blond-and blue-eyed-girl-next-door fashion. She had not come this far without a struggle, and a fierce determination to overcome some early tragedies.

Her mother died when Therese was just a child, and she was left to pretty much raise herself for awhile when her father, distracted by grief and then later the loss of his business, gradually sank into an alcohol-fueled depression.

Until her grandmother moved in with them, she ran loose on her block for a time, unsupervised and neglected. Several other neighborhood moms, one in particular, Viola, stepped in and provided the direction she needed to restore her dignity. They washed and combed out the snarls in her hair, provided some hand-me-down clothes, and made sure she had a healthy diet and was in school every day.

Viola also protected her from bullies, from those who made fun of her manners, or lack of, and schooled her in the rules of etiquette.

She could hear Therese's future in her voice and see it in her demeanor. When a playmate told her she couldn't play with her anymore because her mom said she was unkempt and poor, Therese replied, "Well, then, tell your mom that's fine because if you're like that, I don't want to play with you, either." When a bully splashed mud on her skirt, she marched over to his house and demanded that his parents pay to have it cleaned or buy her a new one.

Therese played often with Viola's own daughter, Tiffany, and Viola could overhear their conversations. Even then, Therese was determined, resourceful and independent, announcing to Tiffany one day that, "Some day I am going to own my own business."

"You are a bright and promising child," she remembered Viola telling her. "Right now you have everything you need that's important – food, clothes and especially love. Your dad will pull out of this. We are here for you. Because you are going to be somebody."

Viola also provided something else that was priceless. Therese searched desperately and unsuccessfully for a photo, any photo, of her mother. It was Viola who came up with a faded snapshot she had taken of Therese and her mother, on their front porch.

Therese would never forget her kindness, her support and faith in a bright future, her intervention in deflecting the embarrassment and humiliation of those early years. It was a pay-it-forward lesson she would take with her into adulthood, an example she tried to practice every day at the café.

Her father did pull out of his despondency, although he suffered from continuing health problems. As a second-generation American, he instilled in her a love for her family's new country, with stories about the Pilgrims, the American Revolution, the noble principles of the Declaration of Independence and the Constitution, its stature in the world, and especially its traditions of equality, generosity, opportunity and exceptionalism.

She gave up a lot – college, friends, a career – and worked restaurant jobs to help support her dad until he died. She was back in school now, nights, part time, working on a degree in hotel and resort management, with grand plans to extend the Rainbow Café's offerings into high-end catering for weddings, corporate events and private parties.

Therese was married once, briefly, just after high school. It was such a mistake that she was embarrassed that anybody might find out about it. So they didn't.

Later, she worked for a time in her father's book store, where she met Winthrop, an Oxford graduate and the author of a hit series of murder mysteries set in the British Cotswolds, during a book-signing tour.

They hit it off from the start.

"Come with me," he said. "I need somebody to help manage these signings."

"Yes you do," she observed, after looking at his schedule. "You are double-booked in three of your next eight stops. You can't be in Chattanooga and Tulsa next Tuesday at the same time."

On an impulse, she dropped everything and joined his tour. It traversed the US for a month, and then Europe for another, ending in the Cotswolds, where his parents threw a huge welcome home party for the returning celebrity.

They probably would have married, were it not for yet another tragedy. Perpetually preoccupied and absent-minded, Winthrop was struck and killed by a black cab while crossing a London street shortly after the homecoming. He had been in America just long enough to forget that in Britain, the traffic pattern is reversed, and he was looking the wrong way.

♣ ♣ ♣

Back in America, trying to shake a feeling that she was cursed when it came to personal relationships, she landed another waitress job, at a place simply called "Joe's." The buzzing and flickering neon sign that dangled precariously from one rusting chain over the door said, also very simply, "Eat."

Some would have called it a dive. It was a relic from another era, in an aging building in an aging block near the river, on the oldest side of town.

But it survived, largely due to Therese's personality and because the grumpy owner mostly stayed out of sight in the kitchen. More than one businessman customer told her, "If you are ever looking for another job, I will hire you in a minute." Therese turned down several such offers, biding her time, waiting for an opportunity to have a place of her own.

The donation jar started under the previous owner. It was unlabeled, and customers fed it generously, in the American tradition, thinking it surely must be for some worthy cause. They were annoyed and some even were angry when they learned that the aging and ailing café owner was putting the money toward her electric bill.

"She should be ashamed, she's giving donation jars everywhere a bad name," Therese groused. She knew that the owner's clumsy, awkward, ham-fisted approach to customers probably explained why the café was not doing well.

There were enough complaints that the jar eventually disappeared.

And then the opportunity came. The owner, who had taken over the café when her husband died, took her aside one day.

"I'm putting the place up for sale," she said. "As you know, my heart has never really been in it. I'm a septuagenarian myself. It's time to get out and finally retire. You are so good at this, Therese, such a natural, I will give you the first chance to buy it."

At first, Therese dismissed the idea as out of reach. Then the word spread among customers, who knew that Therese had ambitions to open a place of her own.

Partly as a prank, one of them put up a new jar and taped a sign on it asking customers to "Help Therese Buy This Place."

She was embarrassed as the small bills and coins began to accumulate, knowing full well the jar could never raise the money needed to buy out the owner.

But then came the first miracle.

One morning when Therese emptied the jar, she found an astounding surprise, a note.

"Therese, stop by the Horizon Heights National Bank and see the manager, Juval Platt," the printed note said. "He has some news for you."

Therese tossed it off as part of the joke, but then had to reconsider a few days later when Juval himself called. He was a café regular, and his tone was urgent.

"Therese, I need to see you. It's quite important. Stop by as soon as you can."

♣ ♣ ♣

Juval pulled up a chair for her. It was obvious from his hesitant manner that he was as bewildered as she was.

"I don't know where to start," he said. "I know that you would like to buy the café. You will find that there is a $50,000 deposit in your personal account. Don't ask me where it came from, because I don't know. It's enough certainly for a down payment, and a loan will be no problem, given your reputation."

Therese gasped and started to get up from the chair.

"Is this part of the joke? This is going too far. I don't think this is very funny."

"It's not a joke. It's legitimate. The money was wired to us. We tried to determine where it came from but the sender's identity is hidden behind a shell company and a trust. Whoever this is, went to great lengths to remain anonymous. But I assure you the money is real."

Therese learned that there were some rules. She was not to talk about her windfall, which was not a problem since she knew next to nothing. In the future, if she was able, she was to pass her good fortune on in some way, pay it forward in generous, humane gestures of her own. If things didn't work out, or if she squandered it, well, she would have to live with herself and "what might have been."

"This is for real?" Therese's head was spinning. "Who would do such a thing? Why would they do such a thing? "

She walked on air back to the shop.

Within days under her ownership, the café was renamed, and within weeks was remodeled. There was a glitzy new sign depicting a leprechaun, a rainbow and a pot of gold, and the donation jar became a fixture again at the end of the counter. Therese moved into the apartment above the café.

Her regulars presumed she landed a bank loan to finance her dream, and she said nothing to make them think otherwise. She did thank them for their donation to her "cause," and told them she put the money toward the new sign.

The rainbow name and emphasis were in honor of Therese's mother, who loved rainbows and told Therese they were signs of good luck.

"I saw one the day before I met your dad," she said. "There was one just before I knew we were going to have you. And another when we were trying to decide if we could buy our first house."

But her mother died when Therese was six of a short but debilitating illness. To soothe her, her father told Therese that her mom left a note.

"My dearest Therese," it said, "I have to go away, because God has called me. He told me that since I am such an expert on rainbows, he needs me to help him decide where to put the next ones. I will be thinking about you always, be a good girl and listen to your daddy. I love you so much. Mommy."

The typewritten note became a cherished comfort to Therese, even after she learned when she was 13 that her father had written it. She still carried it in a side pocket in her purse, along with the faded snapshot, the only vestige of her mother.

On the day she reopened, a customer gave her a small leprechaun figurine as a good luck and café-warming gift. Eventually, that would grow into a collection of leprechauns, all perched in various poses on shelves behind the counter. They were gifts from appreciative café regulars who picked them up on their travels around the country and the world.

On close inspection, some of the figures were not leprechauns at all, but gnomes, goblins, trolls, fairies, sprites or elves. Therese did not discriminate; she was an equal opportunity pixie collector.

One day Juval Platt came into the café carrying an enormous enlarged photo of a spectacular rainbow.

"It's so big," she said. "What am I going to do with this?"

"Well, my thought was that it could frame the doorway," Juval said. "Then we could cut out the material under the rainbow and customers would literally be walking under the rainbow to enter here."

Therese had to agree it was a novel idea.

The café was one big room, with a long L-shaped counter and stools set against the back wall. Behind that was the kitchen, a tiny office, closets and restrooms. Booths and tables lined the other three walls. Therese kept it all going with the help of some part-timers.

Despite her painful past, Therese's customers never saw anything but a sunny extrovert. She attracted and kept customers through the sheer force of her personality. She was cheerful, chatty, enthusiastic, compassionate and funny, always ready to listen and help while they unloaded on her a litany of family and job problems, girl and boyfriend and marriage troubles, personal woes of every kind. Every day she dealt with a cross-section of people, with their pain and anguish, their joys and successes.

"Maybe I should have been a psychologist," she sometimes mused. "Although a good peach cobbler is also a very refreshing antidote to a lot of things."

She sometimes was asked how she could keep up her spirits amid the discord, disagreements and heartbreak that seemed to be everywhere.

"I decided long ago that I would not let my tragedies define my life," she said. "Lots of people have a tough time of it. You can sulk and whine and complain, or you can pick up the pieces and move on. A good sense of humor helps. Especially a sense of humor."

And her Irish wit was on display there every day.

She liked to tell customers that her parents were hippie radicals, and that she was carrying on the family tradition by running her own cafe counter-culture.

"Counter-culture, get it?" she would say, winking at customers across the counter, some of whom did not get it, while suppressing a crack about their counter-intelligence. She might try again with a story about the penguin who walked into her café one day and asked, "Have you seen my brother?"

"And I say, 'I don't know. What does he look like?'"

The café became her life, her social circle. She looked on her regulars, that cluster of eccentric characters, as her family. Most of them were there every day, usually in the morning for what they called "Therese's Breakfast Club," but many also popped in-and-out throughout the day.

She did not lack for admirers. Therese developed an effective technique for handling Lotharios of all stripes – straying husbands, oversexed delivery people, aggressive customers, rowdy street construction crews.

"She turns you down with such charm and good humor that you're not even disappointed," said one admiring suitor. "You feel like it's an honor to be rejected with such style. She's probably got guys standing in line looking forward to being rejected."

But she was not above flirting a little, especially with the macho firemen from the station just down the street, or the neighborhood cops, all of whom regularly received complimentary peach pies and cobblers. And with Rex Warnevar, the handsome owner of the ice cream shop next door.

Among her favorites were the golfing groups who came in after a round. Sometimes the rapid-fire taunts and jibes between them brought gales of laughter from other customers.

"Hey Therese," one of them would say. "This coffee tastes like mud."

"It should, it was ground this morning."

Or, "Hey Therese. There's a fly in my soup." "OK, I'll get the fly spray," or "Shhh. The others will want one too."

Even irritable employees, unpleasant and picky diners and miserly tippers could not get her down. Many of her customers became good friends.

It was not unusual for Therese to pick up the tab for customers who appeared to be down-and-out, or sometimes just for people who seemed to be having a bad day, or to cover for employees with personal problems and inevitable absences.

The café became the heart of the neighborhood, a warm and inviting gathering place for both newcomers and regulars.

Part of the charm was the jar. The adage that Americans are the most generous people on earth was proved every day at the Rainbow Café. The jar was fed constantly and generously by the many people who stopped by.

Therese often reflected on America's reputation for unbounded charity.

"It's embedded in our national DNA," her father told her. "We are inherently so grateful for our good fortune at being born here into this land of freedom, justice, liberty, plenty and opportunity, that we want to spread our blessings."

Generous was not a big enough word for the gesture that made Therese the first beneficiary of the mystical pot of gold.

Chapter 3

THE BANKER

J uval Platt was a fixture in the neighborhood and one of the regulars at the Rainbow Café. Therese had been one of the first to sympathize with him years earlier, coming to his defense when he unwittingly became the butt of jokes and ridicule after he appeared in commercials sponsored by his parent bank.

The bank's advertising agency apparently thought it a good idea to portray one of their branch managers as a friendly, small-town fatherly type always ready to help customers find happiness. Juval was chosen.

In the commercial, a dewy-eyed, smiling young couple were sitting across a desk from Juval, signing their new home loan papers. Juval, the portly, balding, friendly neighborhood banker, peered down at them benevolently through wire-rimmed glasses perched on the end of his nose. As they rose to leave, Juval embraced them in a hug.

He accompanied them to the door of his office, and it was then that it became apparent that the woman was quite pregnant. The camera closed in for a tight, sentimental shot as the three clasped hands, and it also became quite apparent that neither of the lovebirds was wearing a wedding ring.

The reaction was swift and merciless in the surrounding conservative community.

"You are condoning promiscuity and co-habiting before marriage!" said one. "What kind of example is this to set for our children?"

"What's next?" barked another. "Are you going to loan money to people who want to open a house of ill repute?"

"I'm moving my money somewhere else, where Christian ideals and values are honored and respected," said still another.

There were letters to the editor. One of them included a crude cartoon showing a bank teller opening an account for someone who looked very much like the devil, over the caption, "My kind of bank!"

Even Pastor Twittle at the nearby Abiding Redemption Church had something to say about the commercial. Although he did not name the offending establishment, everybody knew who he was talking about.

"Do not patronize evil establishments that encourage sin, wickedness, debauchery and depravity!" he thundered from the pulpit. "They are an abomination and disgrace before the eyes of God!"

The ad was a flop, and inflicted a severe black eye on the bank. It soon disappeared under the avalanche of ridicule and negative publicity.

The bank tried again with still another commercial featuring Juval. In it, a ragamuffin little girl, barely able to see over the counter, appeared at the bank wanting to open one of its special accounts aimed at encouraging thrift among children. After faithfully depositing a quarter a week all year, the little waif would have enough at Christmas to buy her widowed mom a present.

But she only had a dime, and as the teller reluctantly turned the teary-eyed child away, grandfatherly Juval strode over to save the day by giving her the additional 15 cents.

But instead of bringing a smile and a tear, the bank was hit instead with another backwash of reproach. While some viewers thought the tear-jerker ad quite sweet and cute, others were critical that it didn't go far enough.

Again, the ad backfired loudly and became a lively subject for discussion all over town and even in the letters to the editor. For a lot of people, generosity apparently had to be measured quantitatively, commercials were taken quite seriously, and they had to have larger happy endings.

"Oh, c'mon," said one critic. "Would it kill them to just give this broken-hearted little girl the whole measly $13 as a reward for her devotion to her mom and for her good intentions?!"

Wrote another: "Are they sure the board of directors would approve of that excessive display of generosity? At least give the kid a lollipop and a little stuffed animal, too, or are they afraid of starting a stampede of urchins?"

A third sent a cartoon image of Ebeneezer Scrooge wagging a bony finger at Tiny Tim and scolding, "Fifteen cents here, fifteen cents there, pretty soon you're talking real money."

The bank itself also received a lot of negative mail.

"Aren't you concerned that the bank examiners are going to want to know where that 15 cents came from?" said one critic.

That commercial soon disappeared also. Juval was retired as a spokesperson. The bank decided it couldn't win and turned instead to placing bland, generic ads in the Horizon Heights *Herald*. But both commercials had aired enough times to become common knowledge among the café regulars.

When Juval appeared one morning soon after for his daily coffee and doughnut, each of the regulars filed solemnly in a line past his stool, dropping quarters next to his cup. Another morning, he found a slice of devil's food cake, with a sign saying, "For the manager of the devil's bank!"

Juval began to think he would never live this down.

After a few days of this, Therese called a halt to it. She began to scoop up the quarters and drop them in the jar.

"From now on, Juval is only accepting $10 bills," she announced with great fanfare. "And all of it will go into the jar."

The hazing stopped. Juval thought his reputation would be restored with a new series of commercials starring him as the friendly banker reminding people that they should move unneeded money from their checking accounts to savings, where they would earn a princely one percent.

But then that started it all up again.

Juval did enjoy immensely his own clandestine ability to help people achieve their dreams. He had been a middleman in Therese's good fortune, but he had his own roster of people he had helped, sometimes with a bank loan, sometimes by other means.

One of his beneficiaries was Luigi Costicello, an Italian immigrant who came to America with nothing but the clothes he wore. He took any odd job he could find – road construction laborer, orchard field hand, ditch digger, hod carrier for masons on construction sites. He met Juval Platt when he was hired to mow Juval's lawn. Juval, out of shape and overweight, was averse to mowing his own.

It was an oppressively hot summer weekend, and Juval, from the comfort of his screened porch and his tall lemonade decorated with a little umbrella, could not help but notice how meticulous Luigi was in tending the huge lawn, which stretched 70 yards down to the river.

Luigi had insisted on bringing his own push-mower, disdaining Juval's offer to use his riding model.

"I am an artist," he said. "And artists must work with their own tools."

Juval watched admiringly as the artist went to work on his Bermuda grass canvas. He was painstaking in picking up every stray leaf, his mowing rows were so neat they could have been plotted by an engineer with a laser tool, every invasive grass that dared show a blade was pulled out by the roots. And for a finishing touch, Luigi mowed the huge back lawn in a cross-hatch pattern so meticulous it could have been mistaken for the outfield at Yankee Stadium.

Juval invited him onto the porch when he was done and offered him a lemonade. His wife brought out some cookies and cakes.

"You do such a thorough, painstaking job," Juval said. "I admire that."

Luigi blushed and stared at his shoes.

"My dad, he always tell me, when you do a job, you do it right. A correctly mowed lawn is my signature, my sign I leave behind saying I am an artist, I bring beauty to the world, in my own way."

The two talked for a while on the porch, and Juval learned that Luigi had been in the country for a time under a green card, living with a sister, was looking for any work he could find, and intended to apply for citizenship as soon as he could. Juval offered to be his sponsor if his sister did not or could not.

The "signature" that Luigi left behind at Juval's house was noticed by his neighbors. Soon, Luigi was mowing the lawns at most of the houses on the block. Word spread around the neighborhood and it wasn't long before Luigi had more business than he could handle.

"Come see me at the bank," Juval said one day.

Luigi arrived in an-fitting suit and waited patiently while Juval tended to another customer.

"I have an idea for you," Juval said. "Would you want to start your own company, hire people to help?"

Luigi was momentarily stunned.

"How can I do that? I have no money for mowers, more people."

"The bank will set you up with a business loan," Juval said. "I am so impressed by what I have seen of your work that I think you will be a risk we are happy to take."

And so Luigi's Luxurious Lawns was born. He soon had a pickup truck and trailer, two employees and several new hand-push mowers. The old-style mowers became part of his signature, were featured in his advertising: "We do it the old-fashioned way!"

Also becoming part of his "signature" was the discreet but distinctive script "L" that he left behind on every lawn, carved into the grass in a remote corner.

Before long, Luigi was a citizen and able to bring the rest of his family – his wife and three daughters – to America. And within a year he had repaid the bank loan.

Juval was surprised to see him waiting in the bank lobby one day.

"I need to tell you something," Luigi said. "I want to pay back my good fortune, my 'American Opportunity.' So I want to tell you that I have organized several other landscape companies, and we are going to patrol the city for vacant, overgrown lots and keep them attractive and presentable, maybe even plant some flowers."

When Juval told Therese about Luigi's generous gesture, she grinned. "That's what Americans do," she said. "Even the brand-new ones."

♣ ♣ ♣

Juval's lawn was becoming an incubator for new businesses.

A tall white pine on his property had been snapped in two by a lightning strike, and he hired a local nursery to dispose of it. They sent Paul Hagward, a chainsaw expert in more ways than one.

Juval asked him to cut up the fallen piece into firewood for the family-room fireplace. Hagward had a better idea.

"I can make something out of that for you if you like," he told Juval. "It would be a shame to waste it."

"What do you mean?"

"Well, I'm pretty good with this saw, so how about I carve it into an alligator for you? It'll be beautiful, and the talk of the neighborhood. Only $50."

Hagward showed Juval some photos of other carvings he had done. Impressed, Juval agreed, and went back into the house. For hours he could hear the saw buzzing and droning as Hagward trimmed branches, cut the piece down to the size he needed, and coaxed the creature out of it. When Hagward came to get him, Juval was astounded at what he saw.

The lifelike alligator was so menacing that Juval instinctively took a step backward. Its mouth was partly open, showing rows of sharp, conical teeth, and its sinister eyes seemed to be sizing Juval up. The posture was tense, as if ready to strike, there were rows of scales along the back, a tail almost as long as the body.

"I can come back tomorrow and paint it for you," Hagward said. "Blackish grey. Guaranteed to keep ne'er-do-wells, vagrants, burglars and aluminum siding salesmen away."

"Better than a watchdog," Juval said, laughing.

Hagward proposed another idea. For an extra $50, instead of removing the remaining stump, which was about six feet high, he would provide another creature.

"I'll make you a raccoon," he said. "When I come back tomorrow."

Again, Juval was delighted to accept.

Hagward appeared early the next morning. After a few more hours of buzzing and droning, Juval went out onto the lawn to check on his progress. Hagward had carved a large rectangle into the stump; inside it was the perfect likeness of a raccoon.

And not just one. Three raccoons, a family, stacked one atop the other.

"I got a little carried away," he said. "Couldn't stop myself. I can put masks on them tomorrow and touch them up a little with some paint. Three for the price of one."

Juval was happy to pay the money, and wondered if Hagward did this kind of thing regularly.

"Oh, yeah, I have a bunch in my basement, rabbits, owls, skunks, porcupines…"

"You should open a studio and sell them there."

"Naw, can't afford it. I just do it mostly for friends."

Juval persuaded him to come see him at the bank, and within a month Hagward was set up in his own garage-studio. He sold half of his basement inventory on the first day.

Over the years, Juval had developed an unerring "feel" for people. He could tell after a brief interview who were the good loan risks, who were not. But too often the good risks were talented people with no means of their own, no assets or collateral to back up a loan.

Juval believed talent, determination and ambition were assets just as precious as real estate or stocks and bonds or jewels. But his loan committee demanded something more tangible. Sometimes they would back Juval in his faith in a person, but not always.

So for special cases, he set up his own loan committee, which consisted of himself.

He financed a muralist who made a business out of painting beautiful nature scenes on ugly blank urban walls. Likewise a home brewer whose beer became so popular among his friends that Juval helped him branch out and start his own micro-brewery. And a geocacher whose imagination and GPS talents were so impressive that Juval set him up as a treasure-hunter, specializing in parties and gatherings featuring scavenger hunts.

His choices had never failed him. But for some of them, he never would have been able to persuade his board of directors that they were worth the risk.

So Juval Platt had a secret, a dangerous one. In a way, he was another version of the jar at the Rainbow Cafe, covertly financing people like Therese who otherwise might not be able to pursue their dreams.

But if his secret was ever discovered, the odds were pretty good that he would go to jail.

"It's for a good cause," he kept reassuring himself. "It's worth the risk. Chances are that before anybody would ever find out, I would be able to cover my tracks."

As a branch-bank manager, he was privy to bank records that other employees were not. He knew that among the bank's many deposits was a forgotten $50,000 account belonging to a wealthy elderly widow now confined to a nursing home. This is what he used to finance loans for projects like the chain saw artist, the muralist, the geocacher and the microbrewer.

The "loans" from the account were repaid so rapidly, the bank records showed such regular churn activity, that it was never in danger of being declared dormant and thus turned over to the state. And there were no heirs who might have complicated things. Even so, Juval kept constant watch on the health of the widow.

Occasionally, Juval's projects overlapped. Payments made to satisfy one secret loan would be used to finance another. The irony of this was not lost on Juval.

"This is a sort of pyramid scheme," he had to admit to himself, "but a successful one, and for worthy causes."

Sometimes Juval used his "secret fund" for needs more basic than business startups. It was not uncommon, for example, for a struggling young single mother to puzzle over the anonymous $500 she found in an envelope in her mailbox, or for a financially-stressed elderly widower to find an unexplained $400 in his checking account.

When pressed, Juval would shrug it off as a bookkeeping error.

"You probably just forgot it was there," he'd say.

But Juval knew there might be a day of reckoning ahead.

He confided as much to Therese. He had come to trust her judgment and discretion, since they harbored a mutual secret.

"My God, you are walking such a tightrope," was her reaction. She was aghast at the risk he was taking to help other people, and resolved to help him find a way out of the trap he had set for himself.

After thinking about it for a time, she decided it might be worth it to turn to the jar for help, a reversal of the way she had been contacted.

"Why not?" she said. "I'll write my own note. I guess we should try to find out if this mystery person has any limits, if there's any two-way communication."

Her note, explaining Juval's predicament, was addressed to "Whoever you are." It lauded his generous heart and altruistic aims, described his many successes, his fear that bank examiners might one day start sniffing into suspicious records.

And it said that because it was becoming too risky to go on with his project, Juval might have to discontinue his off-the-books philanthropy.

The pot at the Rainbow Café, which had made Therese's own dream possible, made an honest man out of Juval. He could continue his campaign with a fresh, unencumbered $50,000, the reply note said.

And the bank restored to its original state a long-abandoned $50,000 account that had fallen through the cracks for years.

But rather than take a deep breath and a sigh of relief at his reprieve, Juval began to wonder if there weren't more such "abandoned accounts" out there in the system's many branches.

"Stop!" Therese counseled sternly. "Stop while you are still ahead. Stop while you are still not in jail."

Chapter 4

THE EDITOR

Juval was not the only one of her regulars in need of rescue and reclamation. Hank Lyson, editor and publisher of the Horizon Heights *Herald,* who had a precarious grip on the basics of running a business, was another. If Juval Platt had a soft spot for people who needed a loan, Hank had one for anybody who owned him money.

"Hank is in some trouble," Rex Warnevar told Therese one morning. "No surprise, given the way he runs his business. I don't see how he can last much longer."

Therese had to smile to herself. Rex, who owned The Sundae Pew, the ice cream shop next door, didn't seem to be in any position to criticize someone else's business practices. Rex was in and out of the café all day, schmoozing with

Therese and his coffee buddies at the counter. He always sat in the same spot, where he could keep an eye on the pedestrian traffic outside, ready to head out the door the moment one of them made a move toward his shop.

Therese sometimes wondered how his own business was faring, given that he didn't seem to spend a whole lot of time there.

"What happened?" she said. "I saw Hank yesterday and he seemed OK."

"He should spend more time on his real newspaper and less on his phony ones," Rex replied, shaking his head.

Hank's office was up the hill in the next block. The weekly paper included a small job-printing shop, which helped pay the bills, but Hank was so lenient in his billing practices that the business was constantly on a financial precipice.

The paper served a crucial function. It covered its side of town and the Rainbow Café neighborhood like nothing else could. Nowhere else could you read about the fire at the Granger house that destroyed Tom's priceless collection of antique pencil sharpeners, or about the pot-luck supper to raise funds for a new baptismal font at St. Sebastian Church, which had spurted a leak at an inopportune time and left everybody wet except the baby.

Without the *Herald* you would not have known that Ace Chevrolet was moving to the old Hickstrom Building, or see a legal notice proclaiming that Marmaduke Dahlstrom was no longer responsible "for any debts incurred by anyone other than myself," or know that Trudy's dress shop would now be closing earlier on Wednesdays.

Reading between the lines could tell you a lot about what was happening in a small town. It was quite obvious to discerning readers, for example, that Marmaduke's marriage might be in some trouble. And it appeared that Wednesday now was Trudy's car-pool day to take the kids to soccer practice.

And you wouldn't find in any metro newspaper a full, free account of the Byers-Cunningham wedding, including a detailed description of what the bride wore ("The new Mrs. Cunningham was stunning in a sheer A-line lace quarter-sleeve gown with a sweetheart neckline..."), plus names and gown descriptions of all five bridesmaids, a full list of the 82 out-of-town guests attending, and a detailed elaboration of honeymoon plans ("The bride and groom will be motoring to visit the Corn Palace in Mitchell, SD and points west...")

The *Herald* did not have a large staff. Two, to be exact. Hank was the editor, and Mrs. Lyson was the society editor and part-time reporter.

Hank's problem was that he was a competent journalist but not much of a businessman. He had extended so much credit to customers who were lax in paying that eventually they stopped ordering their letterheads and billing statements and flyers from Hank because they felt so guilty about all the money they already owed him for past projects. Some *Herald* subscriptions had not been paid for in years.

And Hank was loathe to call anybody and remind them that they had owed him $450 for three years now.

The business was handed down to Hank by his father. But Hank really would rather have been a land surveyor or an auto mechanic or maybe even a farmer, than a newspaperman.

He did admit one day to Therese that the newspaper was in jeopardy, on the brink of bankruptcy, and in the face of overwhelming debt might have to put the paper up for sale.

The word was out on the street soon that a national chain expressed interest in buying the *Herald.*

Therese was not the only one alarmed.

"You know what happens after that," Rex Warnevar said. "They swallow it up, it loses its unique local identity and voice, and it becomes plain vanilla like all the rest of the papers in their stable."

But his heart of gold suited Hank well for his "hobby," a sideline that no one except Therese and Rex knew about.

So she always brightened whenever Hank came through the door. He was in his 50s, tall and slender with a mustache, and wore a green eyeshade and suspenders as an affectation, just like the gruff, stern editors in the old movies about newspapers. He liked to share his "surprises" with her, and lurked outside until he was sure she was alone.

"What do you have there this time?" Therese said, peering eagerly at his briefcase, where she could see part of a newspaper in a side pocket.

He pulled it out to show her, but glanced around first to reassure himself that they were alone.

She smiled at the headline, in huge type across the top of the front page.

LOCAL SCIENTIST CREDITED
FOR ALZHEIMER'S CURE

Hank grinned sheepishly.

"Too much?"

Therese smiled through the beginning of a tear and shook her head, no.

"She'll love it."

The story described in some detail how a team of researchers at the nearby medical college, applying theories first advanced by Maybelle Hunnicutt, former lead researcher, had announced a breakthrough that fellow scientists were heralding as the crucial piece needed to bring down the scourge of Alzheimer's. High on the page was a large photo of Maybelle.

The rest of the front page and those behind it looked suspiciously like those of last week's edition of the *Herald*.

Maybelle, 78, now retired, had until her illness been another regular at the Rainbow Café. Ironically, she now was savaged by the very disease she had devoted her professional life to eradicating. Her husband, Raymond, had succumbed to the same debilitating affliction ten years earlier.

"I'm on my way over there now," Hank said. Maybelle, a patient at the nearby New Horizons extended care facility, was in and out of dementia, and he hoped to catch her on one of her better days. A nurse had tipped him off that Maybelle probably did not have much time left.

"This will mean so much to her, even if it's not true," he said.

Hank's voice trailed off and he wiped away a tear himself.

Therese put a comforting hand on his arm across the counter.

"You're doing a beautiful thing," she said. "Surely God cannot be upset at a last-minute lie that brings so much comfort and release. Just be sure nobody else sees it."

The next day she pumped him for the story.

Hank smiled, the kind of sad smile somewhere between melancholy and gratification.

"The whole family was there in the room, children and grandchildren, other relatives, friends. She was barely conscious.

"At one point they were all called away by a doctor. I showed her the page, read her part of the story, and she smiled.

"I just wanted her to die happy. She had devoted a good part of her life to this cause. So what's the harm?

"When the family returned a minute later, she was gone. There was such a beatific smile on her face..."

"What a beautiful lie," Therese said.

♣ ♣ ♣

Therese first became aware of Hank's "hobby" on a morning five years earlier. Over breakfast, he pulled that week's edition of the *Herald* from his briefcase, but with it spilled out another, with a startling headline.

"Evidence of Aliens Found in Rockland" it said, referring to a nearby town. A second headline elaborated: "Fabyak's 'Wild Tale' Not So Wild Now?"

Therese was intrigued. "What's this all about?"

The story beneath described how authorities were baffled by a huge circle that had appeared overnight in a farm field, all the vegetation within it destroyed by a strange secretion that scientists could not identify, except to say that it did not appear to be of earthly origin.

The story also recalled an event from ten years earlier, when farmer Victor Fabyak disappeared for five days and then suddenly reappeared. He claimed he had been abducted by aliens, spent five days aboard their flying saucer, and that he had been given a message for earthlings.

"They warned us that we'd better learn to get along with each other," Fabyak claimed. "They said they could see from wherever they came from that life forms down here always seemed to be fighting each other."

He was savagely ridiculed not only by his family, friends and neighbors, but also by the press. There were cartoons showing Victor sitting with three-headed green creatures, he was pilloried on late-night television, and began to receive hate mail. His house was pranked by teenagers, rocks were thrown through windows, and garish alien-scarecrow type figures appeared on his lawn.

Victor retreated into his house and seldom emerged, except to retrieve the paper from his front porch or go to a store. But even there he was subjected to constant stares, whispers, smirks and finger-pointing.

Hank grinned ruefully.

"Victor is not well and I thought it would be nice if he could feel vindicated in his last days. He's the only one who will see it."

Victor Fabyak was an old friend of both of them; for years he had stopped by the café during his weekly trip to town, arriving on a farm tractor, his only means of transport other than an aging draft horse. Victor was widely admired for his philanthropy. He sponsored Little League teams and bowling leagues, he underwrote the costs of the annual canoe race on the river and provided the prize money, he loaned his heavy farm machinery for all kinds of civic projects – playgrounds, athletic fields, the new riverside park.

Therese became an accomplice in Hank's campaign to help others truly rest in peace. She was well-placed at the café, the neighborhood social center and gathering place, to hear all of the local news, and fed him tips on people who might be deserving of his editorial largesse, or a "Hanking," as she came to call it.

Hank turned out his secret special editions working nights at his printing shop, dreaming up fictitious headlines intended to bring some final solace to deserving and worthwhile neighborhood figures.

"I hear Billy Flynn is not doing well," Therese told Hank another day. Billy, a retired fireman, years earlier had saved a four-year-old girl from an apartment blaze. The girl had gone on to a successful career in state and national politics, and the edition Billy would see of the *Herald* had the girl, now a U.S. Senator in Hank's version, on the brink of becoming vice president of the United States.

Not all of Hank's fabrications were quite so grand.

Another beneficiary, Walter, a self-effacing plumber whom Therese and Hank both hired occasionally, learned on his deathbed that he had been elected to the National Plumbers Hall of Fame. Grandmother Lorraine, who had taught ballet to her granddaughter, was told just in time that Gracie would soon be auditioning with the New York City Ballet. And Maurice, a local watercolorist, went to his rest assured that he was a finalist for the Wildlife Artist of the Year award.

Hank's loose relationship with the truth, combined with access to a printing press, enabled him to spring phony newspaper surprises on friends now and then.

Café regulars knew that Juval Platt, the banker, was an admirer of the infamous D.B. Cooper, the hijacker who bailed out of a plane over the Pacific Northwest in 1971 with a small fortune in ransom money from the airline, most of which was never found. Juval insisted to anyone who would listen that Cooper must still be out there somewhere, although there had been no sign of him since.

"What do you think of this?" Hank asked one morning with a huge smile, plopping a copy of the *Herald* on the café counter in front of Juval. "A souvenir for you."

The familiar news sketch of Cooper accompanied the story, which said the FBI discovered that a man believed to be Cooper died, alone and penniless, in a Portland homeless shelter in 2001.

He was separated from the money during the drop, the story said, eventually made his way back to Seattle, and under an assumed name was hired as a flight attendant on the same airline, determined to try his stunt again. But he was fired after arguing violently with an unruly, tipsy passenger who was wandering up and down the aisle trying to sell subscriptions to a fanatical religious magazine.

"As for the money," Hank's version continued in a flight of imagination, "the bundled loot thudded into the yard of a convent, in front of a group of startled nuns. The sisters considered this a sign from heaven that they should use it to expand their charitable acts. They opened a series of soup kitchens in the inner city, with enough left over to erect a shrine on their grounds to St. Therese of Lisieux, patron saint of aviation causes, including flyers, air crews, pilots and parachutists."

Juval was delighted with the spoof, especially the headline, "D.B. Cooper Story Hits the Ground Hard."

"This makes as much sense as any other theory I've heard," Juval said.

He hung it over his desk at the bank.

"You should have seen my alternate version," Hank told him. "Old D.B.'s parachute gets hung up in a tree, a female Sasquatch comes by and rescues him, and they're found living in a cave together surrounded by little Sasquatches. Or is it Sasquatch-i? No sign of the money."

Therese and the regulars at the counter laughed with him.

Encouraged, Hank produced a few more spoofs for friends.

For Jacob, a retired underwater archeologist, the headline blared that the legendary and controversial Lost City of Atlantis had indeed been found. According to Hank's *Herald,* bathysphere explorers found it on the ocean floor just off the Azores in the Atlantic, exactly where Jacob always figured it would be. Scientists were astounded to discover among the ruins a building that appeared to be a sort of fast-food drive-in for chariots.

Winston Arnold, a remote descendant of Benedict Arnold, read in his *Herald* that new research showed that his vilified but misunderstood ancestor had not betrayed anyone but had simply gone over to the British because he was tired of military rations and had become quite fond of bangers and mash, black pudding and steak and kidney pie.

Hank got more mileage out of the Sasquatch legend with Brandon, an avid hunter, who was shown on his *Herald* front page posing in a selfie with his arm around the shoulder of a blurry, hairy image said to be that of Bigfoot, taken during an encounter in a remote forest. The story said Brandon's new book, providing evidence that Sasquatch/Bigfoot and other so-called mythical creatures were indeed very much real, was climbing the best-seller charts and about to be made into a movie.

The *Herald* account went on to say that investigations now extended to the other side of the world, prompted by fresh sightings of Bigfoot's cousins, the Yeti and Abominable Snowman. In another burst of creativity, Hank added to his bogus story a report that an aging, well-fed, overweight, pot-bellied Yeti had been spotted in the Himalayas, one that headline writers were calling the Abdominable Snowman.

"It needed an extra touch of believability," Hank said in relating the story to Therese, "so I added a crude sketch. I gave him a cane, too. He looked like a shaggy elderly golfer."

Therese could not suppress a giggle. And this gave her an idea.

"Hank, why don't you produce these spoofs for sale? Not just as practical jokes, but as tabloid-size souvenirs or conversation pieces, such as for birthdays, anniversaries, graduations, athletic honors and career accomplishments, whatever... You know, 'Ed Smith Scores Hole-in-One' or "Linda Jones is Club Champ.'"

So soon Hank was churning out milestone and trophy front pages. He gave Therese one for over her counter reading, "Rainbow Voted World's Greatest Café!" Rex got a 'Cairo Chronicle' front page for his ice cream shop proclaiming, "Cleopatra Declares Rum Raisin Her Favorite Flavor; Sales Soar"

And that gave Therese yet another idea.

♣ ♣ ♣

After mulling it over for a few days, she walked up the block to the newspaper office and tried it out on Hank.

"Listen," she said. "You are so good at creating these fictitious front pages, how about branching out into actual historical events, before there were any newspapers, or any mass media at all? Print souvenir-type pages as if a newspaper reporter had actually been there.

"I can see the headlines now: 'Huge Meteor Wipes Out Dinosaurs.' 'Little David Slays Mighty Goliath.' 'Noah's Ark Ties Up Ashore; All Safe.'"

Hank beamed.

"It's a natural!" he said, warming to the idea, trying out a few of his own: "'China Building Wall to Keep Illegals Out' and 'Trojans Fall for Giant-Horse Hoax!'

"Thank you! Why didn't I think of that? I could maybe sell multiple copies to schools and churches as study aids, or elsewhere just as jokes and conversation pieces!"

He kissed her on the cheek. She blushed. Therese left him to his fertile imagination.

Soon he was showing her test copies.

"Columbus Discovers Vast New Land!" The story below described his historical voyage in three little ships, how his crew nearly mutinied, how he returned with gold, spices and captives.

There were several sidebars to the main story.

In one, the Vikings in Scandinavia pooh-poohed Columbus' claim, pointing out that Leif Ericson had done the same thing centuries before, and demanded an investigation.

In another, under the headline "Indigenous and Indignant," the chiefs of several Native American nations laughed at the claim.

"What do you mean, 'discovered'? said Shaking Leaf, an Iroquois. "We've been here the whole time."

Hank's bogus papers began to sell much better than the real thing, as souvenirs and framed wall "art."

He began advertising them nationwide.

"Egypt Erects Strange 3-Sided Structure," was one.

"What's Going on at Stonehenge?"

"King Tut Entombed With Great Fanfare"

"'So Long,' Moses Tells Egyptians"

"Igluk Invites Clan to Gallery Showing of His Cave Paintings"

That last was accompanied by a review in the "Neanderthal *News*":

"Igluk's stick drawing of the hunter pursuing a deer with his bow and arrow bursts with life and energy," it said. "Minimal, candid, frank and brutal, the image flows effortlessly along the purity of its cave-wall canvas. The fleeing deer evokes pain, fear and suffering, yet the work as a whole balances the delicacy of life while asking us to think about our own values and the need to get in touch with our feelings."

Hank was perhaps most proud of his edition on the Crucifixion, complete with a crude drawing of the proceedings, which did not endear him to some of the local churches.

"I have to tell you I did that one while looking back over my shoulder," he told Therese. "I was expecting to be hit by a bolt of lightning at any minute. And now I find that some church schools are using it as a teaching aid."

There were four stories on the page, each authored by a different reporter – Matthew, Mark, Luke and John. One was an interview with Pontius Pilate, another briefly described the transgressions of the two thieves who also were crucified that day, there was a recitation of Jesus' own "crimes," and then a description of burial plans.

And three days later, a special-edition bulletin: "EXTRA! EXTRA!!"

Hank was so giddy with his newfound success that he branched out into tabloid journalism spoofs:

"Inside Caesar and Cleopatra's Love Nest!"

"Spartacus Comes Out of the Closet"

"Juliet Was Pregnant! Did Romeo Know?"

"Adam and Eve Evicted; She's Out Shopping for Clothes"

Hank now was so busy and having so much fun putting out bogus newspapers that his real newspaper and printing businesses were still being neglected. What had started as a kind but deceitful gesture to ease the final days of Maybelle Hunnicutt, a friend, had become a publishing conglomerate.

Nobody was keeping the books. Bills still were going unpaid. Everybody knew the *Herald* accounts were a shambles.

This time the note Therese found at the bottom of the jar said there was money for Hank to help right the ship, if he agreed to hire a new editor, a bookkeeper and a bill collector.

And there was more. A sizable and anonymous donation to the Alzheimer's Foundation in Maybelle Hunnicutt's name.

Another to an international center studying the possibility of extra-terrestrial life, in memory of Victor Fabyak.

And others to Billy Flynn's old fire department, to a plumbers' union, a ballet corps, and a wildlife art group, each in honor of other neighborhood figures honored with one of Hank's bogus front pages.

Chapter 5

The Comedian Cleric

Over at St. Sebastian's, Father Dunne was in trouble with the bishop again. Stiff, strait-laced, conservative parishioners were complaining once more, this time because he had told a story from the pulpit about a nervous young minister who invited everyone to the conception after the wedding ceremony.

Father Dunne's relationship with the bishop was closer than he would have liked, mostly due to complaints about his refreshing sermons and what some saw as a scandalous sense of humor.

But almost everybody except the bishop loved Father Marcus Aurelius Dunne, because he seemed to project a beam of light, humor, laughter and goodwill whenever he approached.

One morning, Therese had her back to the door but knew without turning that it was Father Dunne, stopping for his daily peach cobbler and coffee after Mass, when a voice said, "Did you hear about the pirate who wanted to sign on as a crewman aboard Noah's Arrrrrgk?"

Ready as always to trade barbs with the popular priest, she fired back, "Another pirate story? What's it going to cost me this time? A buck an ear?"

Father Dunne roared. The best part of his day, so often taken up with deathbed visits, funerals and sordid confessions at St. Sebastian's, was his morning break at the Rainbow Café and his continuing but usually futile effort to match wits and puns with Therese.

His illustrious name was bestowed by his father, a professor of history at the state university, a specialist in the Roman Empire, who named his four sons after Roman emperors.

Marcus' siblings were Augustus, Vespasian and Hadrian, and his long-suffering mother, having lost the battle to have a voice in the process, was at least grateful that her husband passed over Caligula, Nero and Caracalla.

Father Dunne proclaimed that he was proud to bear the name, since one of Marcus Aurelius' most quoted sayings was, "Life is short. Do not forget about the most important things in our life, living for other people and doing good for them." And he lived the maxim every day.

Short and portly with mischief in his smile and mirth in his eyes, Father Dunne was yet another in the beguiling group of regulars who made Therese's life a joy, whose eccentricities spurred her to bound out of bed in the morning, eager to open the doors and welcome what a new day might bring. For Therese, he was one of her leprechauns come to life, an essential ingredient that made her café friends a family, with both its fun times and trials.

Father Dunne was the archetype of her regulars – an intriguing backstory, and always ready to help someone in need, pitch in for a worthy cause, make somebody feel better, ease someone's pain or sorrow, make the world a better place. But he had something special that some of the others did not: a lively sense of humor, constantly on display, as much a part of him as his nose.

"The most precious of all the senses God gave us is the sense of humor," he often said with a twinkle. "It helps us bear all of the other crap he sends us."

If anyone ever looked the part, it was Father Dunne. He was approaching 60, and with a perfect halo-circle of graying red hair just above the temples, and his otherwise gleaming bald head, he could have passed for a medieval monk.

"I can picture you sitting at a high bench, spectacles perched on the end of your nose, illuminating ancient religious texts," Therese kidded him.

For church functions and socials, he often did play the part, donning a rope-belted brown robe and sandals and circulating among the crowd with a tray, offering parishioners what he claimed were goat-cheese tarts and flagons of mead.

He looked so much like St. Anthony of Padua, patron saint of lost items, that his friends at the café thought it hilarious that he sometimes spent hours looking for things he misplaced.

He once spent the better part of a day looking for his glasses, which eventually turned up in the choir loft, and was a frequent passenger in the golf carts driven by parking garage attendants as they circled the aisles from floor to floor with patrons who couldn't remember where they parked.

The other café regulars looked up to Father Dunne, not only for his stature as a priest but because he often was the first to seize on one of the rainbow jar's charitable causes and help push it through to success. If he thought the situation worthy enough, he might even give the project a plug from the pulpit during his Sunday sermon.

Joshua Clarver, the trashman troubadour and the choir director at his Baptist church, became one of Father Dunne's closest friends, and bristled at those who might think they made an odd couple.

"Too many wars have been fought over religion," he told them. "We're all trying to get to the same place, so what's the problem?"

♣ ♣ ♣

Father Dunne had confided to Therese that he was worried about the fate of his parish. Besides an alarming recent rumor that the whole neighborhood was under the microscope of the city's planners, the aging church was in need of major repairs, if not replacement.

Worse, in an era of declining attendance, there was rampant speculation that St. Sebastian's might be the next casualty of consolidation, which might mean a transfer for Father Dunne.

"What a loss that would be," Therese sighed. "The church, Father Dunne, are central pillars in this part of town."

His reputation also rested in large part on his legendary sermons. People from other parishes across the city sometimes bolted on Sunday to St. Sebastian's instead, just to hear for themselves if what others said about Father Dunne was true. Methodists and Presbyterians often were seen in attendance. Even an atheist or two stopped by occasionally to check him out.

They were not disappointed.

His sermons were always larded with amusing anecdotes. One of his favorite seasonal stories was a tale about a Christmas pageant at St. Sebastian's where first-graders re-enacted the Nativity scene. When the Three

Miniature Wise Men appeared, bearing gifts, St. Joseph met them at the manger.

"What did you bring?" St. Joseph asked of one of them. "I brought gold," was the answer.

"And what did you bring? He asked of the second. "I brought myrrh."

"And you?" he inquired of the last little boy. "What did you bring?"

And the miniature wise man, struggling with a word he was not familiar with, improvised: "Here, Frank sent this."

His congregation never seemed to tire of his stories, even though they had heard them countless times. Many of them were old classics, but he always gave them a local twist:

"Father Dunne, this is agent Jones from the IRS. Just checking. Did Arthur Ferguson give $10,000 to the parish?"

"No, but he will."

And: "One day I told little Lexie that I heard that God had seen fit to send her little twin brothers. And Lexie said, 'Yes Father, and He knows where the money's coming from, too. I heard my daddy say so.'"

He had a story about little Gracie, who said she loved to sing the song about the Christmas sheep.

"What do you mean, Christmas sheep?"

"You know, Fleece Navidad."

Father Dunne was revered among the young people of his parish, especially high schoolers and students at the nearby football-crazy college, whose incoming freshman class was treated every fall to his legendary "pigskin sermon." Sophomores, upper classmen and alumni laughed along with them every year as he launched his description of an epic game between the Saints and the Sinners.

"Coach God has fielded an awesome offense this year," he began. "In the backfield are the four evangelists, Matthew, Mark, Luke and John. Up front are the Seven Graces: Temperance and Virtue are the tight ends, and the linemen are Patience, Knowledge, Reverence, Charity and Love. The defense is just as formidable.

"Now, you might think that no one would have a chance against this mighty lineup, but Coach Satan should not be underestimated. Look at the defensive front line Satan has put together, the Seven Deadly Sins: Envy, Gluttony, Pride, Lust, Sloth, Greed and Anger, buttressed by a defensive backfield made up of Profanity, Adultery, Murder and Dishonesty..."

Then he slipped into a play-by-play description, broadcast style, of the action: "Matthew takes the handoff, he's trying to sweep left on an end-around play that looks a lot like the old Green Bay Packers power sweep, but coming up fast to stop him with blood in their eyes are Pride and Anger. Oh, my! They've been taken out with brutal blocks by the archangels Michael and Gabriel. What a collision! Oh-oh, that must have hurt! Pride is very slow in getting up..."

♣ ♣ ♣

Father Dunne was a quite unusual cleric in other respects.

He was a frequent visitor at the nearby children's hospital, bringing laughter and joy to the sober surroundings.

Dressed as a clown, with a huge foam stethoscope around his neck, he examined the young patients in their beds, claiming that he could hear organ music, or that their spleen was "expleening" their problems to him.

He always got giggles when he placed the stethoscope on their calf and made mooing sounds, or told them that since their body didn't seem to be living correctly at the moment, it must be the fault of their 'liver' and he'd have to adjust it. Or he'd produce a huge foam wrench and announce that he had found the problem: "Your belly button just needs to be tightened, or otherwise your butt might fall off."

Therese was one of the few who knew that Father Dunne once worked a gig as a stand-up comic at a sleazy comedy club across town, a stint that ended abruptly when the bishop got wind of it.

"Oh, my. How did that come about?"

"Well, the club owner was a former parishioner, and he apparently enjoyed my sermons so much that he asked if I'd be interested in subbing a couple of nights for one of his regulars. He billed me as 'The Minister of Mirth.'

"And I thought, what the hell, excuse the expression, why not? But I warned him that this would not be his usual fare – no dirty jokes, smutty double entendres, lewd comedy, but good, wholesome humor with a Christian twist. I looked on it as sort of 'mission outreach' -- maybe it would do his shady patrons some good.

"I had only one stipulation. I did not want to follow or precede a pole dancer."

Therese had to smother a giggle.

"And how did that go?" she said, lips pressed tightly together to hide a grin. She was having a hard time picturing this, a standup priest-comic trying to entertain boisterous, profane drinkers in a smoke-filled room while half-naked dancers looked on from the wings.

"Well, I lasted one night before the diocese got a complaint and that was the end of that. The bishop did not share my liberal interpretation of 'Christian outreach.'"

"I'm not surprised. What was your routine like?"

"A lot of it was stuff I just carried over from sermons. Purely innocent fun like the shepherd who trained his sheep to do ewe-turns, and 'Did you know that Jesus drove a Christler,' or how God must have been a capitalist because of all the prophet sharing, dumb stuff like that."

Therese struggled to keep the creeping grimace from overtaking her face. She was beginning to see another reason why his nightclub comedy career was short-lived --

Father Dunne, unlike Samson in the Bible, was not exactly bringing down the house.

"One of my favorites was the little boy who was very anxious about being late for school and kept saying, 'Please God, don't let me be late. Please God, don't let me be late.' Then he tripped and fell, and on picking himself up and dusting off his clothes, looked heavenward and said, 'But don't shove me either.'

"But I did get a pretty good laugh from the old one about the guy in heaven who visited his baseball-crazy friend in a dream and told him that he had good news and bad news. The good news was that there was indeed baseball in heaven. The bad news was that he was scheduled to pitch on Sunday.

"I had one about a minister in Washington who answered a phone call from a concerned woman who wanted to know if the president was going to be there on Sunday. The priest told her, 'No, but God will be.'"

Therese did manage a grin at that one.

"I also liked to talk about all those people who suddenly get religion toward the end of their lives. 'Cramming for the finals, are we?' I liked to say.

"And then there was the little boy who was quite proud that he had mastered the Golden Rule. I asked him to explain it. 'Well, Father, it says, 'Do one to others as they would do one to you.'

"Kids were a great source of material. Like the little boy who told me he couldn't wait to grow up and become an adulterer."

Father Dunne said he was ready to give it up anyway because he was running out of material.

"I had some other stuff I could use, but I didn't think it was appropriate, for example, to be telling the one about the minister who mixed up the announcement about the taffy pull at St. Peter's."

Therese did not hear or abide many off-color jokes, but even she could pretty much figure out what that one was all about.

"The club and I reached a mutually agreeable parting of the ways," Father Dunne said, "prompted, of course by the bishop's distaste for my side gig. Apparently the clientele there was not ready to accept salvation via comedy anyway. They could not quite reconcile the image of a man of the cloth being followed on the stage by a stripper who was not wearing any cloth at all."

But Father Dunne's sense of humor could not protect him from some mounting problems.

Like most everyone else in the Rainbow Café neighborhood, he heard the rumors that the growing city was looking for space to house its expanding facilities, and that his and nearby blocks were under scrutiny.

Equally distressing, he just recently had delivered some additional grim news to parishioners. Unless the parish could come up with its share of the money to repair or rebuild the aging church, the diocese said it would have to be abandoned and absorbed by another parish.

Parishioners steeled themselves for an announcement, wondering which would come first – condemnation of the block for a civic improvement, or the disappearance of the church anyway amid a financial crisis.

That was the bad news.

The good news followed soon thereafter. The Rainbow Café's patrons -- Protestant, Catholic, Jewish and Muslim alike -- inspired by an anonymous bequest through the donation jar, helped produce enough to put the church's own long-struggling building fund over the top.

The diocese was so impressed that it decided the new church would become the nexus for a new St. Sebastian parish that would now incorporate two other nearby endangered parishes.

"Well, what do you know?" Therese told Father Dunne. "How perfectly fitting. If there's going to be a miracle, why not do it for a church?"

Chapter 6

The Cupcake Lady

Neither of them knew it at the time, but they were about to launch a cupcake empire.

It all started when Harriet Harterton, another of Therese's regulars, brought a tray of her amazing cupcakes to an after-hours party celebrating the rescue of St. Sebastian church.

"Harriet, these are divine!" Therese exclaimed after a first bite. "They are heavenly! What's your secret?"

Harriet grinned shyly. She was used to getting compliments about her confections, but she was especially flattered by praise from Therese, who knew something herself about baking.

Therese was doubly impressed, because the cupcakes not only tasted heavenly but were themselves works of art. Harriet painstakingly embellished each one with colored frosting swirls and peaks, glitter, piping, sprinkles, colored balls, even edible butterflies, flowers and tiny animals.

Harriet could provide cupcakes, and cakes, too, in whatever color scheme you preferred – sports team colors, high school and college themes, flags of countries – for the cake itself, the frosting, or both.

"These are so pretty that it's a shame we have to eat them," Therese said. "They taste even better than they look."

Harriet, a retired tax accountant, was already a cupcake legend in her nearby apartment building. Her neighbors were used to answering a knock at the door and finding Harriet there, still in her apron, holding out a tray of her famous cupcakes.

She made regular cupcake rounds, especially when she got wind of a birthday in the building, or an anniversary, or unexpected company, or a party or a shower or tea. She was a regular visitor at the nearby police and fire stations, too. And sometimes she was at your door with her tray for no other reason than pure, unabashed neighborliness.

Harriet sold her tax practice eight years earlier when she reached 65. Her husband passed away three years ago, her son was overseas in a diplomatic post, and in her loneliness and melancholy turned to an old hobby, baking, for solace and for something to keep her occupied. She secretly harbored a dream – her own cupcake shop.

Few people knew it, and Harriet certainly didn't talk about it, but long ago she worked as a checkout clerk in a big supermarket chain. She was fired when the store discovered that she sometimes "overlooked" and failed to ring up all of the items on the belt, particularly if the customer appeared to be impoverished and on a limited income.

She got away with her own private welfare program for quite some time, but was brought down when management discovered that when the Rescue Mission people picked up their usual 13 turkeys for the Thanksgiving meal for residents, they somehow only paid for six.

"Harriet, we are not without heart and compassion; indeed, we gladly would have donated some turkeys, but this behavior is a little much," said the manager, struggling to suppress a smile.

But that was long ago, and did not prevent Harriet from succeeding later in several high-paying jobs with big accounting firms, and then her own practice. One employer told her they were quite aware of her "shady past" but chose to look on it as an endearing quality.

"What's in these?" Therese asked, holding up a cupcake and winking, knowing full well as a fellow baker that she probably would not get a full answer. She knew that many expert bakers, herself included, might tell you the basic ingredients, but seldom would reveal their secret process or mystery ingredient.

She remembered friends of her grandmother asking for her recipes, and then complaining when they did not turn out as well as hers. They always accused her of deliberately leaving something out.

"Oh, these are just something I whip together every now and then," Harriet said modestly.

Therese persuaded her to bring a tray to the café as an experiment, and added cupcakes to the dessert menu. The response was so enthusiastic that they became permanent.

Then, while walking through a nearby mall one day, Therese passed by several specialty bakeries. Her jaw dropped at some of the prices. A single cupcake was steep enough, but some "designer models" were priced at well over $100 for a dozen.

She bought one and tried it. It did not taste as good as Harriet's. It did not look as good either.

"My God, girl!" Therese said to herself. "You have to get out into the world more often. At these prices, pretty soon you'll need a bank loan to get a cup of coffee and a cupcake."

And this gave Therese an idea.

As a trial, she turned one of her booths over to Harriet, who set up shop there to take orders. Soon, customers who tried her menu cupcake were ordering by the dozens from her booth.

The traffic soon became too steady for a booth to accommodate. Rex Warnevar offered a temporary solution.

"I have an empty room I don't use," he told Therese. "It's a storage space now, but could be repurposed for a cupcake shop, with a separate entrance.

"Cupcakes and ice cream," he said, laughing. "A perfect combination, unless you're on a diet."

Harriet's new business soon outgrew those quarters as well. Once again, the sign on the Rainbow Café jar asked for some help, this time in setting up Harriet in her own shop. And once again, an anonymous note in the jar pushed the drive to the point where Harriet was able to move into an empty storefront nearby.

"We need a name," Therese said. "Something catchy, unique, descriptive."

That turned out to be harder than they thought.

"I give up," Harriet said when she stopped in at the café the next morning. "I spent the whole night researching names. You won't believe how many cupcake stores are out there. I can't use my own name because there's another Harriet out there somewhere doing the same thing. I tried a long list of common names, but struck out every time. I tried using unusual names, still no luck. Do you know that Hepzibah's Cupcakes, as well as Nefertiti, Hildegard, Hannelore, Dagmar and Gertrude are all taken?

"I'm learning that bakers are an extremely clever and creative bunch. There's even a John Dough out there somewhere, and a 'Let Them Eat Cupcakes.'"

"And a Nebuchadnezzar's Cupcakes, believe it or not. Maybe we should forget this. There are too many people in this business, some of them no doubt inclined to think of suing for infringement."

Therese tried to reassure her. "I'm sure we can come up with something. Yours are so different, so unique, so local, they will find a place."

"I even tried some ridiculous things," Harriet said, "thinking that people would see the humor in it. But no. I thought of Yummy's Non-toxic Cupcakes, but had to reconsider when it dawned on me that another Yummy's Cupcakes might be upset for implying that hers were toxic."

Therese laughed. "You're making too much of this. Let's brainstorm a bit."

But in the end they had to settle for something safe, not quite so catchy, unique or descriptive after all.

"Cupcake X," read the new neon sign blinking in the window.

Once settled in at her own digs, Harriet began to research how to expand her repertoire of designer cupcakes, experimenting beyond the traditional.

But there were problems.

She thought of baking cupcakes the size, shape and color of peaches and pears and bananas, and even a watermelon, to share for parties. She considered carrot-shaped cupcakes, onions, mushrooms, peppers, various other vegetables, but gave that up and had to agree with Therese: "I doubt few people will want to buy, much less eat, a cupcake that looks like an onion or a banana."

And all those unusual shapes meant she would need her own oddly-shaped baking molds and cups. "What do you even call something like that?" she said, laughing. "It's not really a 'cup' cake."

"It's really an actual cake," Therese said. "So why don't you just call them that?"

And thus Cupcake X expanded into imaginative designer cakes, as well. Harriet's fertile mind experimented with cakes in the shape of toasters, teapots, typewriters, tombstones, toboggans and even a Taj Mahal.

Soon she was taking special orders on these as well as other custom designs. Her line of cakes for people in the skilled trades became especially popular – wrenches, hammers, circuit breaker boxes, concrete blocks and paint cans. Sporting goods were another big hit – bowling balls and pins, footballs, pickleball racquets, billiard racks heaped with pool balls, baseball gloves, even cornhole bags.

She tackled just about anything. For Juval Platt she created an old-fashioned hand-crank adding machine. For Juval's protégé Paul Hagward, she made a chainsaw, which he displayed in the front window of his new shop; it brought her a lot of referrals. At a Rainbow Café party celebrating the opening of Luigi Costicello's landscape service, she even made a large cake in the shape of a push lawnmower.

"The handles were a special challenge," she told Therese. "I used a couple of sawed-off broomsticks and then frosted them."

One line of new models became exceptionally popular.

Rex Warnevar persuaded her to design some risqué shapes for stag parties and bridal showers, assuring her that they would become a sensation. He was right.

"They are among my best sellers," she told Therese, blushing. "I have to keep the samples out of sight under the counter. And shaping them is, ah, well, interesting."

"I can imagine the process," Therese said, giggling.

When the gang of regulars at the café got wind of her expanded line of merchandise, they suggested to Hank Lyson at the *Herald* that he print a new window sign for her Cupcake X shop.

"Ask about our XXX cupcakes," it said.

Harriet chose not to display it prominently. But she didn't need to. Anyone so inclined soon knew where to get cupcakes shaped like certain body parts.

But the old traditional standbys, creatively decorated, continued to be her best sellers.

One elderly gentleman, who became quite enamored of her, took his elaborate cupcake home and told Harriet that he kept it in a glass case on his mantel. "It's too pretty to eat," he said. "It belongs in a museum."

"Well, if you keep it in that case long enough, it will look and taste like other fossils," she said with a grin.

It was not long before Harriet's imaginative creations caught the attention of newspapers, TV crews and magazines. She became somewhat of a local celebrity, the host of her own local TV show, "The Cupcake Queen," and wrote a book.

But eventually it became too much for her to manage ("I'm in my seventies, I'm supposed to be retired, you know,") and sold out to a big bakery chain that paid her handsomely to retain the name and the use of her image, and then proceeded to franchise it.

One morning she came into the Rainbow Café and handed Therese a substantial check made out to her.

"I am forever grateful for what you and your customers and especially that magic jar have done for me," she said. "I am asking no questions, I don't want to know the secret, but I want you to see that this money goes somewhere to help somebody else who has a dream."

Therese smiled ruefully. "Well, that's the first time that has happened. Now what do I do? I don't know the secret, either."

After signing the check, she slipped it into the jar.

"Let's see who countersigns it, if anybody," she said, laughing.

It stayed there for two days and then was replaced by a small notecard bearing only a smiley-face emoji. Next to it was the check, shredded into tiny pieces.

By this time, the Rainbow Café regulars were well aware that something peculiar was going on, and began to wonder aloud at the counter about the anonymous benefactor who lived in a jar. But they backed away from more speculation when it became evident that Therese not only didn't seem to know any more than they did, but didn't want to talk about it, either.

Chapter 7

The Collectibles Shop

You could say that a leprechaun introduced Therese to Adeline Enders. Therese was on an errand and walking past her store, Adeline's Annex, three blocks from the cafe, when the little ceramic figure in the window caught her eye.

It was one she had never seen before, and she was something of an expert, since her own collection of leprechaun figures, frowning down at customers from that shelf at the Rainbow Café, numbered almost fifty now.

So Therese stopped in, and an instant friendship was created. Adeline had that effect on people, but then, so did Therese.

The shop was filled with figurines, dolls, music boxes, collector plates, teacups, crystal, Christmas villages and ornaments, a potpourri of knickknacks. It was the kind of place that required careful navigation through the aisles, lest you wind up going home with a damaged item you had not intended to purchase at all, which did not happen often because you wound up buying so many other items that Adeline said, "Oh, forget it."

"Can I help you?"

Adeline, petite, blond and still a beautiful woman in her 60s, came out from behind the counter carrying a blown-glass figurine of a praying mantis. She set it down gingerly amid a collection of similar glass and crystal figurines – dragonflies, bees, even aphids and spiders.

"Some people love these things," she said, wrinkling her nose. "Me, I like insects as long as they stay outside. Except butterflies and ladybugs. They bring good luck. They are always welcome."

"I'd like to see that leprechaun in the window," Therese said, smiling. "You have a lovely shop. I don't get out much, but even so, I can't believe I've never been in here."

Adeline fetched the item, and Therese inspected it carefully. "I've never seen this artist before. I'll take it."

"It's a new line I've added. They come direct from Ireland. You collect leprechauns?"

Therese told her the whole story – her Irish heritage, the rainbows, the Rainbow Café and her collection of the mythical and mischievous little creatures.

"I was Adeline O'Callahan before I met my husband," Adeline said, beaming. "I must surely stop by."

And she did. Often. Adeline became another of Therese's 'regulars,' a fast friend with a shared ethnic background and a common interest in the problems of running a small business. And in leprechauns. Adeline became her best source for adding to her collection of imaginary little people. It now was evident where some of her customers were finding the figurines they contributed to her collection.

Adeline, too, had an unusual back story, one leading from social work to the world of collectibles. She had a degree in sociology, and had worked in a county social welfare office for a time, until she met Alec Enders, a reporter with the big nearby metro daily newspaper.

"Well, you know how that goes," she said. "Sometimes you just have to follow your heart."

Therese nodded, but grudgingly. Following hers had not worked out so well.

Adeline and Alec had a son, and they settled into a happy suburban life. When the boy, now a missionary in South America, started school, she needed something to fill her newfound time. One day she saw an ad in the local paper by a woman selling collector plates – porcelain plates beautifully adorned with artwork.

She bought one, then another, then another, even though the woman who delivered them to the house was dour, cold and abrupt.

Alec met her on several of her visits.

"She has the personality of a turnip," he told Adeline. "If she can do this, then surely you could do it much better. Why not consider something like this yourself?"

Adeline mulled it over for a few weeks, and then the decision was made easier when she learned her sales contact was leaving the business.

"Surprise!" Alec said.

And it set her off on a remarkable journey. What started as a hobby became a new career.

Starting with several hundred dollars in figurines and collector plates, financed through a credit card, she began by placing a few ads in national publications aimed at collectors. It started slowly, a figurine sale here, another collector plate shipped there, all by mail order run out of her house. Within a year the house was overflowing with inventory.

"We have to do something about this," Alec sputtered, surveying a basement rec room that had become a stock room. The pool table was buried under merchandise soon to be sold and replaced with more. The bar in the corner that he had so painstakingly built could not be accessed anymore without moving twelve cartons of collectibles.

So she moved the business into a small retail space in town. In another year she was moving into larger quarters in a shopping center a block away. Then she had to move again. What had started with $200 in merchandise was now a one-woman combined mail order and retail colossus with annual sales of more than $1 million.

"This is absolutely remarkable," Alec said, awed by the accomplishments of his amazing wife. "After all, you are not selling furniture, or appliances, or automobiles. You are selling little stuff."

With the Internet, a whole new world of opportunity opened up for her. She attracted customers from all over the world. She started a newsletter to stay in touch with all of them and the circulation had recently reached 10,000. She had to take on some help.

It was a business, like Therese's, built on the strength of one woman's personality.

Alec, by now an editor at his paper, came by after work to help with back-office chores like bookkeeping, advertising, mailings and inventory. He usually found her either waiting on customers or pounding away on her computer keyboard.

What are you doing?" he asked one day.

"Writing to a customer."

This was not usual. She spent long hours on the phone and writing e-mails and letters. Alec could see that she was on page three already with this one.

"How can you spend so much time writing letters and talking to customers? How do you get anything else done?"

"Never you mind. You worry about your newspaper and I'll worry about this."

He couldn't argue with her success. Somehow she managed all of it with one clerk-employee, a part time person, and another part-timer – her husband.

Her customers adored her. To many of them, she became a friend and counselor. Some days she spent more time on the phone or writing e-mails sympathizing with a distraught mom about her teenage son's sudden peculiar behavior, or counseling a troubled woman about her husband's failing health, than she did on business affairs.

For some of her long-distance friends, like Emma, a lonely, homebound elderly widow in Cleveland, who called her every day, she seemed to be her sole contact with the outside world.

Alex grumbled about this, too, then slinked away, admonished, when she replied, "You are not in charge here. I am. So go away."

Adeline told her remote customers like Emma chatty stories about the artwork they were buying or local news tidbits or about her own family and neighbors. They wrote back or called with long details about their own lives.

Anxious to tell others about their newfound friend and her charming shop, they spread the word, and now there were family chains across the country where aunts and uncles, grandparents, nieces and nephews plus their friends, were all eager customers on her swelling mailing list. Many of them, especially those who liked Christmas villages and other collectibles issued in a series, bought the entire series as soon as she notified them that it was available.

It was the same with customers who came into the store. Most of them soon became friends. Adeline's new friends brought their friends. They all brought their spouses and children and grandparents. Like Therese, Adeline was a magnet. People stuck to her.

Adeline became a major figure in the collectibles industry as sales reps spread the word about her flourishing little shop of whimsy. At trade shows and on buying trips, other shopkeepers whispered and pointed in her direction, and often came over to brush shoulders with this retailing celebrity or pick her brain on marketing techniques. She was always willing to share.

"You are a legend and an inspiration to those of us just starting out," said the new owner of Amedee's Collectibles in Louisville. "What's your secret?"

And her stock answer always was, "Be nice to people. Most of them are carrying silent burdens. Give them a place to set them down for a while."

She was so successful in a difficult, competitive business that several of the companies she bought inventory from were pressuring her to expand, offering to help her create a small chain of Adeline's Annex stores.

So because Adeline was such a force of nature, so self-reliant and unflappable, Therese was surprised to see her come into the café one day with a long face.

"The landlord is raising the rent. Again. This time it's unreasonable. He must think the sky's the limit. Maybe I have to move, or buy my own space, or take those guys up on their offer to help me go wider."

By now the patrons of the Rainbow Café were used to being solicited for worthy causes, but this was a little beyond their capacity.

But with the help of another anonymous note from the jar, Adeline was able to cover the increased rent for a couple of months while she decided on her next move.

As weeks passed, Adeline became less enamored of expanding the business.

"Times are changing," she told Therese. "The internet has drastically altered peoples' buying habits. The competition now is so intense that it's becoming a struggle. And Alec and I are not getting any younger. We're just going to try to hang on where we are for now. We might even consider selling to a big store out east that wants to expand across the country."

And then the decision was made much easier.

Late one day, Adeline noticed a handsome, graying, distinguished-looking man browsing among her display cases. He was in a tailored suit, looked quite professional, but was taking a long time, moving idly among the cases, glancing in her direction every now and then. She realized finally that he was just killing time, waiting until she was alone.

When a last customer finally left, she moved toward the door to light the "Closed" sign, and told him that she was sorry, but she was locking up for the day.

"That's all right," the man said. "If you are Adeline, I need to talk to you privately."

He introduced himself as William P. O'Farrall, an attorney with a prestigious law firm in Cleveland.

"I represent the estate of Emma Parneloff," he said.

Adeline gasped. That's why she had not heard from her friend Emma for a while, why nobody answered the phone of the elderly, homebound widow.

"It seems," O'Farrall continued, "that Mrs. Parneloff has left to you a substantial portion of her assets, specifically, two million dollars. I am here to carry out her wishes. I need to have you sign some things." He pulled some papers from his briefcase.

Adeline groped for a chair and sat down, numb.

"I don't know how much you know about Mrs. Parneloff," the attorney continued, "but she was the heir to a considerable estate left to her by her husband, who was a pioneer in the early days of internet retail commerce.

"She has a son, a missionary who has taken a vow of poverty, of course, so most of her fortune will go to several charitable trusts she created over the years, mainly to aid the missions. But you were identified in her will as a dear friend who helped see her through some difficult times."

Adeline was stunned, speechless for a few moments. Then she told O'Farrall about her long friendship with Emma, a long-distance relationship that had grown into something that both of them cherished.

"In today's vernacular, I guess you could say we were Besties."

Her foremost concern now was for her friend.

"Did she die peacefully?"

"Oh, yes. A short illness. I was with her. And she said, 'Make sure my dear friend Adeline knows.' So here I am."

♣ ♣ ♣

Adeline could not wait to share the news with Therese. She was waiting at the door when Therese opened up the café in the morning.

"This is hard to believe," Therese said. "Did you see this coming?"

"Oh, no. I knew she had money, but nothing like this. She talked now and then about her son and her favorite charities, and I just assumed it would all go to them."

Then Adeline unloaded her own bombshell.

"Listen, Therese, I know you must have something to do with the wonderful things that are happening through that donations jar, even though you deny it, but even if you don't, you must have a way of contacting whomever or whatever is behind it."

She looked for some reaction from Therese, but got only a blank look and a slow, back-and-forth sideways shake of her head.

"No matter. I just want you to know that Alec and I have discussed things thoroughly. We are going to sell, at a good price, and also because of Emma, we will be comfortable now for the rest of our lives. We want to add a million dollars to whatever beautiful causes the jar sees fit to promote next. This will also repay the financial help we got in being able to stay in the store."

It was Therese's turn to be stunned. She struggled to get her head around the potential ramifications of Adeline's gesture.

Later, as she arranged with Juval Platt to park the money temporarily in the bank and in safe investments, Therese wondered how to initiate a two-way communication with the jar.

"How else?" said Juval, laughing, whose bank had become the financial conduit for dispensing some of the Rainbow pot's many blessings. "Through a note, of course." He reminded her of his own two-way exchange with the jar, when it bailed him out of his risky private loan venture.

Therese thought it peculiar yet heartening to hear the jar being referred to as if were an actual living, breathing thing.

She left in the jar a short, penciled note explaining the new influx of available funds. She was disappointed the next morning when she found it was still there. But then she noticed that it now bore two smiley-face emojis.

Chapter 8

The Veteran

Therese met Jeremy Cooperton when she found him sleeping in the doorway of the Rainbow Café when she opened up one cold morning.

She roused him, brought him inside, sobered him up with six cups of coffee and the first real breakfast he'd had in months, and sent him upstairs to her apartment to shower and clean up. Then she gave him a job as a dishwasher.

Made presentable, Jeremy, 73, was a handsome six-footer with a square jaw, a shock of long, graying hair in a ponytail, and a slight limp. Therese could see pain and anguish in his eyes, but also kindness and empathy.

Jeremy had lived a tough life. Abandoned as an infant on the doorstep of a police station, he grew up in an orphanage that later was in the headlines for stories of staff abuse to children. He was adopted as a teen by a miliary couple who gave him the only home, and love, that he ever knew. He became especially close to his adoptive father, an Army officer, and when he died in Vietnam, it was another blow from which he never quite recovered.

There was a short but successful career as a salesman, a brief marriage and two daughters, but much of his later life had been spent in a haze of alcohol and drugs. Now he was living on the streets, estranged from his daughters, bouncing from one part-time job to another. He might have died if Therese hadn't found him in the doorway first.

Jeremy wouldn't talk much about his past life. He sometimes asked for an hour or two off, usually on slow days, and was quite reticent about what he did with it. When he returned, his trousers often bore dirt and grass stains.

She asked him about it.

"I was visiting some very special people," is all he would say.

Concerned, Therese followed him at a discreet distance one day, and to her surprise found him at the St. Sebastian cemetery, adjacent to the church. He was wandering among the graves, stopping here and there to kneel before one, making notes in a little book he carried. Before moving on to another, he placed a hand on the headstone and bowed his head.

She tried to remain hidden, but as she turned to leave, he caught sight of her.

"So now you know," he said.

"I'm sorry for trailing you," she said, "but I was worried if you're alright."

"I'm OK," he said. "It's some other people you should be worried about. The ingrates, the people who disrespect our country and its flag and its veterans, especially the obliviot celebrities, ignorant kids and celebrities who think it's OK to kneel while the national anthem is played."

He gestured toward the tombstones.

"Well, I'm making it a personal campaign to find every veteran's grave here, kneel instead in *gratitude,* and also find out something about him or her, maybe a birthday or date of death."

Therese looked puzzled.

"Then I send any next of kin I can find a note like this."

He showed her a card with a veteran's name on it, branch of service, date of death, and a message: "Even though I didn't know him, I want you to know that I visited his grave today. He is not forgotten."

At the bottom was his own name, nothing more.

"What a remarkable thing you are doing," she said, "bringing such consolation and comfort to families that have suffered such a loss."

She hugged him fiercely.

"How do you find them, the families I mean, the kin?"

"It's not hard. Parish records, cemetery records, obituaries. Helpful websites. Government agencies. And the tombstones usually have birth and death dates, at least the years. The old custodian, Ezra Prufong, used to help me, he knew everything about this place and everybody here."

Therese was blown away by this one-man campaign of gratitude and recognition. When he confided that he was paying for the cards, research and postage himself, she resolved to give him a raise.

When she left, looking back, he was kneeling before another grave.

♣ ♣ ♣

Therese learned more about Jeremy when a scruffy, bearded man in threadbare military fatigues showed up looking for him. He was about Jeremy's age, and looked as if they had gone through the same trials of life together.

"I'm Tom," he said. "I heard my friend Jeremy is here. Is that right?"

When Jeremy emerged from the kitchen, the two exchanged smiles and fist bumps.

"How you been, man? We've been looking for you for two weeks."

The two became friends in a homeless shelter. Tom was a vagabond, a wanderer; he hitchhiked around the country, rode the rails, lived in hobo camps. Soon he would move on to another shelter.

"I don't like to be tied down," he said. "I like the wide-open spaces, where I can live a real life, a real adventure. Maybe I'll write a book some day. Like the old song says, 'Don't Fence Me In.'"

But before he moved on he wanted to locate his old friend.

"Jeremy one day just wandered off," Tom told Therese, "and the word was out on the street to be on the lookout for him."

Another friend apparently had seen him wandering aimlessly in the Rainbow Café neighborhood. Jeremy had spent more than one night in doorways.

After that, Tom came around often to the café to see Jeremy, who now was staying nights in a rehabilitation center sponsored by St. Sebastian's. One day Therese caught Tom alone, and pumped him for more information about Jeremy's background and story.

"Nobody knows much about him," Tom said. "He didn't say much. It seems he had a successful career at one point. Before his life fell apart, he apparently had been in Vietnam."

That would explain a lot, Therese thought to herself.

"He did talk a lot about his adoptive dad, his hero, got very emotional about it. He had this obsession, this reverence, for anybody who served in the armed forces. He was pretty vague about his own hitch. I don't think he saw much action, but over the years he apparently had heard a lot of stories from veterans like me about guys they had served with and how some of them died. He would pump them for all the information he could get – addresses, names.

"Then he would track down these families and write letters to them. He would tell them that he should have written long ago, but had some personal problems, and that he wanted them to know now that he had been with their son, or boyfriend, or husband, whatever, when they died, and describe in some detail how they died heroically trying to save their comrades, or wiped out a sniper that had their squad pinned down, or maybe even single-handedly obliterated an artillery position. He'd sign it with just his first name."

Therese interrupted. "What a wonderful thing to do."

Tom blinked slowly, and looked at her with the saddest eyes she had ever seen.

"Not really. Trouble is, he just made this stuff up."

"What?!" Therese gasped and stared at Tom in disbelief. "He made it up?"

"Yeah. He had such a profound respect for veterans, he had such good intentions. But he was a fraud.

"He actually went to a family's house once, not too far from here. He asked me to go with him, for reinforcement, you know. He insisted I wear my old uniform, said he couldn't find his and it didn't fit anymore anyway.

"So he tells the family he knew the guy, spent the last moments with him after a deadly firefight, and that his last words were, 'Tell mom and dad I wanted them to be proud of me.' He even pressed into their hands a pocket-sized Bible, claimed it was found on him."

Tom's eyes were wet. Therese clutched a tissue.

"And that's not all of it," Tom continued. "He told them their son had died while protecting his friends, when in reality for all we know the guy had been cowering in fear back in a rice paddy somewhere. He was gambling that they had not heard a different story from someone else."

Therese breathed deeply and shivered in disapproval.

"I told him more than once, 'Jeremy, this is so dishonest, so dangerous, so cruel. What if they ever find out the truth?'

"And every time he'd say back to me, 'Well, what's wrong with what I'm doing? At a time like this, why not tell them something inspiring and uplifting, something they can carry with them forever, a beautiful legacy? Why not tell them something that will make them feel even a little bit better?"

♣ ♣ ♣

Therese learned from Tom that there was even more to the Jeremy Cooperton story, more than his war-story whoppers.

"Like I said, he was obsessive about veterans, going back to his adoration of his adoptive father. Sometimes he would roam airports and bus stations and train depots, and whenever he spotted a guy or gal in uniform he'd approach and press a $20 bill into their hand and say, 'Thank you soldier, have a good meal on me.'

"He had money from somewhere, he must have had a good job once, was quite secretive about it, maybe even had a trust fund from his parents. Plus, he worked all kinds of temporary jobs, but some days I'm sure he gave away more than he earned.

"He hitchhiked more than once to the Vietnam Memorial in Washington. Somehow he'd find the names of local families who'd never been there, whose sons and daughters names were engraved on the wall, borrow a photo from them, make a rubbing of the soldier's name, and then send them a beautifully framed remembrance souvenir -- the photo and the rubbing.

"He even started a small mail-order business doing this – all out of his own pocket – and then turned the whole thing over to a veterans' group after times got tougher for him. And wouldn't you know it, he didn't lose any money doing this. Grateful families sent him more than enough to cover his costs.

"Until just recently, he would scan the newspaper for obituaries of older servicemen and women, and then show up at the funeral home or service or gravesite in a fatigue jacket, just to add moral support to the family. If anybody asked, and sometimes they did, he would claim he had been in boot camp or stationed somewhere with the guy and describe him as an exemplary soldier.

"Like I said, he was obsessed.

"He carried a bugle with him – somewhere he had learned to play the bugle – and if other arrangements hadn't been made, he would volunteer to play 'Taps.' Have you ever heard 'Taps' played in a graveyard at twilight, the notes lingering mournfully over all those tombstones? It's chilling. It's unnerving."

Tom glanced wistfully at Therese, who was beginning to see Jeremy in a new light.

"What a story," she said. "There's only once piece missing. No, two pieces."

♣ ♣ ♣

She pried out of Jeremy what he knew about his estranged daughters, their names – Laura and Lynne – their last known locations, and tracked them down in Milwaukee.

After that last argument so many years ago, when he stalked out angrily after another confrontation over his drinking, they lost track of him. Over the years they searched, chasing down a lot of false leads, and had just about given up when Therese reached them.

"Oh my God," Lynne said. "We'll be there tomorrow."

Therese met them at the airport and filled them in as best she could on what she had heard about their father's missing years, how he had turned himself around and become so dedicated to veterans and their causes.

"That sounds so much like him," Laura said. "He admired his dad so much. I wish we had found him earlier. We tried everything..." Her voice trailed off.

Back at the café, Therese hid the girls in a back room.

"I have a surprise for you," she told Jeremy, leading him by the hand from the kitchen. When the middle-aged "girls" appeared, daughters and father fell sobbing into each other's arms.

Therese locked the door and turned the sign to "Closed."

"I'll be next door," she told Jeremy. "The place is yours for the morning."

♣ ♣ ♣

Rex was surprised to see her.

"You don't come over here very often."

"Hope you don't mind," Therese said. "I need to hang out here for a while."

Rex listened to Therese's story and then turned to look out the window. He was quiet for a few seconds and then turned to face her, his face red and angry.

"I'm sorry," he said. "But I was in the Marines, and he should be court-martialed or whatever the proper punishment is now for the lies he told."

"What?!"

"That is so cruel, so dishonest. Those families should know the truth. What if they pursue this, inquire into missing medals? Find out it's all bogus?"

Therese glared at him, anger rising in her throat.

"Well, apparently they didn't! You are such a by-the-book arsehole! You have no soul!"

She stalked out.

♣ ♣ ♣

Jeremy and his daughters made the most of the week they stayed.

He learned about their lives, their husbands and families and careers, and his grandchildren. He planned a trip to visit them, to elaborate on where he had been all those years, to catch up.

It was not to be.

When Jeremy died shortly thereafter, from the effects of long years of abusing his body, the girls agreed he should be buried among the veterans he so honored, and returned for the funeral.

Therese told them how Jeremy had spent his final days still helping veterans, organizing packing parties at St. Sebastian's, where parishioners and others prepared care packages to send to local servicemen serving at posts around the world.

Therese made sure each package contained coupons for free peach pies at the Rainbow Café, redeemable when they returned.

She described again for the girls how their father had straightened himself out, gave up the alcohol and drugs, "because I want my daughters to be proud of me."

Unlike some of Jeremy's tales, this one was the truth.

Tom was gone now, too, drifted on to another wide-open space somewhere, so she told them the tales that Tom had related to her, how Jeremy had brought so much comfort, even if dishonest, to so many families whose sons had also fought in Vietnam.

Laura and Lynne exchanged startled glances.

"What?" Therese said, alarmed. "What?"

Laura replied slowly, in a raspy voice.

"He was never in the military. He was 4-F. Probably drugs and alcohol. And OCD. He told me once he felt guilty that he had never served."

Therese thought Jeremy's story so touching that sometime later she put a new note on the jar asking for donations to erect a plaque to Jeremy, "Forever a Friend of Veterans," at the cemetery where he now rested with the people he so admired.

She wrote to his daughters, telling them that a Hank Lyson newspaper story about Jeremy's campaign had caught the imagination of the public.

Citizens began to turn out in droves on Memorial Day and Thanksgiving to kneel at the tombstones of veterans, in gratitude and respect. Media everywhere noticed, and Jeremy's crusade, propelled by veterans' organizations, soon was being emulated across the nation.

And she was able to tell them that thanks to the jar, and an anonymous donor, her cemetery plaque idea had been expanded into a large memorial sculpture of Jeremy, kneeling, hand on a headstone, and that a generously endowed Jeremy Cooperton Scholarship Fund was now open to children of local veterans.

In the days to come, Therese often recalled Jeremy and his story, and his creed: "Why not tell them something they can carry with them forever, a story of a beautiful legacy?"

"Beautiful lies," Therese reflected. "Jeremy would be astounded to see what has grown out of his dedication to veterans. This story is better than any of his whoppers."

Chapter 9

The Troubadour

You could hear Joshua Clarver coming from two blocks away. He had a glorious baritone voice, a vast repertoire of gospel, spiritual, folk and traditional songs, and was so content in his work that it made his clients smile. His work consisted of driving a cumbersome garbage truck down neighborhood streets and alleys, collecting trash.

It was heavy, hard work, but he had the physique for it. Joshua was 6-5, muscular, with huge hands that could conceal a baseball. He was about 55, Therese thought, a bald spot beginning to show on his scalp.

On this particular morning he was serenading his clients on Therese's block with "Swing Low, Sweet Chariot," and by the time he had reached the alley behind the Rainbow Café, was lamenting loudly that "Nobody Knows the Trouble I've Seen".

To nonbelievers who might object to his religious selections, he grinned good-naturedly and switched to "Nearer My God to Thee," implying that if they did not change their agnostic ways, they would wind up in a region even farther down than the Titanic.

Therese looked forward to his arrival. Sometimes he stopped for breakfast or lunch, usually on days when he forgot his lunch bucket. And sometimes he entertained her noontime crowd with a selection or two. Given the leprechaun environment, his choices usually tended toward Irish ballads like "Danny Boy" or "Galway Bay."

He also entertained Therese's regulars with stories about his many trash "finds," the keepers, the pristine items he kept. Most were commonplace items – toys, games, paintings, sporting goods, tools, furniture. But not all.

"I found an old roll-top desk on the curb, left there by the family of an old Bible-thumping firebrand politician who died. When a helper and I got it home, inside a hidden compartment we discovered a substantial porn collection.

"Another time, there was a bronzed toilet plunger and a plaque attached with some guy's name on it. I had to wonder what was going on there.

"I found a wedding photo album with some disgusting substance smeared on it. I could guess what that was all about.

"Another day I found one of those fancy funeral urns in a trash bin. It had a name on it, but when I tried to return the urn and the ashes to the family, they did not want them.

"Guess he did not quite qualify as a 'loved one.'"

Somewhere in his past, Joshua had received a pretty good education. He was literate, erudite, familiar with great music, art and literature, and the history of the town. He made no apologies for his career path choice.

"I'm independent, got my own business, I'm outside, doing essential work, get to meet some great people, the pay is OK, and I'm doing my bit to help save the planet," he liked to say. "Not a bad life. And the Greenies love me.

"You might even say I'm an urban anthropologist," he told Therese in a burst of dubious embellishment. "Or urban archeologist, maybe, sifting as I do through human customs, beliefs, diets and habits, exploring and sometimes preserving much of the city's flotsam and jetsam, a connoisseur, as it were, of useless or discarded objects."

Therese grinned. She thought that was a bit of a stretch, but admired him as one of those she liked to call "genuine human beings."

"He's one of those guys who's happy in his own skin, content with a job he loves, no pretense of trying to be someone he's not," Therese told Hank Lyson one day as they watched Joshua wheel a trash bin away while crooning *Dirty Old Town*, which had become his theme song. "If you offered him a better job, he probably wouldn't take it."

Joshua had endeared himself to the neighborhood in other ways. Therese and others called him the guardian angel of the streets.

A little boy had crawled head-first into a hole under a garden shed to hide from a playmate during a back yard game, and was trapped there. Neighbors gathered to try to help, and when Joshua heard the frantic screams of the mother, he drove up onto the lawn and into the back yard. He cautiously maneuvered the fork lift arms on the front of the truck until they were under the shed, then hoisted the structure high enough for the boy to scramble out.

He offered to pay for the damage to the lawn and shed, and the mother said, "Are you serious?"

He had saved another child in an intersection by bolting his truck through a stop sign and ramming a speeding car that surely would have hit her. The motorist sped away in his mangled vehicle, tail pipe dragging and a rear wheel wobbling, before anyone could get his license number.

"Well, there is some justice," Joshua said. "He's probably uninsured and is going to have to pay for that mess himself."

When he noticed a schoolyard bully extorting lunch money from a terrified little boy, he stopped the truck, confronted the bully, forced him to turn over the money plus his other ill-gotten gains from a morning's "work," and then turned it all over to the recess teacher.

Joshua was married, but everyone agreed that it was a very odd pairing. His wife, Chantelle, was a concert pianist who had won national and international competitions and now played with the city symphony.

Therese wanted to know how they met.

"I was in her block, singing some traditional gospel songs, and she was out on her lawn working in some flower beds," he said. "We struck up a conversation, we got to talking about music and our backgrounds, we both have roots in the South and in black churches. Turns out she is an expert in gospel and spiritual music, wrote a book about it, and well, one thing led to another.

"What a scene at our wedding. Some of my fellow 'sanitation engineers' formed an honor guard outside the church with their trucks while a string quartet contingent of her orchestra mates played 'Here Comes the Bride' inside. I think her relatives and friends were mortified, appalled. We even made the papers."

Therese could not help but laugh.

"How does she explain this to her friends?" Therese asked, regretting immediately what she had said. "I mean..." she stammered.

"It's OK," Joshua said. "I – we – get that all the time. People seem to expect that some day she's going to dump me, excuse the expression. We *are* sort of an odd couple, I suppose, but maybe not any more so than Oscar and Felix. Or vegetarians and carnivores, or extroverts and introverts."

He laughed at his own comparison.

Joshua's knowledge of art, music and literature sometimes served him well on his trash route.

"I found a painting leaning next to a trash bin," he told Therese one day. "I set it aside, looked it up and discovered that it was by an obscure Renaissance artist and worth something like $25,000. Next time I was on the block, I told a lady in the driveway what I had discovered and said I'd be bringing it back. When I did, she gave me $1,000, which I donated to a local arts fund."

Joshua once figured in a notorious incident that scandalized the city.

He detected a particularly repugnant odor in a dumpster, and discovered that it contained a human torso.

"I had to stop work while the cops searched every trash bin in the neighborhood, and then across the city," he recalled. "They were looking for the remainder of the remains, I guess."

The victim eventually was identified as a drug dealer who apparently had displeased someone higher up in his merchandise disbursement chain.

"Maybe I'm in the wrong business," he quipped at the time. "I should open a body shop."

Therese often slipped him a piece of peach pie out the back door to the alley when he didn't have time to stop in. He was always grateful and sometimes reciprocated with one of his found treasures. Indeed, he had provided the centerpiece for her collection of whimsical imaginary figurines.

"This is for you," he said one day, steering in a handcart bearing a life-size figure of a leprechaun, freshly banished, apparently, from someone's garden or yard.

"My word," Therese said. "Where in the world am I going to put that?"

"Wait, there's more," Joshua said, disappearing again out the back door. He returned with another, a leprechaun twin.

Therese put them both on display out front, near the door, with a "pot of gold" between them, a perfect complement to her rainbow theme. She was not concerned that they might obstruct traffic, considering that for a leprechaun, life-size is maybe three feet high.

"Why do people discard such playful things?" Joshua said. "I'll never know why they put stuff like that out with the trash."

Setting aside such items paid off several times. He found antique furniture, old advertising signs, sheet music and much more. Even an old Cracker Jack box that had never been opened fetched $100 at the auction house he brought it to. His garage was becoming so cluttered with such stuff that there was no room for his car anymore.

Joshua confided privately to Therese one day that the work was becoming too hard, with all of the bending and lifting, and that he might have to give it up for someone younger, stronger, maybe take on a partner, work fewer hours.

And Therese had an idea.

The Rainbow Café jar soon had another new sign: "Help Joshua Open His Antiques and Second-Hand Shop."

This time the note helped provide the financing Joshua needed to rent a small space nearby. His colleagues at the café collaborated to create a name for his new venture, one they thought would convey the idea that these were not just ordinary discards, but trash with a certain dash.

And so Joshua's Junque Shoppe was born. But he decided to keep his day job, too, for now.

The regulars also contributed significantly to Joshua's growing inventory. This was their chance to clean out their garages, basements and attics of unwanted but still usable items.

Hank Lyson gave him some old wood-block letterpress type. Juval Platt provided a crank-handle adding machine. Harriet Harterton kicked in a dozen antique cookie molds. Adeline Enders contributed her old vintage Underwood typewriter. Father Dunne found in the church basement an old wall-hung, two-piece telephone set.

Since for years he had been stashing away "items of potential interest," Joshua already was primed to open up shop with substantial inventory. There usually was a story behind each of them.

"Golf clubs," he said, glancing mischievously at Hank Lyson, a golfer. "Lots of golf clubs. Probably as many as you would find at the bottom of a typical golf course pond.

"Musical instruments. A tuba so banged up, probably by a hammer, that it was unplayable. Which probably was the whole intention.

"Old comic books, baseball cards. Every old guy's nightmare revisited, that his mom threw out his collection when he left for college,"

That brought a grimace from Juval Platt, remembering again his first experience with a financial reversal. He was certain that among the lost treasures of his youth was a Mickey Mantle rookie card that his dad had given him.

♣ ♣ ♣

Therese had just opened up one Sunday morning, anticipating the usual after-church crowd, when a handsome couple came through the door.

From a distance the man looked vaguely familiar, and then with a flash of recognition she exclaimed, "Joshua, is that you?!"

It was Joshua, trashman troubadour, in a suit and tie, and on his arm was a beautiful woman, stylishly dressed.

"Wow, Joshua, you clean up pretty nicely," Therese said. She had never seen him in anything other than his grubby, trash-truck work clothes. Joshua grinned sheepishly.

"One must always dress so as not to embarrass one's companion," he said. "I want you to meet my wife, Chantelle."

"I've heard so much about you," Therese said. "Joshua speaks of you with such admiration and respect."

"He'd better," Chantelle said, blushing and grinning. "And he talks about you like you were Sojourner Truth, Harriet Tubman, Wonder Woman and Florence Nightingale all rolled into one."

It was Therese's turn to blush.

"We're on our way to church," Joshua said, grinning and dusting off his lapels, "and I wanted to stop and run an idea past you.

"You and this tribe of eccentric characters who hang out here have done so much for me that now I want to do something for you."

Chantelle, beaming, clutched his arm.

"What would you think, if someday soon, the two of us did a concert for the folks in this wonderful neighborhood, who have done so much for me? I'm told I'm a pretty good singer, and Chantelle here, well, she has some chops on the piano."

"Chopsticks, too," Chantelle said, grinning.

Therese was flabbergasted. But only for a moment.

"That's a wonderful idea!" she said. "And so generous of you. Leave it to me. I'll set everything up."

As they moved to leave, Chantelle paused at the end of the counter.

"So this is the famous pot of gold at the Rainbow Café," she said.

She held the jar up to her ear, listening.

"It's like holding a seashell up to your ear," she said.

"Only instead of the ocean, I hear angels singing."

♣ ♣ ♣

At the high school five weeks later, Joshua and Chantelle took the stage in the auditorium before a full house.

Some were café regulars and neighborhood friends quite aware of the pair's abilities, but many had seen Therese's posters in windows around town and read Hank Lyson's story in the *Herald*.

They performed for an hour and a half, gospel and spirituals mixed in with popular tunes and folk music. Even some classical music and opera.

The evening ended with a standing ovation and an encore tribute to the neighborhood, "Dear Hearts and Gentle People," with the entire audience joining in on the rousing chorus.

Without asking their permission, Therese arranged to pass the hat, and a substantial sum, subsequently enhanced considerably by a note from the jar, was donated to the school for a music scholarship in the name of the two performers.

Word soon spread about the talented couple. Both began to enjoy their new sideline careers as entertainers.

Joshua was able to seriously consider giving up the trash route.

"As soon as I can find a buyer, it's time to recycle myself," he told Therese.

Chapter 10

The Leprechaun Band

The experience with Joshua and Chantelle reminded Therese of something she had been thinking for a long time.

"What this place needs is some music."

So that gave her an idea.

She knew Rex played the guitar. She could hear him occasionally, strumming in his back room on slow days. Hank Lyson worked his way through college partly by playing the fiddle in a country band. Few knew it, but Adeline Enders played the accordion as a youth in the heavily-Irish suburb she grew up in. She also could play a harmonica at the same time.

"You are a wonder," Therese told her at the first rehearsal. "Why am I not surprised?"

Joshua, of course, had a marvelous voice, and Chantelle was a piano virtuoso. The question was if they would be willing to transition, off and on, to a country music sound.

"We would love a change of pace," Joshua said.

"I miss my down-home roots," Chantelle added.

Father Dunne, never ceasing to amaze his friends with his overlapping talents, showed up, too.

"You know, back in my seminary days, I played a pretty mean banjo. I could do some licks on a washboard, too."

Then, sheepishly, he added, "Not that we did much partying." Winking at Therese, he added, "It was all to raise money for Christian charities, of course."

And when Juval Platt heard what was going on, he showed up at their first practice with a novel instrument none of them had seen before. It was called a stump fiddle, and consisted of a short pole with an assortment of noise-making devices attached to or hanging from it.

"Can't have a real country band without this," he said, pounding his strange "instrument-on-a-stick" on the floor.

Juval's home-made contraption, common in rural, farming and lumbering areas of the Upper Midwest, had not seen much use lately. He inherited his skill, and the stump fiddle, too, from his father. But in no way was it a fiddle. It was many instruments in one.

"My dad always said it was a country symphony, all by itself" Juval said, beaming.

Its central feature was a stick, three feet high or so, repurposed from a former life as a shovel or pitchfork handle or broomstick, Half of a tennis ball was fastened to the bottom as a cushion.

Attached to the stick were a pair of screen door springs stretched over two face-to-face pie tins, an old coffee can holding an assortment of nuts, bolts and beer bottle caps, a bicycle horn, a triangle, a cowbell, a block of wood, sleighbells, and a cymbal -- the lid from the coffee can, nailed loosely to the top of the stick. When the contraption was bounced on the floor in time with music, and its various elements struck with a drumstick, it set up an entertaining cacophony all by itself.

"I've led a sheltered life," Therese quipped. "I had no idea this thing existed, or could produce such sounds. Or maybe noise is a better word. It's percussion and string in one instrument. I hope it doesn't drive people away."

And so, after dismissing a brief thought that maybe she should reconsider the idea, a Rainbow Café band was born.

What to call it? There was no dearth of suggestions.

"How about "The Café Clutch?" Joshua said.

"Latte Da," offered Hank Lyons.

"Six Appetizers and an Entrée," suggested Harriet Harterton.

Among some others were the Rainbow Café Irregulars, Decaf Drips, Cuppa Cappuccino, Counter Culture, and The Coffeebean Counters. "Hills Brothers and Sisters" was turned down because of possible trademark complications; same for the Starbucks Seven. They finally settled on The Rainbow Leprechauns, which Therese thought was quite appropriate.

But they balked at Therese's idea that they should all look the part. Father Dunne, always willing to test the boundaries of decorum, diocesan and otherwise, was the only one who agreed to don a green frock coat and short pants, a fake red beard, a green top hat, and pointy shoes with gold buckles.

"You look like you're all set for Halloween," Therese said, laughing with the rest. "Or maybe St. Patrick's Day."

Thus costumed, Father Dunne became the emcee for the group. He had an ulterior motive – he was gambling that nobody would recognize him in his musical attire and therefore not be able to report him to the bishop.

The new septet, after several rehearsals, began to play outside the café on Saturday afternoons, entertaining shoppers at the weekend sidewalk sales, when the street was closed to vehicle traffic. Word spread, and soon they were accepting gigs at venues around town, including the Shamrock Bar and a place called Pickups and Pitchforks, a country music tavern just outside the city limits.

Therese backed them not only financially but logistically. She scheduled and managed their growing list of gigs, but exacted a promise first.

"I have first dibs on your talents," she said sternly. "I suspect I will need you here sometimes."

And the popularity of the Rainbow Leprechauns did begin to grow as word spread about the novel country band featuring not only the usual guitar and fiddle, but a trashman vocalist, a symphony musician on the piano, an elderly gift shop proprietor adept at both accordion and harmonica, a banker with a unique musical instrument that defied easy description, and an actual leprechaun on the banjo who doubled as the emcee.

It was not long before the septet faced a problem common to bands and combos everywhere.

One night a man showed up asking if he could join them for a number. He carried a tuba.

"They call me the Traveling Tubadour," he said earnestly. "I carry this around everywhere, just in case, you know..."

Rex turned him down gently.

"I'm sorry," he said, "but there's really no place for a tuba in our country band."

After the man turned away, disappointed, Rex told Therese that such offers were a common problem for all kinds of music groups.

"I heard of one classical string trio that was approached by a woman asking if she could join them with her bagpipes.

"Can you imagine?"

♣ ♣ ♣

When the jar coughed up money to pay for a trailer to haul the Leprechaun band's equipment around, speculation about the mystery "angel" heated up again.

Therese's customers, when she was out of earshot, guessed endlessly about the jar's anonymous benefactor and tried to make connections. It was hard to hide that once a "cause" was posted on the jar, significant things often started to happen.

Therese emptied the jar first thing every morning. It was an open jar, accessible to anyone, but she knew none of her patrons would do such a vile thing as steal from a worthy cause. But it also was open to anyone who wanted to drop in a note. The notes she found usually were concealed -- creased carefully, sometimes stapled, into the folds of a $10 bill.

Her regulars all knew their generous contributions to help bail out Hank Lyson's newspaper and print shop were not nearly enough. Someone was behind Harriet's new cupcake venture and Joshua's Junque Shop. They knew their jar donations were far short of being enough to finance the impressive Jeremy Cooperton memorial sculpture at the cemetery.

And when Father Dunne at St. Sebastian's added to the flames by announcing in the church bulletin that the cemetery had been blessed with an anonymous endowment in memory of Ezra Prufong, and again later when he revealed that the church itself had been spared a ruinous fate, they concluded that somebody with deep pockets must be behind it all.

"I need to invent a cause," quipped Rex Warnevar. "Then I need to die so I can see what might happen."

Therese avoided joining the speculation. She assumed that since her own terms had asked for secrecy, that rule applied to every jar note. Even so, she knew the jar's role in the café's philanthropic ventures was not much of a secret anymore; after all, customers knew a down payment that made it possible for her to purchase the café had to come from somewhere, and in retrospect, what could be more likely than the pot of gold at the end of the counter at the Rainbow Café?

"It's got to be you," Hank Lyson chided privately one day. "Who else could it be?"

Therese threw up her hands in irate denial.

"I have no idea. You know me. I don't have that kind of money. I'm just a shopkeeper. I try to keep a close watch on that jar, but I'm not out front here all of the time either. A lot of people come through here every day.

"Hey, I don't know why, but I am just the messenger."

Chapter 11

The Immigrant

Jean-Paul Stoquet, the Rainbow Café's assistant chef, maintenance man, and sometimes waiter, was more American than a lot of people who were native-born. Therese loved stories about successful, happy immigrants, and his family's tale was both remarkable and entertaining.

Jean-Paul, 64, thick black hair graying at the temples, but still as fit as a bodybuilder, was a true patriot, even fanatic. His father, Etienne, had filled him with wondrous stories about America, especially one he had lived himself, when he was a little boy – the liberation of Paris toward the end of World War II.

Etienne had been with his parents among a mob of tearful, cheering Parisians lining the Champs-Elysees as Free French forces, American and other Allied troops marched down the avenue before continuing their pursuit of the fleeing Nazis.

Etienne had caught one of the Hershey bars thrown to children from an American Jeep; he always insisted to his son that after years of Nazi occupation and deprivation, it was the best thing he had ever tasted.

He also had little regard for Gen. Charles DeGaulle, the French wartime leader-in-exile.

"He gave the Americans and the allies such little credit for the liberation of his country and Paris," he told his son. "Without the Americans and the others, we all might be speaking German today."

All of his life, Etienne had read and heard stories about America, from relatives and friends who visited or emigrated.

"To hear him tell it, the streets were paved with gold and money grew on trees," Jean-Paul remembered fondly. "For him, it truly was the land of opportunity. All the men were seven feet tall and handsome, the women were charming and beautiful, the kids smart and obedient. You could start with nothing and become a millionaire on your own merits. And he'd never even been there. All he knew was what he read and what other people told him.

"He had a somewhat exaggerated view, I guess, except for the land of opportunity thing.

"But as I got older I realized he was right. In this country there are no limits to opportunity and ambition. I think about all those people who came here from somewhere else, and yet are still free to be Irish or Polish or Jewish or whatever, and to practice their ancient customs and traditions and religions, and yet are proud to call themselves Americans, too. What a country.

"For many of them, especially the displaced, they can finally say, 'At last we have a country of our own – the promised land.'"

Therese needed little help in stoking her own fires of Americanism, so she liked to prod Jean-Paul for more of his stories.

One of his own best childhood memories was of standing on a beach with his family and others in France on a summer day in 1969, and staring at the sky. They were listening by radio to an unprecedented, unfathomable event – the American space ship Apollo 11 was about to land men on the moon. He recalled that when Neil Armstrong's unforgettable words, "That's one small step for a man..." came crackling through the ether, his family and friends erupted with cheers.

"They set off fireworks and partied all night," he said. "My father was so proud you would think he had been born in Milwaukee. On that day, we were all Americans!"

"I would love to go there some day," Etienne had confided often to his son. "I want to go to America, where they do these marvelous, incredible things." But because of family circumstances and the expense involved, he could never realize his dream.

Jean-Paul eventually did make it to America, was warmly welcomed, became a naturalized citizen, and raised a family. He was so proud of his accomplishment, which he ascribed to his father's dream and encouragement, that he told anyone and everyone who would listen how fortunate they were to have been born where they were. Customers at the Rainbow Café were bombarded daily with stories about his father, back in France, and about the wonders and influence of America.

"You should see it," he often recalled. "All over Europe, at public events, you find people singing along with John Denver's *Country Roads*. In English yet, some of them struggling to pronounce 'West Virginia' and 'mountain mama.'"

Working with the Chamber of Commerce and officials at city hall, he appointed himself the town's official greeter in welcoming new people, especially immigrants, to the neighborhood and America, just as he had been. They responded by giving him a quasi-official title – ambassador to newcomers.

He presented each immigrant with a uniquely American "Swag Bag" -- a welcome package consisting of an American flag to display, a pocket-size version of the Constitution, and a book relating a litany of American-immigrant success stories – Andrew Carnegie, Irving Berlin, Cary Grant, Albert Einstein, Bob Hope.

There were coupons from local merchants good for a hot dog and a baseball game and even a complimentary test drive in a Chevrolet. A coupon for a peach pie, courtesy of the Rainbow Café, substituted for the apple one in the familiar commercial.

Sometimes Jean-Paul's over-the-top ambassadorship and patriotism became embarrassing.

Every Flag Day, he decorated his house and yard like some people decorate for Christmas. Star-spangled bunting and colored lights festooned the house, American flags sprouted all over the lawn. On the porch, an animated life-size figure of Betsy Ross was busily sewing stars and stripes onto a piece of cloth.

An animated Thomas Jefferson figure recited passages from the Declaration of Independence out by the sidewalk, and on the roof, an animated display of the familiar painting of two Revolutionary War drummers and a fifer, complete with *Yankee Doodle* audio, marched along the roofline.

That was just the warmup.

Three weeks later, on the Fourth of July, the dress rehearsal behind him, Jean-Paul put up the lights again, with additional flourishes. Patrick Henry appeared beside Betsy Ross on the front porch, bellowing, "Give me liberty or give me death!" and Paul Revere, on a mechanized horse circling the lawn, shouted warnings that the British were coming.

Five doors down, Roger Pimby, an executive with a British import-export firm, was not as amused as his neighbors.

And every year on July 4, Jean-Paul paid for a spectacular fireworks display out over the nearby river.

"This is too much." his long-suffering wife protested to no avail. "We are going broke buying and maintaining and doing all this stuff. This place looks like Disney World, or the Las Vegas Strip on steroids."

Jean-Paul once made an attempt to leave the decorations up year-round, but neighbors complained vociferously that the blinking lights and animated voices were setting off burglar alarms, keeping them up too late, and upsetting their pets.

Jean-Paul first showed up at the Rainbow Café in answer to Therese's ad for a handyman. She decided she needed some help in caring for the aging building, especially after noticing that the musty odor in the basement seemed to be getting worse. From the top of the steps – she would not go down there if she could help it – she could see a small puddle of water on the floor.

Jean-Paul for years fixed problems for his neighbors – plumbing, electrical, roof leaks, drywall repair, painting. He retired recently as a bus driver for the city, and decided to hire himself out for odd jobs to supplement his pension and Social Security.

So far it had not been very lucrative, and that's why he found himself at Therese's doorstep.

Jean-Paul was a perfect fit for the cafe. Among his many talents, he had culinary skills, which satisfied another of Therese's needs ("A French chef!" she could boast somewhat misleadingly to customers). He also could wait on tables if necessary. It would be only part time at first, but Therese could see the arrangement becoming permanent if business continued to be as good as it had been. And he was a hard worker.

"You have more American traits than some people who were born here," she marveled one day, watching him move from one expertly completed job to another. As a first-generation American, he had drive, ambition, patriotism, generosity and kindness, and worked long hours, past quitting time, until the job was done.

But he had no sense of humor. None. Therese's stream of jokes, puns, stories and wisecracks landed on barren ground, brought no response.

The café regulars adopted him immediately as one of their own. They admired him for his uber-patriotism, and as proof of their affection, kidded him mercilessly about his background and his father "back in the 'Old Country.'" And they rode him constantly about his utter lack of a sense of humor.

"What's the matter?" said editor Hank Lyson. "Don't they allow a sense of humor where you come from?"

"You're not allowed to stay here if you don't have a sense of humor," quipped Father Dunne, an expert practitioner in the art himself. "If the authorities find out, you might be deported."

"I hear you can buy one on Amazon," Rex Warnevar added, with a wink in Therese's direction.

"Oh, leave him alone," she said. "What's wrong with you guys? You should be ashamed. He's a better American than some of you are."

Jean-Paul saw no humor or affection in any of this ribbing from his friends.

"They probably are jealous," Therese said, noting that Jean-Paul's chiseled good looks had set more than one female customer's heart aflutter. And she told him, "Listen: You should take this as a compliment. They would not be ribbing you unless they were quite fond of you. This is what Americans do."

On his third day on the job, following up on Therese's worry, he brought up some bad news from the basement.

"Water's getting in from somewhere. The leak seems to be behind a wall. I'll need my tools to get at it, and somebody to help me move some things around."

That would not be Therese. She had been down there only twice, once as an employee and again with a building inspector when she bought the place. On both occasions she was repulsed by spiders, cobwebs, sinister shadows, musty odors and the dark, dank dampness.

"I have nightmares about being trapped in that place," she said. "I would not be surprised to discover that werewolves and vampires and extraterrestrials live down there."

"Perhaps I could bring my son Jacques to help me," Jean-Paul said suddenly, smiling. "I am training him to be like me, how to do many jobs, perhaps become, how do you say it, a Jacques of all trades."

Therese was halfway back into the kitchen. She stopped, turned and glared at him, fists on her hips, shoulders hunched in mock astonishment.

"Wait a minute!" she said. "Did I hear right? Did you just make an actual joke?"

Therese sometimes found Jean-Paul staring wistfully out a window. She knew his aging father, at 86, was not well, and was on his mind constantly. He had not seen him for several years. On his last return visit, they met in Paris, and his father insisted they take a train down to Normandy.

Standing amid the row upon row of grave markers in the American Military Cemetery, Etienne wept.

"This is a holy place," he told his son. "I have been here many times. All these soldiers died to save the world from a madman. And they died in MY country."

Jean-Paul's stories about his father moved Therese, to the point where one day she said, "I have an idea."

The sign on the jar asked customers to help bring Etienne Stoquet to America for a visit, his first ever, and probably his last. The jar filled faster than usual, and then the fund was topped off in a few days by a new note.

Hank Lyson was impressed, and wrote a story for the paper. More contributions poured in.

"I'm not surprised," Therese said

Jean-Paul met his father in New York, where the first stop was the Statue of Liberty.

"You know, this was a gift from the people of France to the United States," Jean-Paul said.

"Oh, yes, I know. I am told that some of our ancestors, including my grandfather, a metalworker, helped build and shape it before its trip across the Atlantic."

The two then set off by bus for a grand tour of America. Washington, D.C. and its monuments. The Great Smokey Mountains. Florida and the Kennedy Space Center, then New Orleans, where Etienne did his best to haggle with a shopkeeper in Louisiana French and reminded everyone who would listen that the U.S. had bought the Louisiana territory from France.

Then it was on to Texas and Wyoming and cowboys. Then the Kansas and Nebraska prairies and amber waves of grain. The Great Lakes and the Upper Midwest of the Rainbow Café, where Therese and the regulars staged a party for the visitor so smitten with America.

The Leprechaun Band played its first gig there. They were pretty good with "America the Beautiful," stumbled a bit over the unfamiliar "LaMarseillaise," but finished strong with some popular country and folk songs, especially "Country Roads." Etienne sang along lustily to them all.

Next were the Grand Canyon, the purple mountain majesty of the Rockies and the Sierra Nevada, Yellowstone,

Yosemite, the Pacific northwest and the Pacific Ocean – from sea to shining sea.

Hank's newspaper story about the aging Frenchman who finally had realized his dream to come to America was picked up by the wire services and went viral, capturing the imagination of the public. TV networks loved the story, local stations along the route hyped the celebrity's arrival. At every stop, Etienne was showered with gifts and feted at dinners and luncheons. By the time the tour was over he had become an honorary citizen of 19 cities and towns.

Jean-Paul snapped photos all along the way for a family album. He especially prized the one of Etienne in the bleachers at Wrigley Field in Chicago, munching on a hot dog.

Etienne was overwhelmed. Just before Jean-Paul saw him off at the airport in Los Angeles, Etienne learned that Jean-Paul's congressman had succeeded in getting him a congressional citation as "a special friend of America."

Etienne hugged his son, kissing him on both cheeks.

"Thank you," he said. "This has been the best time of my life."

Then, glancing at passengers hurrying to make their connections, he added dolefully, "I guess it's time to go. *Au revoir.*"

Jean-Paul smiled sadly. It was not likely they would see each other again.

A woman rushing by, late for her gate, stopped abruptly when she recognized Etienne from all of the news coverage. Glancing at Jean-Paul, she picked up intuitively that this was a farewell.

She plucked the American flag pin from her own lapel and pinned it on his.

"Come back soon!" she said.

Etienne beamed. "What a country."

Chapter 12

The Ex

Well, hello there, Tessie!" Therese shuddered. It was a voice she knew all too well, a voice she had hoped she would never hear again.

She turned slowly from behind the counter, where she was putting the finishing touches on a pie, and there he was again.

Older, older beyond his years, balding prematurely, overweight, his once-handsome face beginning to sag into jowls.

Junior Tourneaux. Her ex-husband.

In high school, they were a cliché: Junior was the star quarterback, and she was the lead cheerleader. They married soon after graduation, intending to legitimize their surging teenage hormones.

It was a mistake. He turned out to be such a loser that she wondered later what had possessed her, what had enticed her to hitch her wagon to such an undependable, fickle, colossal dud. In her case, youth and inexperience probably were the answer to an old question: Why are some attractive, personable, bright women attracted to such zeroes, only to discover their mistake too late?

Junior turned out to be junior in every way: maturity, honesty, responsibility, morals. She never liked his name anyway.

"Everybody should have their own individual name," she told her father, "and not be perpetually in the shadow of someone else."

He declined his parents' offer to send him to college. Instead, he worked a series of nothing jobs, supplemented by Therese's meager income as a waitress, began to hang out with his street cronies, got into alcohol and drugs.

He ridiculed her dreams, her aspiration to run her own business some day. He made constant fun of her idealistic Americanism, laughed at her romanticism and what he felt was her naivete.

"The world ain't like that," he told her. "It ain't all sunshine and roses. There's a lot of bad stuff, out there, too."

He was living proof of that.

He insisted on calling her Tessie, a nickname she detested. Within a year, she discovered that he was cheating on her.

When he came home late again that last night, reeking of a scent that was not hers, the door was locked and his suitcase was out on the lawn, open, his clothes soaking up the rain.

He broke a window trying to get in, but found himself staring down the barrel of a .20-gauge shotgun, Therese's father on the other end of it.

That was the last time she saw him. Until now.

She took back her old name and set off in a new direction. Her father, after a long struggle with the church, succeeded in getting the marriage annulled.

♣ ♣ ♣

"What do you want now, your jerkship?"

"Now, now, Tessie, don't be like that, don't get upset. I just stopped by to say hello."

"Well, you've said it, so goodbye. Get the hell out of here! Don't let the door hit you in the ass on the way out."

Jean-Paul, in the kitchen, and Joshua, at the far end of the counter, her first customer of the morning, tensed at Therese's tone: They had never heard her raise her voice in anger, much less use even a mild profanity.

Joshua shifted silently to another stool, closing the distance between them, just in case. Jean-Paul appeared in the kitchen doorway, a long boning knife in his hand.

"Actually, I was wondering if you could help me out here a little," Junior said. "It took me awhile to find you. I heard from an old classmate of ours that you were here and doing pretty well."

He looked around the café admiringly, at the gleaming countertops, comfortable booths, the leprechaun collection, the rainbow painting.

The new cash register.

"What do you need now?" she hissed in a whisper, embarrassed that Jean-Paul and Joshua might be hearing their exchange. She shot him a look of such utter contempt that anybody with any self-respect would have slunk back out the door.

"Just a hundred or so, to help me get home. My dad died and I have to get there by tomorrow. I don't have anybody else to ask."

Junior didn't look much like he was grieving.

"I'm sorry to hear that. *He* was a nice man," she said in a voice that meant, 'How did someone like that sire such a piece of...'

She turned to the cash register, pulled out some bills, and slipped him $200, hoping Joshua and Jean-Paul did not see it. She kept some extra money under the cash drawer so she could cash personal checks for customers on occasion.

"Goodbye and good riddance," she said. "You know, I think of you often. It reminds me to take out the trash. This show's over, you know. Has been for a long time."

"I promise to never darken your door again," he said with a condescending sneer, bowed sarcastically, and left.

Therese, her face red, turned to face Joshua and Jean-Paul.

"My ex-husband. The biggest mistake of my life. I gave him $200 to get rid of him."

Joshua started to say something, but Therese cut him off.

"I don't want to talk about it."

♣ ♣ ♣

She hoped she had seen the last of him. But she knew it was a slim hope. She was right.

Two weeks later, Joshua, his trash truck idling in the alley, came bursting through the back door.

"Therese, you're not going to believe this!"

"What?"

"Your ex. He's up in the next block with one of those mobile street-food trucks, selling coffee and pastries!"

Therese felt the rage rising in her like molten lava in a volcano.

Ripping off her apron, she stormed out the door and headed up the street. Joshua followed at a distance. He didn't want to miss this.

She found Junior standing idly alongside his cart. He was not very busy.

"You used my money to go into competition with me!?" she shouted. A passerby paused briefly at the commotion and then hurried on.

"Well, I figured if you could make a go of it doing this, then I certainly could, too. Rented this rig for a week and thought I'd try it out."

His sneering contempt brought back so many horrid memories that she did something that was very out of character.

"You are such an asshole that I can't find a more fitting word. You are the reason God made the middle finger."

She flipped him one and stormed back down the street.

Joshua, watching from a discreet distance, shook a clenched fist and shouted, "Yes!"

♣ ♣ ♣

Junior did not fare too well in his new endeavor. Joshua stayed and watched for awhile and saw only one sale, one coffee. And that customer asked for his money back; the coffee was weak and tepid.

He heard another potential customer tell Junior he was in the wrong part of town.

"Nobody needs you when the Rainbow Café is just down the street," the elderly man said.

Junior reddened and gave him a finger of his own after he turned away.

A week later, when Joshua stopped at the back door of the café on his usual trash run, he found Therese just inside, sitting on a peach crate, wiping her eyes with her apron. Like all of her regular customers, he was quite protective toward her, as a vulnerable single woman in an often precarious business.

Joshua was old school, and not much concerned that some people might look on this attitude as sexist.

"What's the matter?"

"He came back, when nobody was out front. He helped himself to $400 from the cash register."

Joshua did not need to ask who "he" was. She looked so sad that he wanted to hug her.

"I will get you your money back," he said, emphatically, winking. "I have some influential friends in this business, as you probably know, people who frequently suffer from bad publicity, if you know what I mean."

On his next run a week later, he assured her that Junior the Jerk would not trouble her again.

"Oh, my, what have you done?" she said, alarmed.

"Oh, no, not that," he laughed. "Let's just say he has been enthusiastically encouraged to move his base of operations elsewhere and to not ever show his face around here again."

He handed her $400.

"He already spent two hundred of it. My friends and I decided to make up the difference for you."

This time it was she who wanted to hug him. So she did.

"And thank you to your friends, too. And no, I am not anxious to meet them."

Therese later learned that Junior's business, with a week's receipts of $5.75, ended as abruptly as it had begun.

Before the intervention by Joshua's "friends," her regulars, taking turns, had stationed themselves near Junior's cart, and whenever a potential customer approached, pulled them aside and whispered a warning.

"Botulism was a word I heard used quite frequently," said Hank Lyson, with an evil grin.

And as for endings, she also learned that the senior Mr. Tourneaux, said to be recently deceased, apparently had experienced the first resurrection in 2000 years.

Chapter 13

Bethlehem Street

The Rainbow Café's donation jar did not specialize exclusively in grand, sweeping, philanthropic causes like scholarships or church rescues or cemetery endowments. Sometimes it was just a neighborly gesture of kindness and friendship.

Such was the case with Molly and Mike Malone and their Christmas tradition.

At least it started as a small gesture.

"It just won't be the same this year," Molly confided to Therese over her morning coffee and oatmeal. "Maybe it won't be the same ever again. Michael just can't do it anymore."

Molly was one of her oldest and dearest friends in the neighborhood, going back to Therese's waitress days. She was in her 60s, gone totally gray, and at four-feet-six made Mike, a six-footer, look like a pro basketball player.

The day she opened her new café, Molly was the first one through the door, carrying a box containing 24 rainbow-themed coffee cups.

"A little housewarming – I mean café-warming gift," she said.

She and Mike were popular regulars. Whenever Joshua Clarver saw her coming through the door, he'd launch into a verse or two of the familiar Irish ballad.

Molly loved to be flattered with comparisons to the celebrated Molly Malone, but this day the strain of the situation was evident on her face. Fidgeting with her cup, she looked wistfully out the window, where a soft snowfall signaled the arrival of an early winter storm.

"He can't get up on a ladder anymore and he shouldn't be exerting himself like that anyway."

Michael Malone was a legend in his neighborhood. Every year for 40 years, his house at 3615 Bethlehem Street had been lit up like far more than a mere Christmas tree.

He began planning and updating in July, replacing bulbs, adding new lights and features, plotting a grid. These days it was taking him all of two weeks to prepare for the Big Reveal, the magic Friday after Thanksgiving, when the entire neighborhood gathered for the official local opening of the Bethlehem Street Christmas season.

At precisely 7 p.m. Mike flipped a switch, and his display flooded the street with a red-blue-green-yellow-white holiday glow.

Some lights twinkled. Some blinked on and off. Some just glowed quietly in the spirit of the season. There were lights around porch posts, around windows, lining the rooflines and sidewalk, swooping along the landscape bushes and coiled around tree trunks and branches. The windows of the Malone home glowed with the warm, inviting light of electrified candlesticks.

Decorative, animated figures filled the lawn – snowmen, carolers, a Nativity manger scene complete with Three Wise Men and the recorded lowing of cows and bleating sheep. There were angels, shepherds, and even a floodlight "star" concealed high in a tree, shining a heavenly light on it all.

And on the roof, an animated Santa unpacking a sleigh, one foot already in the chimney, while eight anxious reindeer pawed at the snowy roof. Underlying it all, a constant loop of soft Christmas carols from Mike's elaborate sound system.

Immigrant Jean-Paul Stoquet's neighborhood, with its flamboyant July Fourth/Flag Day panorama of lights and patriotism, was only a few blocks away.

"Good thing you don't both do your thing at the same time," Therese told Molly, laughing. "You might shut down the city's entire electrical grid."

When accompanied by a soft winter snowfall, the effect of Mike Malone's show was magical. The entire neighborhood basked in the glow of his creation. The effect was so overwhelming that most neighbors gave up trying to compete, although one year, two neighbors ganged up for a practical joke. George on one side spelled out in Christmas lights across his porch, "Me, Too," and on the other side, Fred's message read, "Ditto."

Others might put up a feeble wreath or a scruffy, tattered lawn angel, but the consensus seemed to be, "Why try to compete with THAT?"

One neighbor wondered if their little corner of the world might even be visible from outer space.

"Maybe we shouldn't be doing this," he quipped. "What if we're telling the aliens where we are?"

But Mike was 78 now, fragile and ailing from a lingering and as yet undiagnosed illness, so the news of his condition was devastating to the neighborhood.

"Mike is crushed," Molly said. "He has always put so much into this. He's thinking about hiring somebody to do it, but we just can't afford that. Not now."

Their son, Grady, and a grandson lived too far away to be of any help.

Therese was worried not only about Mike, but Molly, too. The strain, both physical and financial, of Mike's illness and the thought of having to announce the end of a long tradition, obviously had been weighing on her.

"What a shame," Therese said. "But I have an idea."

She sent Molly home with a fresh peach pie for Mike, and with a secret message she should pass on to the neighbors. Therese put a new sign on the Rainbow jar, but instead of asking for money, this one solicited volunteers to help save a neighborhood ritual.

On the Friday morning after Thanksgiving, seven regulars from the Rainbow Café showed up to help on Bethlehem Street. They joined eight homeowners from the 3600 block, and working from Mike's planning grid, strung lights, inflated lawn figures, erected displays and climbed ladders to restore Mike's vision of Christmas Present.

Here and there were a few new touches, such as the life-size Ebeneezer Scrooge frowning irritably from the front porch entry, and the Tiny Tim figure trying to make it up the steps on crutches. And a more modern addition: a cartoon grandmother being run over by a reindeer.

Molly had arranged to keep Mike away for most of the day, at a doctor's appointment and a shopping excursion. They arrived home just after dusk, too dark for Mike to see what had transpired while they were gone, or to notice or hear his neighbors and friends partying in the house and garage after a long day of exertion.

As they made their way slowly up the front sidewalk, Molly pushing Mike in a wheelchair, Therese emerged from the front door and came toward them.

"Welcome home," she said, as his friends materialized around her. She handed Mike the remote switch device.

He looked puzzled for a moment, until he caught sight of the strings of lights along the eaves. He beamed as the surprise dawned on him. Mike flipped the switch, and the house and yard exploded into a colorful and camera-friendly Christmas panorama, bathing the scene in light. Maybe it was not all quite as precise as Mike would have done it, but close enough.

Molly caught Therese's eye and mouthed her gratitude. "God bless you."

Mike died in the spring, and after the funeral a note appeared in the Rainbow Café jar announcing the formation and endowment of the Bethlehem Street Foundation in Mike's memory. It provided funds, if residents were willing to provide the labor, to maintain and update Mike's Christmas tradition.

At Christmas, not only did Mike's house look as impressive as it always had, but the neighbors took it up a notch, jumping in with their own decorations and displays. Fred and George, on either side of the Malone house, abandoned their "Ditto" and "Me, Too" pranks and joined in the effort.

The only house on the block not fully decorated was the vacant one for sale, but the neighbors dressed that one up, too.

The decoration fever spread to two adjoining blocks, where neighbors splashed their houses, too, in a blaze of twinkling color.

Word about the neighborhood with the spectacular Christmas displays spread. People from all over the city came to see Bethlehem Street as part of their own Christmas tradition. Television crews and newspaper photographers loved the event, and one year Mike Malone's Holiday Light Show made one of the national evening news shows.

Neighbors discovered that there was another built-in benefit to the new Bethlehem Street Foundation. After the usual expenses for replacement bulbs and displays, there always was enough money left to help pay everybody's December electricity bill.

♣ ♣ ♣

Lighting his house for Christmas was not Mike's only hobby. He had nearly finished restoring a 1953 Cadillac El Dorado, the family car he remembered fondly as a boy, intending eventually to pass it down to his son and grandson.

But Molly, faced with mounting medical and nursing care expenses for Mike, had been forced to sell it.

Then one morning, as Molly opened the living room blinds, there it was again, gleamingly restored, parked in the driveway.

A note, unsigned, taped to the steering wheel said, "Thank you for all the happy memories you have provided down through the years for our community and our neighborhood."

Chapter 14

Diplomaville

Cyrus Steelfarb, 73, was a modest man, but over many morning coffees, Therese pried out of the aging, successful novelist a remarkable story.

His writing career started as a boy of seven when, influenced no doubt by a raft of B-western movies and TV shows, he set out to recount the adventures of Lance, a wandering, laconic cowboy who was hired as sheriff to clean up a town dominated by an evil, scheming banker and a vile rancher, who were plotting to take over the spreads of neighboring ranchers because only they knew that there was a lode of gold underneath ripe to be mined.

Even then, Cyrus had a proclivity toward convoluted plots.

But after three short chapters, Cyrus tapped out his imagination and trapped his hero and his sweetheart, the local schoolmarm, in such an impossible, ludicrously inescapable quandary that he had to abandon the project. His schoolteacher father, smiling over his shoulder, counseled that his proposed solution ("With a mighty leap, Lance sprang out of the pit") was not going to cut it.

His plotting techniques, ability to plausibly extract heroes from their predicaments, and other writing skills improved over time. He went on to write for the school newspaper and then for the local paper, and might have stayed there, after his father died, were it not for a family friend who helped him go to college. He would not forget the gesture, which shaped the rest of his life.

After college he worked for several newspapers, then with a popular magazine, but found the work stifling and mundane. In his spare time he tried his hand again at fiction, his first love, this time not with westerns but by testing the world of other genres. But his attempt to become a famous romance novelist got off to a shaky start.

"I had read enough of them to figure I had the formula down pat," he told Therese one morning.

His first story involved a pretty young widow who inherits a seaside inn from her aunt, and soon she finds a hoard of old letters, photos and a diary in the attic, and the handsome guest who soon arrives helps her unravel the astounding family secrets they contain. They do not get along at first, but eventually patch things up and get married.

"I think that's been done before," Therese volunteered, refilling his cup.

"I tried again with a lonely bookstore owner with a mysterious past who finds a faded map between the pages of an old book, directing her to a remote area where a hunky young farmer helps her find a legendary buried treasure. They do not get along at first, but eventually patch things up and get married."

"No luck there, either?"

"Naw. So I try again with four feuding sisters who reunite at the funeral of their father to clean out the old homestead, and in an old trunk in the attic discover an alarming story about their prominent family's infamous, suppressed past.

"A studly young neighbor finds out, and threatens to sell the scandalous story to a newspaper, but the unmarried sister, who does not much care for him at first, pleads with him to relent and he does, and they patch things up and get married.

"Let me guess," Therese said. "Nope?"

"Then there was the one about the bridesmaid, the bride's sister, who's always been secretly in love with the groom, and things come to a head on wedding day when all is revealed, but the bride is not really disappointed because she's always had the hots for the young minister anyway and so now there are two weddings instead of one.

"Or how about the rising young corporate executive who meets and woos the beautiful daughter of the shoeshine guy on the street corner when he stops for a shine one day, but then his family disowns him for stepping beneath his class but when it is discovered that the shoeshine guy has millions in investments and owns several apartment buildings they change their minds but the son then tells them to buzz off because they are so shallow and selfish and such patrician, aristocratic phonies and he marries her anyway."

"I'm exhausted just listening to these involved plots," Therese said.

"I was sure I would connect with the one about the stud who returns to his hometown for a high school reunion and reconnects with the old flame who had jilted him, now the lonely librarian, but after a suitable interlude of renewed mutual hostility, they patch things up and get married.

"No dice?"

Cyrus said he gave up after a round of rejections for his convoluted story about the four siblings at another funeral who discover at the reading of the will that their father is leaving everything to the maid, with whom he sired two children that they didn't know about.

"Their dislike for the maid thaws when she proposes a compromise, which is torpedoed by the two new grasping children they didn't know about, who are influenced by the jealous butler, who is wooing the maid in an attempt to get a piece of the action. This time, things cannot be patched up.

"Oh, and there's an old murder to solve along the way, too, so it's sort of a time travel-romance-mystery."

"Whew!" Therese said with a straight face. "After all that, still no takers?"

"Zilch. So, left unfinished was the one about the four classmates at a high school reunion who compare their lives and discover that one owns a bookstore, one is restoring a historic hotel, one is reconnecting with her old boyfriend, and one, just when she is facing financial ruin and bankruptcy, finds an ancient letter written by Abraham Lincoln under the floorboards of the old house she bought to rehab.

"The stunningly handsome chap at the local historical society who she is not very fond of at first places an astronomical value on it and... Well, you know what happens next."

He told Therese that he was especially disappointed that none of these sold because he had carefully placed a cat in each of the plots.

"Your approach probably did not endear you to agents or other romance authors," Therese observed.

"Yes, I suppose not," Cyrus said. "It's hard to come up with anything new in the land of HEA – Happily Ever After."

So he turned instead in another direction, and created a popular series of medical novels for kids featuring Ash

Jones, a blind physician who diagnoses ailments and diseases through his extraordinarily acute sense of smell. Among the titles were *Scents and Scentsibilities*, *Arrivederci Aroma*, *The Shadow Nose*, *The Proboscis Probe,* even a coloring book, *Prissy Patty and the Chocolate Olfactory.*

"You're kidding," Therese said, marveling that a concept built around a nose could be such a hit.

"Kinda like the way a dog and other animals can sense or detect trouble, or illness, or earthquakes, even a human pregnancy," Cyrus said.

"Ah, the sweet smell of success," Therese quipped. "You could have called him Nostrildamus and he could also have smelled out the future."

"Laugh all you want," Cyrus said, "but the money was nothing to sniff at."

Cyrus described with delight how the first in the series featured Lance, a laconic spelunker who was trapped in an underground cave labyrinth with his sweetheart, the local schoolmarm. Dr. Jones descends into the abyss by rope, his nose determines that because of a slight earthquake the caves will be filled with toxic fumes within minutes, and springs Lance and his sweetheart from the pit, not by leaping but by finding a hidden route to the surface.

Cyrus laughed and glanced sideways at Therese.

"Sometimes it takes awhile to perfect a concept."

The royalties from the books poured in at such a rate, and were still coming because of a hit TV series based on the concept, that Cyrus was able to semi-retire and turn his attention to his earlier vow to "pay it back."

He returned to his old hometown and established a foundation aimed at providing scholarships for other needy, talented students who might not otherwise have a chance to attend college.

He immediately butted heads with the attractive high school principal, an "everybody gets a trophy" type, but he soon persuaded her that this might be quite impractical when it came to scholarships and preached the virtues of the merit system instead. She came around to his way of thinking.

"So much so that now she's my wife," he said. "She helps me run the foundation."

"Sounds to me like a good plot for a romance novel," Therese said.

Word spread about the scholarships, and the foundation was inundated with applications. They were awarded to talented people, not all of them young, who went on to become scientists, artists, doctors, engineers, architects and entertainers.

"There were a few failures, disappointments, too," Cyrus said. "There was an aspiring doctor who discovered she couldn't stand the sight of blood. And the would-be veterinarian allergic to animal hair. But we found places for them somewhere else in their chosen professions.

"And not everyone is suited for college anyway. We sent a lot of people to trade schools, too – you know, electricians, carpenters, plumbers – the so-called 'ordinary people' who really are the ones who keep the world functioning. But there was a big string attached – good grades or goodbye."

Beyond just scholarships, the foundation also sought out people who were mired in jobs far below their talents and ambition, folks with great potential who were vastly underemployed.

"I like to say that we are 'repurposing' people," Cyrus told Therese. "There was an underprivileged kid working in a supermarket as a bagger. He had a photographic memory, was brilliant with numbers and math. We sent him to school and he became a successful certified public accountant and then chief financial officer of a huge corporation.

"Another kid, autistic, was a brilliant chess player. We steered him to a school that specializes in helping autistic kids. Now he's a grand master and makes a good living writing books about chess, teaching and coaching others, speaking at seminars. Tournament winnings, too.

"And there are people who never really had a chance in life," Cyrus said. "We need to bring their 'lights' out into the open. People need to fulfill their destiny, be in the right job for them.

"I would seek out these people, and ask them, 'What would you rather be doing than this?' Bright young kids, stuck in nothing jobs. We would steer them to training – trade schools, community colleges, whatever.

"So many good things in life are left undone, so much talent unutilized, for lack of money or opportunity or a push, a friend or mentor like I had, to get the ball rolling.

"Well, it all just exploded from there. A lot of these people, whose talents might otherwise have been undiscovered and wasted, became quite successful, poured money back into the foundation, then their successful sons and daughters did the same, pretty soon it was a small industry in itself, almost out of control.

"We hope other people, other towns, across the county hear of this success story and set up their own funds. So someday maybe there will be no 'financial need' assistance or college loans anymore, because of common access to a great education, founded on the concepts of pay it forward, pay it back, pass it on.

"The woke universities should be worried. A new breed of student comes along that appreciates the old axiom about America being the land of opportunity and freedom and exceptionalism, where there are no limits to how far your ambition and merits can take you."

Cyrus told her he had a dream one night about one of the prominent colleges that had catered to America-haters, anthem-kneelers, anti-family feminists, and advocates of open borders and the welfare state, that now had become a trade school teaching ambitious kids how to become surveyors and tailors, barbers and beauticians.

"Revisionist professors were being laid off in droves," he said.

Therese laughed. "Your prejudices are showing."

Cyrus described how his foundation had become the largest "industry" in the town, the biggest employer. A manager and staff now handled the day-to-day details.

Families began flocking there because of the opportunities, other businesses and services followed, and soon it had a reputation as "The Scholarship Town."

The cylindrical tank on the local landmark, a water tower on a hill outside town, was repainted and remodeled to look like a human head with a graduation mortarboard on top. Lettering below said "Diplomaville."

Therese put up a sign on the Rainbow jar to encourage support for Cyrus' scholarship foundation, and within a week the mysterious jar pledged a substantial annual contribution.

Chapter 15

Crowvid

Not all of Therese's regulars were human. One of her particular, and peculiar favorites was a bird she named Crowvid.

He – at least she assumed it was a he -- became one of her regulars after she found it wounded in the back alley, hopping around with a broken wing, unable to fly. She took it to a veterinarian for repairs, found a cage for it, and then set it up in the back room while she nursed it back to health.

Crowvid got the same attention her other regulars received. He was fed, entertained, counseled and humored. From the vet, and her own reading on the topic, Therese learned that crows are quite remarkable creatures.

"They are super smart, can recognize faces," the vet said admiringly. "They can talk about you to other crows. They remember what you did, good or bad. They will hold a grudge. They can make and use crude tools to solve problems. They can reason, after a fashion."

Therese was impressed. "What do you mean, 'reason'?"

"Well, for example, like in that Aesop's Fable, they understand the concept of displacement. If there is water in a vessel and they can't reach it, they will drop stones into the container until the water rises to a level where they *can* reach it.

"They will leave nutshells on the road and then retrieve the pieces after they have been crushed by a vehicle. And they know to watch the red and green traffic lights to tell them when the coast is clear for retrieval."

"Amazing," Therese said, eyeing Crowvid with a new appreciation. "Maybe I will hire him to keep the books."

"And they can memorize the routine of restaurants, especially the trash days. They also are bandits, thieves. They like bright, shiny objects especially."

Therese looked at the crow again, this time in suspicion.

"That reminds me of an old joke," she said.

"Which is?"

"The crows post a sentinel in a tree while they gather around a juicy piece of roadkill. They feast for 20 minutes, but intermittently, because they have to scatter every time the sentinel warns that a car is coming.

"A huge semi comes barreling through and kills most of them.

"Why didn't you warn us?" the head crow cries.

"Because I don't 'know how to say 'truck'!"

"I should now charge you twice as much for this visit,' the vet said, laughing.

"Well, they'd like that story in Boston," Therese said.

Crowvid hung around in the back while his rehabilitation progressed. Therese released him from the cage now and then so he could test his wings.

After a month or so she realized it was time to release him back into the wild. Carrying him gingerly to the back door, she stepped out into the alley, and after looking around, opened her cupped hands.

Crowvid hesitated, looked up at her, then lifted off. He flew back and forth several times, testing his repaired equipment, then disappeared into a patch of trees. He emerged briefly, swooped down and buzzed her head, then vanished again.

The next day, Therese heard a pecking at the back door. Crowvid was there, dropped a child's cheap beaded bracelet from his beak, and flew off.

"My reward, my thank-you," she guessed, laughing to herself. "This is one smart bird. Polite, too."

After looking up and down the alley, she shouted, "Thank you!"

She began to leave restaurant leftover tidbits in a small bowl atop a post just outside the back door, same time every morning. She received more tokens of appreciation – a bright button, then a coin, a comb, a small dental floss pick.

Some mornings she could hear a fierce racket outside the door as Crowvid, she presumed, fought off other crows who wanted a piece of today's menu.

"Maybe that's why a group of them is called a murder of crows," she speculated.

The visits stopped for a time, and then one day Therese found a Rolex watch on the doorstep,

"Oh, my," she said. "This is too much."

She noticed two crows watching her intently from a nearby utility pole. She sensed that this was Crowvid's goodbye, that he might be entering a new partnership phase in his life.

"Well, at least his heart is in the right place." She waved at them, and shut the door.

Therese's guess was correct. The grounds manager at the golf course across the river knew where to return the Rolex.

Chapter 16

The 911 Operator

S amantha Broadland was alarmed at the tone of the concerned little voice at the end of the line. But she was trained to keep her cool in the most trying of circumstances.

"This is 911," she said soothingly. "What is your emergency?"

"My family is in trouble and needs help," the quavering little voice replied. Sam guessed he was 7 or 8, and was near tears.

"What kind of trouble?"

"My sister, Sarah, is supposed to be getting married and nothing's been done and my dad died and it's awful." The little boy was sobbing now.

Sam was well aware she should not be spending time on a non-emergency call, but it was a slow day so far. The boy had turned instinctively for help to a place he had been taught to trust in time of trouble.

"Where's your mom? Is she there?

"Yes, but she's still in bed and just cries most of the time."

"How about your sister? Is she there?"

"Sarah's at work. At the library."

"What's your name, honey?"

"Eddy."

"Well, Eddy, tell you what. I can't tie up this line for long, but if you will give me your sister's phone number, I will see what I can do to help."

She wrote down a name and number.

"Don't you worry, Eddy, we'll figure this out."

Sam, a pretty brunet in her mid-twenties, had been counseled many times not to get personally involved in the lives of callers. She had been working the 911 phones for five years now, after a rigorous training program, while also pursuing an advanced degree in psychology through night classes.

But this was different, she felt. This family obviously needed some help, too. How could she not do something?

When her shift was over, Sam called the number. After introducing herself she explained what happened. She could hear the hitch in Sarah's throat.

"Oh, my sweet little man. That poor little guy. He's been so traumatized by all of this. We all are."

Sam learned that the situation was even worse than Eddy had described. The owner of the hall where the reception was to have been held had mistakenly double-booked two weddings for the same day, and now, embarrassed, had to explain to Sarah that the other party booked first.

"Listen, can we meet somewhere?" Sam said. "I don't know what I can do, but maybe we can figure something out. I'd really like to help."

They agreed to meet at the Rainbow Café, which was a regular stop for Sam after a shift, and not that far from Sarah's house.

♣ ♣ ♣

Therese always loved to see Sam come through the door. Well-suited for her occupation, she was sunny and cheerful with a reassuring self-confidence that drew people to her. Unfortunately, when it came to men, she always seemed to draw the wrong kind, and at the moment was unattached again.

Sam always had stories about her day at work. Most of them were sad. Some of them were inspirational. Some even were funny. She often had to fight the feelings of depression and despair common among emergency responders working amid stress, chaos and tragedy.

This day she had a story about an elderly widow in a remote area who heard strange noises on her porch, and a window rattling. She was terrified that it was a burglar. When emergency responders got there, they discovered it wasn't a burglar, but a bear, helping itself to the blueberry pies she had set out on the porch to cool.

"Oh, my word," Therese said. "That poor woman."

Sam smiled ruefully. Sometimes the emergencies weren't so dire.

"The worst ones are those who don't quite get the concept, don't get the message, waste our time."

She told Therese of people, usually older adults, who called to complain about children taking shortcuts across their lawn, or others angered by able-bodied people parking

145

in handicapped zones, and even of a resident of a high rise who called to complain that a golfer on a fairway far below did not repair his divots. Some people wanted help with recipes, or answers to *Jeopardy* questions.

"Then there are the ones we call Frequent Flyers," she added. "People who want us to tell them the time, or the weather. Or nutjobs who say snakes are coming up out of the toilets."

But the bulk of the work was rewarding, she conceded.

"We have talked people down from suicide attempts. We have sent help to break up domestic disputes. We have helped find lost toddlers and Alzheimer wanderers. We coach people on how to apply CPR."

She told Therese of a case where there at first appeared to be no one on the other end of the phone, but then she heard a muffled, emotional voice say, "I gave you all the money I had," and was able to send a nearby police unit in time to thwart a robbery.

But there were many tragedies. Especially vivid for Sam was the motorist whose car skidded into a deep ditch during a severe rainstorm. He was trapped in the car while the water rose around him.

"I don't want to hear the rest," Therese said.

Sam took a booth, and Therese realized she was meeting someone. After Sarah came in, between busying herself with other customers, she picked up snippets of their conversation.

"I really shouldn't be involved here," Sam told Sarah, "but Eddy was such a sweet little boy and so concerned about your wedding."

Sarah nodded her thanks, then explained amid a shower of tears how a tragic series of events had unfolded. Her father, a fireman, had been killed a month earlier while helping to rescue people from an explosion at an industrial plant. Her mother was a mess, barely able to hold it together, and the stress of also planning a wedding had overwhelmed her. Little Eddy, even more traumatized, was doing his best to try to keep the family ship afloat.

"I don't know what to do," Sarah cried. "My mother is immobilized, there have been few preparations, guests have been invited. I haven't even told her about the mix-up with the reception site."

Sarah looked off into the distance, shaking her head.

"I always wanted a big fancy wedding. Maybe we should just elope."

Sam took Sarah's hands in her own across the booth.

"We will figure this out," she said to her new friend.

The wedding date, approaching soon, could not be postponed: Sarah's fiancé was an officer in the Marine Corps and they were scheduled to leave for an overseas post.

The two discussed several options while they sipped tea and nibbled on two of Harriet's cupcakes.

Therese heard enough to know she had to intervene.

"I'm sorry to intrude," she said, coming over to the booth, "but I couldn't help overhearing some of this. If you don't mind a little improvisation, I have an idea."

"Remember all those referrals I sent you over the years?"

"How can I forget?" said her friend Melanie, on the other end of the phone. "You keep reminding me. Whatcha got this time?"

Therese didn't see Melanie often, but they stayed in touch. Melanie, an old high-school friend, was a wedding planner in another part of town.

"Say no more," Melanie said after hearing the story. "Lucky for you, I have an empty weekend on my calendar."

"Wedding Wizard," her business card said. The Wizard was used to handling last-minute complications. Three attendants had been hospitalized after a car wreck while on their way to a wedding, so she made do with the remaining two. A minister had a heart attack in mid-service. A caterer failed to show up. A suddenly-unhappy couple called it all off the day of the wedding.

Melanie jumped into the crisis immediately, fine-tuning, tweaking and following up on the church and ceremony arrangements already made. But even The Wizard was stumped and began to panic when she couldn't find a replacement venue for the reception.

"I don't know what to do," she said finally. "It's wedding season, and I have exhausted all of my contacts."

"I can help you there," Therese said. "You leave that part to me."

Sarah's wedding went off with the precision of a military maneuver, fittingly enough. The Wedding Wizard took care of everything. A church ceremony with hundreds of guests. Sarah wore a wedding gown that her grandmother had worn. Sarah's mother did her best to hold herself together.

Everyone who was at the reception that followed agreed that it was one of the most elegant if unusual the city had ever seen.

Therese sought permission to close off the street in front of the café for an evening, but was denied a permit by an overbearing, rules-obsessive clerk on grounds that it would disrupt traffic.

"Oh, no, we can't do that," the clerk protested, reciting a bureaucratic litany of rules, how exceptions only weakened the civic fabric, how the law must be followed at all costs. Therese stalked out and appealed to the mayor with Eddy's story.

She didn't have to go far. She found him at his regular noontime perch – a stool back at the Rainbow Café. Very soon, the apologetic, red-faced clerk appeared at her door with the permit.

With the help of Rex and Harriet, Therese set up a buffet and drinks line on the sidewalk. Guests line-danced to country tunes by the Leprechaun Band, playing from under an awning. Everyone prayed the good weather would hold.

After Therese spread the word, shopkeepers up and down the block produced folding chairs and tables to accommodate the guests. Harriet created a cake in the form of a church that was fit for a royal coronation: A tiny device embedded in the steeple played a loop of love songs.

Hank Lyson's bogus souvenir newspaper front page, "WEDDING OF THE CENTURY!" listed a long line of celebrities and royalty who supposedly were present, and also claimed that the president and the first lady sent their regrets because he had been called suddenly to put out a diplomatic fire somewhere.

The Rainbow Café was closed to its usual traffic, but wedding guests flowed in and out it and along the block all evening.

They were literally dancing in the streets that night.

"After what this family has been through, they deserve a break," Sam said.

Therese looked on approvingly.

"You have done such a sweet thing here," Melanie said. "You saved a dire situation."

"Hey, this is what Americans do," Therese replied.

Sam and Sarah had become great friends since their fateful meeting, so much so that Sam was one of the bridesmaids. And everyone noticed that the best man, a handsome emergency room physician, seemed to be hovering close to her throughout the day and evening.

Earlier, little Eddy had walked his sister down the aisle. He arrived at the service in the front seat of a fire truck, which also carried an honor guard of uniformed firemen from his father's unit. His mother and sister persuaded him, with some difficulty, not to wear the miniature uniform and helmet the firemen gave him. Instead, he was the second center of attention that day, in a miniature tux.

As Eddy handed her off to her soon-to-be-husband, impressive in his dress blues, the Marine dropped to a knee. "I am honored to become your brother-in-law, sir," he said, saluting. Eddy beamed.

Café patrons chipped in generously to the donation jar after Therese relabeled it once again, aiming to help with the wedding expenses.

This time the note in the jar said all of the expenses – flowers, limousines, tux and gown rentals, reception, even the honeymoon, would be picked up by an anonymous donor. Therese gave the money in the jar to Sarah, to add to a college fund she had established for her little brother.

The note also said that henceforth there would be an annual picnic in a nearby park in honor of 911 operators, EMT workers, paramedics, firemen, police officers and other First Responders.

A few days later, Therese was in the kitchen, her back to the door and wrist-deep in peaches, when she heard Sam call her name.

"Therese, you know somebody named Viola Johnson?"

Therese snapped around at the mention of a familiar and cherished name, and came to the door, wiping her hands on her apron.

"I've heard you talk about a woman with that name from your childhood. We answered a 911 call this morning about a fire, and one of the casualties was a Viola Johnson. I know that's a fairly common name, and it was on the other side of the city, but still…"

Therese's thoughts flew back to her childhood and the surrogate mom who did her best to set her on a straight life's path.

"Oh, my God! Is she all right?"

"Hospitalized, from smoke inhalation. Her daughter also was injured."

Therese lost touch with Viola over the years. Twice as an adult she went back to the old neighborhood looking for her, but was told by a neighbor she moved, and thought she now was living with her daughter somewhere. Therese thought she spotted Viola once in a shopping mall, but it turned out to be someone else.

Therese left the café in the hands of Jean-Paul and Harriet Harterer and set off for the hospital.

She found Viola and Tiffany talking to a doctor who was about to release them. They all had changed considerably over the years, but still recognized each other instantly. They embraced in a tearful reunion.

"How did you find me?" Viola said.

"I have a good friend with the 911 people. She made a connection. What will you do now? Where will you go?"

"I don't know. The house was damaged and it will take awhile to fix it up again. Tiffany was visiting but has to leave tomorrow to get back to her job in Texas."

Therese resolved that until then, her old friends would have everything they needed.

"You are coming home with me. You can stay in my apartment as long as you need to. We have a lot to catch up on."

At the café, Viola looked around approvingly, at the framed awards and glowing reviews on the walls, newspaper stories about "the Rainbow Café, the heart of the neighborhood," civic acknowledgements of the many philanthropic causes supported by its regulars, a citation recognizing Therese as "Citizen of the Year."

"See, I told you you'd be somebody some day. And here's something you'll appreciate. Remember the snotty little girl who wouldn't play with you because you were poor? She still lives around there. She's friendless, childless, and utterly alone."

Viola stayed for a few days, until she concluded that the house would still be livable while repairs went on around her.

"Come and see me," Viola said as she embraced her old friend again in farewell. "I owe you so much."

"No you don't," Therese replied, hugging her fiercely. "I still owe you, I will always owe you."

Chapter 17

The Neighbor

Rex Warnevar stopped in at the café one morning with a peace offering. He had been scarce ever since his run-in with Therese over Jeremy Cooperton and the exaggerated heroics of his "military friends." Her insult about having no soul still rang in his ears.

He set on the counter a large basket with a towel over it.

Therese sniffed, nose in the air, partly in her continuing disdain for Rex, partly because of the tantalizing aromas emanating from the basket.

"What is it?" she said haughtily.

He began to pull out plates and bowls, each with an aroma more tantalizing than the last, and put them on the counter: Fried catfish. Collard greens. Black-eyed peas. Cornbread. Sweet potato pie.

"Soul food," he said.

She couldn't help herself. She laughed.

"Apology accepted," she said, dipping a finger into the sweet potato pie.

♣ ♣ ♣

Therese's dislike of Rex went all the way back to her waitress days at the cafe.

She found him to be arrogant, condescending, sexist, annoying and rude. He teased her about the café's eccentric clientele and her obsession with peach pies and cobbler. They got off on the wrong foot his first day of ownership, when he came over from the ice cream shop next door to introduce himself and ask if anybody at the café knew anything about refrigerator coolers.

"Yes, I do," Therese said.

"You?" His tone was disbelief; this was a job for a man.

Her steely look of contempt should have told him that it would not be wise to pursue this tone of skepticism.

"What's the problem?"

"My cooler won't hold the right temperature. I know how to fix a lot of things, but refrigeration is not one of them."

"I'll come over in a minute and take a look."

After a brief inspection, she told him the cooler was too close to the wall, blocking the vents. She helped him pull it away some from the wall.

"For a woman, you seem to know a lot about this stuff."

Rex was a slow learner.

Disguising her irritation, and fighting a temptation to respond with a biting retort, at which she was quite proficient, she pointed out that the Rainbow Café, too, had coolers that misbehaved every so often.

154

"You'd better learn some of this 'stuff' too," she said calmly, looking around. "When you run a small business, especially an ice cream shop, you can't call a technician every time there's a minor problem.

"Although," she added helpfully, "if you do have to call one, you might find that it's going to be a woman who responds."

Red-faced, having been expertly returned to his place, Rex stammered an apology.

"I'm sorry," he said. "I'm sorta new at this. And I meant no disrespect. My mother was a woman, you know."

He grinned shyly, and she laughed.

"Although," she said, "These days you never know…"

After that shaky beginning, they became friends, but it was several weeks before Rex mustered the nerve to show his face again at the Rainbow Café.

After he did, and she became familiar with Rex's story, Therese began to change her mind.

His own ice cream shop had always been the pot of gold at the end of Rex Warnevar's imagined rainbow.

Not that he had any experience in the business. His expertise was in mechanics and technology. From an early age he was fascinated by machines of all kinds, what made them work, and not only what they looked like inside, but what the insides looked like inside.

He had been severely scolded at age six when he dismantled his mother's new vacuum cleaner, and had been introduced to the old-fashioned concept of spanking a year later when he tinkered with the engine in his father's prized and classic Ford Mustang. He followed that up by taking apart a new desktop computer and putting it back together, not exactly as it had arrived, but pretty close.

"I was not a model child," he confided to Therese, grinning. "With five kids, closely spaced, mom and dad were perpetually distracted."

He went to a technical high school, where he excelled in mechanical and engineering courses, and where his teachers pushed him toward college and a career in technology.

But as one of five children, he might have spent his life as an auto mechanic or appliance repairman were it not for a scholarship from Georgia Tech.

After college he served a stint in the Marines, then worked a variety of technical jobs, first for an auto manufacturer, then as a computer designer, then at a social media startup. But amid the tedium of the corporate world, the politics and the bureaucracy, he felt his talents were being smothered under a blanket of monotony.

"I changed jobs so many times that my friends began to call me Rambling Rex from Georgia Tech," he said,

In his spare time, he continued the tinkering and the experiments that had bedeviled his parents. In his home workshop, he toyed with a series of ideas, most of which never went anywhere for a variety of reasons.

His collapsible, disposable umbrella that fit in a purse failed miserably.

"Miniaturization difficulties, it was too fragile, and besides, I discovered there was not exactly a huge demand for such a thing."

He tried again with another stab at an old idea, a flying car.

"Once again, an intriguing idea that never got off the ground."

Then there was his new, revolutionary fabric that could change color, so a blouse could automatically color-coordinate with the skirt.

"'No, no, no!' my women friends scolded me," he told Therese. "What are you thinking? There goes our reason to shop for clothes."

And he thought he saw a need for a handy device to remove the pit from an avocado, but discovered too late that consumers resisted spending $24.95 to accomplish something they could quite easily perform without it.

"The pits are so big they hardly need any help," he said. "And besides, there already was a similar device out there, at $4.95."

But he did have some success with a quiet leaf blower that became an instant best-seller at hardware and home-improvement stores.

"Grateful customers were able to discard their earplugs, and, as with inventions such as wheels on suitcases, asked, 'What took so long?'"

And then, tinkering in his workshop one day, he discovered, by accident – as was the case with many other modern conveniences such as penicillin, potato chips and saccharin – a way to capture an incoming phone junk message, or a spam e-mail, and turn it back on itself, send it back to its origin, at a much higher intensity, so it would fry or corrupt the innards of the phone or computer it came from.

"This apparently was the answer the world had been waiting for," he told Therese. "The media was astounded, on noting the sales numbers, to discover the level of animosity, and even hatred, that had built up in the public mind over the years toward robo-callers, scammers, virus planters and hackers.

"If they had been paying attention, they wouldn't have been so astounded. They had no idea how angry, how furious people were at having to waste so much time changing passwords, securing their accounts, getting new credit cards, having to prove again and again who they were."

Therese nodded enthusiastically, having fought her own battles with online outlaws and telephone terrorists.

"Nuisance robocalls and texts began to vanish," Rex gloated. "No longer must you worry over that call saying your Social Security number has been compromised, or that there has been suspicious activity on your credit card, and if you will just give us the number, why, we will straighten this all out for you.

"Nevermore would you be pressured to buy that additional warranty on your new vacuum cleaner, which always made me wonder anyway why an additional warranty was even necessary unless the company itself had little confidence in its own product."

Rex described how scammers pretending to be a desperate friend or grandchild in need of money had to put the phone down when it began to sizzle and became too hot to hold. The caller from the contest you never heard of, inviting you to claim your prize, became alarmed and then terrified when his phone began to smoke.

When police detective Phil in Philadelphia got his third call in a week from a phony police association charity scam, he not only disabled their phone but arranged for a real police officer to show up at their door.

Likewise, junk e-mail traffic on major servers began to diminish alarmingly, and thankfully.

"The people promising you those hard-to-get premier seats at the concert of your very favorite singer wound up singing the blues over the cost of a new computer," Rex said. "All those people warning you about a virus infecting your computer discovered there now was a fatal worm infecting their own.

"Your package couldn't be delivered, another e-mail said, so if you'll just send us all of your personal information, we'll get it to you immediately. Now you could send them back some bogus personal information with an embedded code that would, well..."

Therese laughed. She was enjoying this immensely. Rex was providing a real service to humanity.

"And my favorite," Rex added, "all those deposed Nairobi princes who would reward me handsomely from the palace treasury if I would just send money to help them get to this country – I guess now they are stranded there permanently."

Rex eventually sold the licensing rights for his patent to a big corporation, but he continued to experiment with other means of harassing and foiling the scammers. When he was out, a sign on his door said, "Gone Phishing for Crooks."

"But I got out just in time," he told Therese. "These guys never sleep. I was hearing that they were working on a blocking device that would block my device."

So then he was 40, financially comfortable and looking for something else to do. He was not married, although there was a divorce in his past. His bachelor status was not from a lack of opportunities. He had turned to body-building as a hobby, and combined with his natural athletic good looks and engaging sense of humor, attracted any number of females.

But it also made him an easy target for gold-diggers and opportunists, and after several disappointing affairs, he decided to sit it out for awhile.

When he saw the for-sale ad for the ice cream shop next to Therese's Rainbow Café, he jumped at it.

His retirement dream had been to create an old-fashioned ice cream shop like the one in his neighborhood when he was growing up. The décor in the previous ice cream store in this location was all-white, the furniture was modernistic, the art reproductions on the walls were by Picasso, Jackson Pollock and Wassily Kandinsky.

"No wonder it didn't succeed," Rex said.

The "ice cream" there was a soft-serve product that customers dispensed out of a machine by manipulating levers, a product and process that true ice cream purists looked down upon in abject horror.

In Rex's shop, white-hatted servers, reminiscent of 1940s soda jerks, dispensed real ice cream into cups and cones – ice cream that had been churned to perfection by hand in the back room. Wise-cracking waitresses snapping their chewing gum brought your ice cream to the table, where you sat on wire-backed chairs.

If you were of a mind, you could order from the soda jerk a strawberry malt or a cherry Coke. The walls were decorated with old Norman Rockwell *Saturday Evening Post* covers, some of them showing kids and benevolent beat cops at a counter, smiling over their ice cream, or cute young couples, and old couples, too, sipping malts through entwined straws.

For seniors, it was not hard to picture Mickey Rooney and Judy Garland there, canoodling in a booth over a Tin Roof Sundae.

In the corner, a Wurlitzer jukebox, for a quarter, cranked out hits going back to the '40s and '50s. Some nights you might even find a few agile seniors doing the Charleston or jitterbug on the small dance floor, or teaching the steps to envious, watching teenagers.

Rex expended considerable thought on just the right name for his new enterprise, but encountered the same problem that bedeviled Harriet Harterton at her new cupcake shop: All the good names were already taken. He finally settled on "The Sundae Pew."

"I like the name," Therese said. "It should appeal especially to the after-church crowd. But aren't you concerned that it's too close to Sundae Phew?"

"Too late now, I guess," he said, picking up on her joke. "At first I wanted to call it Dairy Air."

"What does that mean?"

"You know, a pun on derriere. I envisioned a sign with the word and a dish of ice cream imprinted over somebody's backside."

"That won't appeal to people who already are weight-conscious," Therese said, playing along. "If nobody got the Dairy Air meaning, you might have tried Gluteus Maximus instead."

Rex laughed. He was beginning to appreciate her sense of humor. It matched his own. They were getting along much better after a shaky start.

"Gluteus Maximus. Wasn't he a Roman emperor?" he said.

♣ ♣ ♣

Rex told Therese that his success had allowed him to indulge another of his interests –helping regular, decent, idealistic people he had heard of who did nice things for other people.

"The scientists, the professors, the biggies, they all get their rewards for doing big things," he said. "Nobel prizes. Oscars. MVP awards. Huge trophies. But how about some recognition for the little people, the people who do nice things every day, the little people who do all those big little things? Not that they seek or even need any approval.

"These are the real people, the people who actually make the world go around. Laborers, factory workers, mechanics, farmers, clerks, cops, firemen, nurses, postmen, teachers, truck drivers, shopkeepers..."

He told her about a friend, a promising baseball player in the minors, who gave up his dream of the major leagues so that he could always be nearby to attend to his invalid wife.

"I got him a job in the front office of the local minor league baseball team. He didn't have to travel, he was back in the business he loved.

"I was on a country road somewhere one time, came across this guy standing beside a dilapidated old pickup truck, steam and smoke pouring out from under the hood. He was from a church, delivering meals to elderly rural folks and shut-ins. So I took him to town and bought him a new truck."

Therese grinned and clapped her hands in approval.

"What a great feeling you get from all of this," he said. "I felt like Elvis. Remember he sometimes bought cars for total strangers?"

♣ ♣ ♣

The admiration was becoming mutual, reinforced when Rex himself benefitted from the generosity and friendship of Therese and her regulars. Several of them helped her avert a catastrophe for Rex when he was out of town for a few days at a convention for confectioners.

"Is Rex around?" Molly Malone inquired one morning. "I need ice cream for a big party, but his door is locked. And his "closed" sign is not lit; he always leaves that on when he's gone."

Therese became concerned later that morning when Adeline Enders came by with the same anxious question and observation. Therese decided to check.

Early on, she and Rex had exchanged keys in anticipation of just such an emergency. On opening his door, she was hit with a draft of warm air, much warmer than healthy for an ice cream shop. On checking, she found that the power to his shop was out.

Worried, she checked his back room, where he kept stocks of ice cream not only for his own daily use but also for customer parties and special events. The containers stored in freezers there seemed to be OK for the moment, but she knew it wouldn't be long before a meltdown began.

She rushed back to the café for help. Adeline Enders, Joshua Clarver, Molly Malone, Hank Lyson and Jean-Paul were all there. She organized a "bucket brigade' of sorts, the six of them carrying bulk containers of ice cream back to her own shop, where she rearranged her freezer to make room.

After exploring the problem, Jean-Paul determined that the problem was beyond his help, and called a technician. Rex's coolers were humming again soon, and restocked.

"I have a small complaint," Rex said when he returned from his convention, confronting Therese over her counter. Winking knowingly at Jean-Paul, he said, "The ice cream cartons in my back room freezers are not organized anymore the way I left them. Do you know anything about this?"

"Oh, go fly a kite," Therese said. And then couldn't resist rubbing it in. "By the way, you might like to know that the tech guy we called to fix things was a stunning blonde who looked like a runway model."

Chapter 18

Moms and Pops

Her name was Adrienne and she often came into the Rainbow Café on Saturdays with her dad. She was 12, with bright blue eyes and freckles and a blond ponytail that spilled out the back of her baseball cap.

Therese and Adrienne became great friends after Adrienne and her dad moved into the neighborhood a year ago, and Therese was quite aware that Dave, the dad, was struggling to raise this precocious child by himself. The mother had disappeared long ago with a boyfriend, and her sporadic contacts with the child had eventually evaporated altogether.

"She's probably better off without her," Therese thought, then scolded herself briefly for even thinking such a thing. "That's a terrible thing to say, but I don't care. It's true."

They usually came into the café after her Little League games on Saturday mornings, and then stopped also at Rex's ice cream shop next door. Dave was doing his best, trying to fill her summer days with activities, but he was at a disadvantage when it came to girly things.

On this particular morning, Therese noticed that Adrienne was captivated by the activity going on next door, where a group of girls about Adrienne's age, accompanied by their moms, were trooping into Rex's shop.

"They do that every week," Therese said. "It's a moms-and-daughters club. First they stop at the tea shop down the street and then come over here for ice cream."

When she saw how wistfully Adrienne was looking at the group, how crestfallen, Therese immediately regretted she had said anything.

Her eyes caught Dave's, and his face said it all – regret, disappointment, frustration, failure, resignation, defeat. Her heart ached for the two of them.

"I have an idea," she said, surprising herself at her spontaneity. "Next Saturday, why don't Adrienne and I go to tea? Maybe we can join this club."

"Really?" said Adrienne. "Really!?" Her excitement was so contagious that Dave and Therese laughed with her. Behind her, Dave mouthed a silent "Thank you!"

But when Therese investigated, she discovered that the club was restricted to mothers and their daughters, period. No surrogates.

"This is ridiculous," she sputtered. "What about all those girls out there who have no mother present? Dammit, I'll start my own club."

So she did. She spread the word among café customers, advertised it around the neighborhood and town with posters and in the Horizon Heights *Herald*.

First she sought out women -- single and otherwise -- willing to become proxy moms for girls who had none in their lives. She was gratified by the number of single, separated and divorced moms volunteering to help and participate. But she was astonished about the others.

More than one married mom who already had a daughter signed up. One of them had three of her own.

"Such a beautiful idea," she told Therese. "There should be no limit to sharing your love and good fortune."

Another of the moms had five boys.

"I love them dearly, yes, but I grew up with three sisters and you have no idea how much I miss having someone else around for girl stuff and talk."

Having been there herself, growing up without a mother, Therese knew that the preteen and teen years could be a difficult time for girls – and for moms and dads, too. Conversations about puberty, body changes and rites of passage could be sensitive. Her new group, Doting on Daughters, offered not only a forum for such conversations, but also something priceless beyond that: Sisterhood.

"Not everyone is as lucky as I was to grow up in a loving two-parent family," one of the moms told Therese. "So I guess this qualifies as 'pass it on'."

"Dads!" her ad said. "Is your girl sometimes left out? No mom nearby, for whatever reason? Sign her up for our Doting on Daughters group for teas, shopping trips and outings."

Therese was not surprised at the response, which started as a trickle of inquiries and then became a flood. She heard from single dads, uncles and grandfathers, all calling about their daughter/niece/granddaughter.

The group's activities soon expanded beyond tea and ice cream to play dates, crafts, hobbies, travel, movies, charity work. There were discussions and talks about goals, ambitions, careers and values. There were lessons in manners, and even self-defense. The outings expanded to include biking, skating, book clubs, museums, cooking for kids.

"I've never seen her so happy," Dave confided one Saturday. "Adrienne's made all kinds of new friends and the world is starting to open up to her. You are a saint for doing this."

"Oh, pshaw," Therese said, her face reddening as she repeated one of her grandmother's favorite expressions. She had to admit she enjoyed the sense of fulfillment and satisfaction she felt when she opened the café to the club one afternoon and showed ten girls how a café kitchen functions. Each one took home a peach pie she made herself.

The Doting on Daughters project was so successful that it gave Therese another idea. If daughters without moms was such an issue, what about sons without dads?

Soon there was another group, called Bringing Up Boys. The community responded again, as first a trickle, and then a stream of men, some with boys of their own and some without, showed up to accompany fatherless boys to father-son baseball and football games, camping trips. There were discussions about rites of passage and growing up and careers.

Dads with connections arranged for star athletes to show up for talks and autographs. Dads in the professions and in the trades explained their specialties. Representatives from the military services talked about their lives. Boys obsessed with baseball were sent to baseball camps, those with mechanical leanings got to work on engines and computers. Firefighters and police officers stopped by.

Sometimes the moms and dads groups overlapped, and there were many joint projects, especially on careers. There were coed computer camps, chess camps, and one for kids who loved horses.

The Moms and Dads groups were growing fast. So far, Therese had been able to cope with the help of some volunteer moms and dads.

"I guess I really have started something here," she told Rex.

She was already beginning to worry that this was becoming too much for her to manage when Raine, a happily married proxy mom with a 12-year-old girl of her own, came to her with another idea.

"I am so proud of my Sienna," she said. "The other night we got to talking about Louise, a neighbor who is an expert baker. I mentioned that Louise's young daughter had been killed in an auto accident years ago.

"Well, I could see the wheels turning in her head, she knew all about my proxy mom thing, and I knew what she was thinking. She looks up at me and says, 'Mom, how about if I go over there some day and ask if she will teach me how to bake one of her famous cakes?'

"And I tell her, 'Of course you can, and I am so proud of you for thinking such a thing. I gave her the biggest hug she ever got.

"That gave me an idea. There must be a lot of families out there who lost a child or whose daughters were far away somewhere. How about them?"

And so yet another division of "Therese's Troops" was born, "proxy daughters." And that led to "proxy sons," a big hit especially with families with sons in the military.

As word spread about the success of Therese's efforts, civic groups, fraternal societies and "just ordinary, nice people" began to approach her with offers of assistance and participation.

She knew she was on to something when the original mother-daughter group whose exclusivity inspired her own efforts approached her and suggested that they combine.

Therese welcomed all of them, but it finally became too much.

"I can't do all of this anymore," she lamented to Jean-Paul. "I have a business to run."

The new sign on the jar asked for both financial and volunteer help.

And one day a note in the Rainbow jar told of a generous bequest that would enable the group to fund a paid coordinator, who would continue the efforts with a cadre of volunteers.

♣ ♣ ♣

Adrienne and her dad eventually stopped their Saturday visits to the Rainbow Café. Therese was concerned, until they dropped in one morning to say goodbye.

Adrienne gave Therese a fierce hug. She had been spending a lot of time with one particular surrogate mom, who had lost a daughter in infancy, and had become very close to her.

So had Dave.

All three were moving downstate, to Dave's new job.

"And this is not the first time this has happened," Therese lamented to Rex one morning, grinning.

She told him about a single mom who knew nothing about baseball who wound up coaching her son's Little League team, and was inundated with offers from single dads volunteering to be co-coaches.

"It seems that I have also started a dating service, matchmaking agency and marriage bureau here. Say, do you think I need a license for this?"

Chapter 19

The Pushover

Brady Stollwitz was somewhat of a celebrity in the Rainbow Café neighborhood on two counts. He had a dog named Whisper. Whisper was forever escaping his yard and roaming the neighborhood.

This often sent Brady in pursuit. Neighbors shook their heads, laughing, or complaining, depending on the hour, as Brady combed the neighborhood, shouting, "WHISPER! WHISPER!"

He did not appear to comprehend the absurdity of this.

Count two: Brady was 24 and single, with the innocent look of an altar boy, and qualified as another of Therese's genuine eccentrics because he was such a gullible soft touch, a naïve pigeon, that she sometimes feared for his survival.

He had been out of college for a few years now, but retained a bottomless, ingrained respect for those who sold things door-to-door, like he did to put himself through college. He knew how tough it was to make a living knocking on doors, and told stories about being sworn at, shouted at, doors slammed in his face, pushed off of porches, even escorted out of buildings by security guards.

So now, out in the world with a new, different job and income, memories still fresh of his struggling college days, he indulged a passion to support and shore up fellow-travelers who labored on the streets. So he bought everything he was offered from the door-to-door sales army.

This breed was not as numerous as in the "old days" of shoe-leather salesmen who pounded the pavement peddling encyclopedias, brushes, pots and pans and aluminum siding, but they were still out there. Only the products had changed. Nowadays, among other more traditional things, they were hoping to persuade homeowners that they could not survive without solar panels or hurricane-proof windows or landscaping services.

Brady was overweight, spoke with a slight stutter, was still troubled by his old teenage complexion problems. He combed his stringy, oily black hair straight down over his eyes.

"He must see everything like he's looking through a bamboo curtain doorway," noted Sam Broadland, the 911 operator, with some amusement. She had offered to give him a free haircut, right there in the back room of the Rainbow Café, but he declined.

Brady worked as an inventory control tech at a big hardware store nearby, and stopped every day at the Rainbow Café for lunch. He always ordered the same thing: a cheeseburger with fries. Therese knew from his employer that he was a good worker, with boundless enthusiasm and ambition. As with some of her other regulars at the café, she became almost a mother figure to him.

He certainly needed some protection.

Brady's own mother lived in California, and had remarried after Brady's father died. His stepfather thought him an odd duck, no argument there, and belittled and teased him about his appearance and speech.

So Brady seldom went there, seemed to have few friends, and Therese felt it her duty to help protect him from himself and his fatal flaw.

This day he burst through the door anxious to share the news about his latest purchase. Before he could say anything, Joshua Clarver, at the end of the counter, started in, as he always did when he saw Brady, with his own version of the hit from *Oklahoma!* – "I'm Just a Guy Who Can't Say No."

Rex Warnevar and Hank Lyson, also at the counter, began to laugh, but Therese cut them off with a frown. Everybody knew about Brady's "affliction," but she didn't like to see him embarrassed about it.

"What is it this time, Brady?"

Brady blushed and glanced sheepishly at Joshua.

"Well, she was such a pretty girl, not much younger than me, selling subscriptions to newspapers and magazines as a summer job to pay her way through cosmetology school, that's what I did, you know…"

"Yes, Brady, we know that. You already have subscriptions to almost every publication on Earth. What did you buy?"

He stared at the floor for a moment while Joshua smirked.

"*Knitters Monthly* and *Baptist World*. Then, after a shy pause: "And some others."

"You don't knit and you're not a Baptist."

"I know. But she was so pretty, and working her way through school and all…"

"Well, did you at least get her phone number, ask her out?"

"Her name is Twilla and we're going to a movie tonight. I told her I could give her a lot of sales tips."

"Well at least that's something," Therese thought. Brady needed an anchor, some stable ground to stand on in life, although she wasn't certain a hot girl selling magazines door-to-door was the answer.

"Now, now Therese," she scolded herself. "You don't even know the girl."

Brady's first experience in salesmanship had been a crushing disappointment, at least to him.

Back in elementary school, his class had been assigned to sell sheets of special Christmas stamps, a fundraiser to help eradicate childhood diseases. Looking forward to a day of adventure, a day of no school, of knocking on neighbors' doors, he stopped first at the one right next door, the home of a kindly, elderly widower.

When Brady came home, crying, shortly after setting out on his mission, his mother was alarmed.

"What's the matter?"

"He bought them all!" he wailed.

While his mother stifled a smile, Brady struggled with the contradictory concept of unwelcome generosity.

In college, wiser, he would have loved to have had that experience. Instead, he trudged door-to-door trying to sell an old standby, vacuum cleaners, working on his sales pitch between calls. He learned that he needed to be imaginative, sell himself as well as the product, and developed an approach that usually worked with bored homemakers anxious for a little variety in their day.

He dressed like Santa Claus, even in July, and his opening line was, "Hey! I know I'm early, but a deal like this couldn't wait until the holidays!"

It always got at least a laugh, and often a priceless invitation to come inside, where, relieved of the Santa face, his lost-little-boy looks melted the hearts of even the most cynical homemaker. From there, he turned on the boyish charm and usually left with an order, or at minimum, a glass of lemonade and a piece of home-made chocolate cake. His barometer of a successful day hinged on how well-fed he felt at the end of it.

"I'm not complaining, of course," he told his roommate after one particularly successful sales day, "but I am continually amazed at how many people are dissatisfied with their existing vacuum cleaners."

He knew humor was a great icebreaker, and used it often. The Santa Claus suit got him in the door, and he usually softened up a prospect a little more by recounting an old movie he had seen where two comics were selling vacuum cleaners door-to-door and had accidentally sprayed a chalky white substance all over a woman's priceless painting, called *Sunset*.

When she complained, they suggested she could just call it *Snowdrift* instead.

Most potential customers did not see the humor in that, but even back then, Brady had a tin ear when it came to appropriateness.

Brady's continuing compassion for shoe-leather salespeople had become obsessive-compulsive, and was taking a toll on his finances. He lived cheaply in a small house his mother had bought for him, spent little on himself because his wages were depleted by so many purchases. His credit card debt was oppressive.

"I know he's looking for a second job to help pick up the slack, and that his mother sends him money." Therese told Rex. "He also wants to start his own business some day, but I fear that with his lack of self-control, he's going to be doomed from the start."

Besides subscriptions to nearly every magazine printed, he had two mobile phones with service from two competing companies, often contributed to the campaigns of opposing political candidates, signed petitions for and against a proposed nuclear power plant, bought a new shingle roof and then two years later replaced it with a solar roof, and was well-positioned to provide recommendations on the relative merits of two competing window replacement companies.

His yard was immaculate because two landscaping companies tended it. He re-sided his house a year after a summer crew of student-painters had already freshened it up, and household pests did not have a chance against his two exterminators.

His house was wired with two alarm systems, which the chief of police, who lived two doors down, thought unnecessary. As for personal security, he had been saved by traveling evangelists 13 times and was well-stocked also with Jehovah's Witness pamphlets.

Brady also believed, from a misplaced sense of loyalty, that it was his obligation to fill out every survey sent to him. Technically inadept, he often called help desks for assistance with some of the products he purchased from their traveling salesforce, and subsequently was inundated with messages imploring, "How did we do?" and "How likely would you be to recommend us to your friends?" and "How would you rate our service on a scale of zero to ten?"

And when it came to "Please share your experience with us," his reply in the box provided might have run to 20 paragraphs if there hadn't been a limit.

"Brady, forget this," Juval Platt counseled his gullible friend. "You owe these people nothing. You could spend all day responding to these surveys, there are so many of them."

Juval gave it up as futile when he learned Brady had spent the entire previous day doing just that..

Therese became even more concerned when she learned Brady had broadened his vulnerability and succumbed to the wiles of late-night TV pitchmen. She knew his garage space and basement shelves were loaded with superglues and supersaws, cleaning products, vegetable-chopping machines and other food preparation gadgets, plus devices to locate fish, even though he was not handy with tools and did not cook nor fish.

His latest purchases were diet plans and exercise equipment. He was presently on three separate diets, constantly hungry, but saving a lot of money on food. He had a treadmill, a rowing machine and an exercise bike, but usually was too weak and tired to use them.

Therese also suspected his home was well-supplied with the latest in pillow technology.

She finally had to do something after Rex shared the ultimate Brady story.

"You won't believe this," Rex said, "but I heard he recently bought all new doors for his house." Rex collapsed with laughter, his head face-down on his arms, folded on the counter. "From a door-to-door salesman! How perfect is that?"

Even Therese had to grin, but ruefully. As with Whisper the dog, the irony in this was evident to everyone except Brady.

"Brady, you have almost enough merchandise in your garage to finally open your own store," she told him one day. She paused in thought for a moment, finger on chin.

"That gives me an idea."

Joshua loved it.

"Have you ever considered," she asked him, "consolidating your Trash to Treasures store with Brady, and all that new stuff he has in his garage and basement?"

That's when Joshua finally stopped teasing Brady, and a new store, Second Chance Treasures, was born.

The sign on the jar asked for help to finance the move and the consolidation. It came through again, but there was a condition: Brady had to get some help with his OCD problem.

Therese stopped by for the grand opening of Second Chance Treasures and observed that the shelves were bursting with Joshua's "found treasures" and Brady's seldom-if-ever-used merchandise. She went home with a vegetable chopping device, one of seven models to choose from.

♣ ♣ ♣

All heads in the café turned toward the door when the young woman came in.

She was beautiful, stunning. A model, some guessed. A movie star they couldn't quite place. Blond, tall, poised, fabulous figure, a knockout.

"Can I help you?" Therese said.

"Are you Therese? Can I speak to you privately?" She glanced around nervously, aware that everyone was looking at her.

"My name is Twilla," she said after they retreated to Therese's tiny office.

Therese's eyebrows shot up. "Brady's Twilla?"

"Yes. I know he thinks the world of you and confides in you. I really like him, he helped me a lot with sales advice. He's so different, so direct and honest, so genuine, compared to some of the fakes and phonies I meet. But he's ghosting me. We had one date and now he's ignoring me, won't answer my calls or texts or emails. I thought maybe you could get to him."

Therese liked her immediately. She learned that Twilla was from a prominent family, that her stern father, who had worked his way up from stockroom boy to become the head of the corporation, now insisted that his children have the same up-by-your-bootstraps experience, which explained why she was selling magazine subscriptions door-to-door to pay her way through school.

She learned that Twilla had tried modeling at first, but soon gave it up on discovering that her potential "managers" were more interested in her for other reasons.

"You might not think so from looking at me," Twilla said, "but I have my feet firmly on the ground. I'm not some dumb blonde. I know what I'm doing, I know where I'm going in life, and I'd like somebody like Brady to go with me.

"I know he's different, gullible, naïve, vulnerable. That's part of what's so endearing, what attracts me so much. He needs somebody. So do I. He's also smart and ambitious. Maybe he just thinks a relationship with me would never go anywhere anyway."

She looked away, stared at the floor, frowning.

Therese was reassessing her earlier dismissal of Brady's salesperson protégé as an empty-headed bimbo. This girl had it all together.

"Let me see what I can do," she said. "Lots of other people here love Brady too."

♣ ♣ ♣

Her conversation with Brady was direct and to the point. Twilla was right; he didn't think a nerdy nobody like him had a chance with anyone like her.

"Listen, young man, I don't like cliches, but this one fits: You only get to go around once in this life, and more to the point, sometimes you only get one chance at a relationship that changes and defines things forever after. I've met this girl. She's pretty, yes, but more important, she has a beautiful soul. She's the real thing. Don't blow it. Go after her."

And so one thing led to another, and one day not long after, the Rainbow Café was closed for an afternoon to host another wedding reception. Father Dunne had presided, Joshua was the best man, Therese the bridesmaid, Twilla's mother came in from California, sans second husband, since she was now open for a third.

All the regulars were there, the Leprechaun Band played, the merriment lasted well into the wee hours, long after the bridal couple had departed on their honeymoon to the Florida Keys, which they had read about in one of Brady's many magazines.

They would return to Brady's new partnership in the popular Second Chance Treasures shop, and Twilla's job heading the cosmetics department of a big department store. She was quite successful, since many customers were convinced the products would make them look like her, and went on to create her own line of cosmetics.

Rex and Cyrus Steelfarb, the novelist, who had stayed to help Therese take down the decorations and clean up after the reception, were the last ones to leave.

"Cheers," Cyrus said, grinning and raising his wine glass to Therese. "Here's to Happily Ever Afters."

Chapter 20

THE PLAYGROUND

Playgrounds were Reginald Truffaunt's mission, his passion. Every time he sat on his favorite park bench, he was reminded that among the most satisfying, comforting and reassuring sounds in the world were those of children playing, the happy laughter, the innocent squeals of excitement, the joyous shouts, yells and screams. They were not just the sounds of today, but the encouraging, confident sounds of many tomorrows.

He knew instinctively that playgrounds and play spaces fostered instant friendships, were places where everybody sized up and knew the new kid's name within five minutes, where lifelong bonds often were established.

Not that he had any first-hand experience with it. He grew up in a rough neighborhood where there were few playgrounds, where kids hung out in back alleys and vacant lots and abandoned buildings. He knew that if it hadn't been for his strong, principled mother, a single mom, he might have lived a different life story.

Instead, she saw to it that he attended school every day, learned good manners, and set some goals for himself. Foremost among them was college. He became a teacher at the recently-established Horizon Heights Elementary School, which had replaced an older edifice, and then its principal. He became great friends with Therese through his frequent visits to the Rainbow Café.

"How's the project going?" Therese asked as he sat down at the counter and ordered his usual 'breakfast' – peach pie and coffee.

"Getting there. Taking a while to clean it up. Just a few more weeks maybe."

Reginald's "project" was a vacant lot next to the school, although it wasn't really vacant. On it was a ramshackle house that had fallen in on itself over the years. The lot was overgrown with weeds and a huge briar patch, and was a dumping ground for trash by people too lazy or irresponsible to put it where it belonged.

It was an embarrassing neighborhood eyesore and hazard, and had been fenced by the city at one point, in a futile attempt at safety.

"Since when is a fence going to keep rambunctious children out of anywhere?" Therese said at the time.

One of the first things Reginald did on taking the principal's job was to petition the city to do something about the lot. He was amazed that the problem had not been addressed long ago, given its proximity to the school, until he learned that the absentee owner refused to do anything about the situation.

He grew up in the house, Reginald was told, and hoped to maybe return there some day and build something. He threatened to sue the city every time it moved to clear the lot. He dutifully paid all the taxes, and the city manager told

Reginald that his constant threats of litigation seemed to be a ploy to just gain some time.

"We could just start condemnation proceedings, but he'd fight it, and that's a long process."

So Reginald made it his mission to try to change his mind.

♣ ♣ ♣

"I've got to do something about this now," he told Therese. "I'm 63, and I don't want to leave this mess for the next principal to try to solve.

"So I got the guy's address from the city. I started by writing him letters. I told him about the new school right next door, how some of the kids played there at their peril. Never heard from him."

Therese wondered herself why the lot was so neglected. So did many of her customers, to the point where her "Playground Jar" was building up a fund to maybe at least help clear away the debris some day.

"Where is this person?" she said.

Reginald ran his fingers through his thick, wiry hair, turning gray now, as he assembled his story.

"He lives on the West Coast. I wrote him another letter. Then another last month. Nothing. So I finally decided to go talk to him directly."

"You went to see him?"

"Yeah. Found him in Newport Beach, California, living a reclusive life alone in a big house overlooking the ocean.

"He didn't want to talk to me at first, wouldn't let me in the house. Said he had ignored me for a reason, that he had plans for that lot some day.

"His name is Barnaby Pickett, he's quite elderly, didn't seem to be very well. I told him the situation, how the house was crumbling, a danger to the kids. He perked up a little at that. So I showed him some photos.

182

"Apparently he had not been back there for years. He cried when he saw the photos, the jumble of old lumber and shingles and wiring, the lot filled with overgrown weeds and trash. I could envision what was going through his mind – memories of a childhood, maybe siblings, friends, playing in that yard, what the neighborhood was like when he was growing up there.

"He told me about his mom, a domestic worker from a hardscrabble background who married an abusive man after his dad died. He beat her, beat Barnaby, too, until he got big enough to fight back. When Barnaby found her with another black eye and a broken nose one day, he beat the guy pretty badly and told him to get out. He vanished soon after with one of his floozies.

"His mom made sure that he went to school every day, then to college. After I told him my somewhat similar story, he disappeared for a minute or two, came back with a couple of scotches.

"We sat there for a long time that night, drinking and swapping stories about our childhoods, our families, our moms, our adventures along the way. Turns out he was some kind of big shot, a billionaire, a pioneer in realizing the potential of the internet back in the '90s. He was active in politics, a big contributor to presidential campaigns, at one point was U.S. ambassador to Finland.

"So he asks me, what do I intend to do with the lot. I told him I wanted to make it into a playground, not only for the school, but for all the neighborhood kids. He was trembling a little, spilled some of his drink, and I could see he was probably not going to make it back to the old neighborhood soon, if ever.

"So I pushed a little more. 'What do you think? Can we make a deal?'"

"Who's 'we'?"

"A group of neighborhood friends are willing to help clean up the place and start the process for a playground. What's a fair price for the lot?"

"He walked over to a window and stared out for a long time. When he came back he said, 'How about a dollar? Just to make it a legal transaction.'

"Well, I was floored, obviously. 'Seriously?' I said. He nodded and smiled sadly. 'I've got to stop kidding myself. I'm never going to be able to go back there. After seeing those photos, I think yes, it's best use might be as a playground for kids.'

"When we finally took leave of each other, as I was walking down the sidewalk, I had a sudden thought. I went back up to the house, he was still standing in the doorway, and I said, 'I am going to name this park after our mothers.'"

Reginald finished his story with a wan smile.

"So he wasn't such a bad guy. He just ran out of time to finish his dreams."

♣ ♣ ♣

Back home, he found that the café regulars were taking a new interest in the park. The jar on the counter was filling with bills, and then a note, offering to make up any difference needed.

The city, on hearing of the project, cleared the way by managing the legal transfer of the property to the city.

Juval Platt at the bank started things rolling by putting Reginald in touch with Luigi Costicello, the landscaper Juval had helped set up in his own business. Luigi showed up one day with a crew and heavy equipment to begin the first of the projects he had promised to Juval.

In two days the lot was cleared of the building debris and plant overgrowth and leveled for a new use. Therese provided lunches and refreshments for the sizable group of workers.

Hank Lyson published a story and photos of the progress. Volunteers from the neighborhood pitched in to help. The usual sidewalk superintendents showed up to watch, and Therese circled among them with the donation jar.

Luigi grinned broadly as some of his other friends donated their skills for the project. Volunteer stonemasons, bricklayers, carpenters, electricians and plumbers swarmed the scene. A fountain, lighted at night, soon appeared in the center of the lot, and a pop-up ground fountain was added for toddlers and small children. The landscapers tucked a butterfly garden into one corner.

Benches, low retaining walls, a jungle gym, swings, slides, see-saws and other playground equipment began to appear, provided at cost by a local manufacturer. Even a small shelter house and restrooms.

When it was done, Reginald fired off an e-mail to Barnaby Pickett in California.

"I was going to send you a photo." he said, "but if at all possible, you have to come and see this for yourself."

Accompanied by a nurse-companion, Barnaby was greeted at the airport by Reginald and a delegation of children from the elementary school He bent to hug the little girl who handed him a bouquet of roses.

There was a welcoming program at the school, where Barnaby was given an honorary diploma, and he announced that he was establishing a perpetual care fund for maintenance of the playground.

An arm around Reginald's shoulder, Barnaby wept when he saw what had become of his old homestead. Instead of the shambles he saw in the photo, happy children were scrambling up and down and through playground slides and tunnels, swinging on ropes, chasing and pushing each other on the swings. The squeals were music to their ears.

"It's perfect," Barnaby said. "Our moms would be pleased."

Reginald introduced him to Therese, and over coffee and peach cobbler, Barnaby grilled her about all he had missed – – the school, the town, the neighborhood.

"I am embarrassed that I turned my back on my old home town," he confided.

"My childhood here was not a very happy one. I just wanted to forget those days. I am happy that now I can do something to help, like the perpetual care fund.

"I should have done it earlier. But thanks to my friend Reginald, now I have."

Before Barnaby left town, the two posed for a photo in front of the new playground's centerpiece, a work of art underwritten by a promise from the jar.

It was a life-size bronze sculpture of two moms, side-by-side, pushing two children on swings.

Shortly after the grand opening of the Cicily Pickett/Raven Truffaunt Neighborhood Park, another note turned up in the donation jar.

Juval Platt confirmed that a substantial fund had been created at the bank to help Luigi Costicello in his campaign to convert vacant lots across the city into parks and playgrounds.

The only stipulation was that one of them was to be named the Reginald Truffaunt Neighborhood Park, and another to be named after Barnaby Pickett.

And one day, Reginald found himself sitting again on a playground bench, leaning back with his face to the sun on a beautiful July afternoon, listening to the happy shouts and screams, the peals of innocent laughter, the joyous yells and squeals all around him.

A little boy, about 6, approached his bench. Reginald could see his anxious mother looking on from a short distance away.

"You're here every day, mister," the boy said. "My mom and I wonder if you own this place."

Reginald smiled.

"No, I don't," he said.

"You do."

Chapter 21

An Old Debt

An occasional stranger or tourist might stop by the Rainbow Cafe, but Therese's clientele were mostly a steady stream of her regular eccentrics and other neighborhood folks.

These two coming through the door that day qualified as strangers, out of place in a tightly-knit neighborhood that was somewhat off the beaten path. The older man was lame and stooped, walked haltingly with a cane, but had the deliberate air of someone on a mission, someone looking for an answer. The younger one stood close to him.

The old man peered over the counter at Therese through eyeglass lenses that were as thick as the bottom of a Coke bottle.

"Are you Therese?" he asked. "I'm looking for somebody. A lady in a shop down the street told me that you know everybody around here."

That certainly was true. She had been here long enough to know the neighborhood as well as anybody. She sized up the features of the pair, and guessed that they were father and son.

"And who is it that you are looking for?" Therese noted that he spoke with an accent, European.

"Well, I don't really know," he confessed. "I only know the name of an American soldier who gave up his life in my country so I could be here today. I'm trying to determine if any of his family still live around here. All I know is that this is where he came from."

Therese invited him to sit down, partly because she didn't think he could stand erect for very much longer, even though the son was attentive and never left his father's side. She poured both of them coffee, cut two generous pieces of peach pie, and listened, entranced, to their story.

♣ ♣ ♣

His name was Andreas Manderfield. He was 85, born in The Netherlands, still lived there, and was on a mission on behalf of his family to repay an old debt. He introduced his son, Dirk, about 60, a former airline pilot.

"It's my job now because all of the others are dead," Andreas said quietly. "For many reasons we were never able to follow through on this, but now it must be done before it's too late."

Andreas had been a little boy during the closing months of World War II, but his memories were as vivid as those of soldiers who fought bitter battles across Europe, or waded ashore amid withering fire on remote Pacific islands.

He still sometimes awakened in the middle of the night, terrified, confused and in a cold sweat, convinced that the low drone and buzz of the air conditioning heralded the return of the dreaded Nazi V-1 and V-2 bombs and rockets that disrupted, derailed and terrorized his country and his childhood. Or sometimes he thought he heard again the familiar roar of the American B-17 "Flying Fortresses" overhead, on their way to and from bombing runs over Germany.

"We have not forgotten the war," Andreas said, nervously fingering the handle of his cane, hanging on the edge of the counter. "Many people in my little town still have vivid memories of the war, and deep and lasting appreciation for the Allied intervention."

He turned and clapped Dirk on the shoulder. "And we try to make sure that our children do not forget, either."

In the closing months of the war, when many Dutch citizens were facing starvation because of the German occupation, the bombers returned to drop tons of food parcels on towns below.

"It was so bad in those days that some families had to resort to eating tulip bulbs," Andreas said.

He was only six at the time, but remembered going out into the tulip fields with his parents and other townspeople to help stamp out a message, "Thanks, Yanks" to the fliers overhead.

"And can you imagine this?" he added. "It is not widely known, but the drops were done with the cooperation of some of the German officers, who let these planes pass through!"

But the Dutch remembered best how the Allies liberated their country in several major battles. One of them was near Andreas' town, and many American soldiers were buried in the nearby military cemetery.

"My family and others never forgot the sacrifices that these soldiers, these total strangers, made to return to us control of our own country."

Andreas described how after the war, families in the town each "adopted" a grave, obtained a photo from the family or the U.S. military, and then erected in their homes a small memorial to "their" fallen soldier. They tended and honored the nearby graves as if the fallen were their own sons.

Sometimes the American family would ask that the remains be returned to them, and the whole town would turn out to bid the repatriated soldier a solemn, bittersweet farewell.

Every year on the anniversary of the battle the town commemorated the sacrifices that had been made on their behalf. There were speeches and bands and sometimes family members from America returning to help honor their dead.

After the war, Andreas established a successful life as an engineer, and started a family. He made sure his new family knew every detail of his country's wartime suffering, the debt it owned to the Allies, especially the Americans, and specifically those lying in eternal rest not far from his childhood home.

"My family's soldier was Alton Hempstead," Andreas told Therese. "My father once told me that if any of us ever had the opportunity, we must visit this family in America, pay our respects, deliver our thanks in person.

"So that's why I'm here. I represent my town, my family, not only to give thanks for Alton's sacrifice, but for all those boys who lie in our soil." His voice was raspy.

He looked intently at a tearful Therese, who was struggling with her own emotions.

"I hope you can help. Nobody here we met so far seems to know of the family. My fear now is that they are all gone, too."

Therese searched her mind for any trace of a family named Hempstead, but came up empty. Ezra Prufong, the gravedigger, or Jeremy Cooperton, the veteran who honored veterans' graves at St. Sebastian cemetery, surely would have been of some help, but both were gone now.

Still, she reasoned, how hard could it be to find a family, especially if they were churchgoers or voters or taxpayers?

And she knew someone who would know. She told the Manderfields to stop back in a day or so.

♣ ♣ ♣

Leo Merleson was the mailman for the Rainbow Café neighborhood, and a semi-regular, although he could never linger long while he was working lest some grouch report him to his superiors for dallying along his route.

"Neither snow, nor rain nor heat nor gloom of night nor the Rainbow Café shall stay these couriers from the swift completion of their appointed rounds," Therese chided, while managing to slip him a piece of peach pie or a to-go coffee every time she had a chance.

Leo had been delivering mail in Horizon Heights for 30 years, and built up such an affectionate following that when the post office attempted to transfer him to another route, the outcry was so loud and fierce that it had to back away.

He was known to give the doorbell a special "It's here!" coded ring whenever he delivered a special piece of mail, such as a Social Security check or a paycheck, or a package or mail from a family member. Therese knew he once even went down to the post office late one Christmas Eve to see if the overdue engagement ring that a panicky Mitch Hornmeir was waiting for had arrived in time for his Christmas surprise for Priscilla Montaine. It had.

"Well, I don't know of any family by that name on my route," Leo told Therese in response to her question. "But let me ask around."

A day later he returned with the news that Andreas Manderfield was waiting for.

"My friend Keith, who handles the rural route, tells me there's a guy way out by Woodspur Corners by that name. A daughter lives with him, but that's all he knows."

Therese offered to go with Andreas and Dirk on the journey, not only because they were on unfamiliar ground but because they did not appear to have any means of transportation.

"Thank you," Andreas said. "I came a long way to deliver a message, but it never occurred to me how I might get around once I got here."

They drove for a half-hour into remote farm country that Therese had seldom visited before. They eventually turned off the highway onto a two-lane gravel road that after three miles became a rutted single-lane dirt path. At the end of it was a rusty mailbox that said "Hempstead," a dilapidated old farmhouse, and an ancient barn that had long since collapsed onto itself.

The name of the elderly man who came to the door was Delroy. Alton Hempstead was his older brother. Therese thought she recognized him as an occasional visitor to town. He was about 90, she guessed, in a wheelchair, and so glad to have some company that he invited them in immediately, apparently not concerned that they might be burglars or hucksters or traveling evangelists. Therese noted that he wore two hearing aids.

After introductions, he explained that his daughter, Adelle, lived with him, but he feared his days of independence here were numbered.

"She's a nurse, but gone all day, and concerned about me being here alone so much." he said, "especially because of this." He tapped the arms of the wheelchair. "So she's been looking into an assisted living place closer to town."

Delroy wheeled himself over to the stove, poured them all some tea, and then, cupping an ear, listened intently as Andreas explained the circumstances, how his father had corresponded with the Hempstead family after the war, sending photos of their adopted grave and accounts of the annual tributes.

But eventually the contact was broken as time took its toll of those who remembered the war firsthand. Delroy's family had the assurance, at least, of knowing that Alton's grave was tended in perpetuity, and there was a family and town across the ocean who remembered and honored him, too.

"So I am here to find Alton's family," Andreas said finally. "I am here to fulfill my father's ardent wish, and acknowledge our debt."

Delroy's eyes had filled with tears as Andreas related his story. He was seven when his big brother went off to war. Therese reached a hand across the table to comfort him, recognizing that this was bringing up many old memories, some fond, some not.

"Well, you are obviously too late to find most of them," he said, wiping his eyes. "But they *are* here, yes." He gestured out the window toward an expansive but untended back yard. Behind the collapsed barn, they could see a number of tombstones under a huge, spreading oak tree.

"That's a family plot. This land has been in our family and farmed for more than two hundred years, and we choose to bury our dead here. Except for my brother, we know he is buried overseas, and we decided to leave him there after the war."

It was hard to stop Delroy once he got started, but neither Andreas nor Therese had any inclination to do so once he began a rambling tale about his family and his older brother. They heard stories about growing up during the Great Depression, accounts of Alton's academic and athletic accomplishments, heard the awe and admiration in his little brother's voice.

"He enlisted the day after Pearl Harbor, like a lot of guys did. The last time I saw him was just before he shipped out for overseas."

Delroy's gaze returned to the little cemetery.

"All the rest of the family is there. Our father. Our mother. Three sisters and another brother. I'll be joining them there one day soon, no doubt. My children and grandchildren and their cousins will be inheriting this place. They plan to make it a family retreat, so those graves, too, will be tended forever."

Andreas rose from his chair.

"May I go out there?" he asked, motioning toward the family plot.

"Oh, yes, by all means."

Delroy showed them to the back door. He led them down a ramp in his wheelchair, then Andreas, Dirk and Therese followed him along a well-worn path toward the little graveyard.

Therese had not noticed it earlier, but Andreas was carrying a large envelope that seemed to be of some weight, since he kept shifting it from one arm to the other. At the plot, he produced its contents.

"My family would be honored if you would agree to place this here among your other loved ones," he said.

He pulled from the envelope a bronze plaque inscribed, "In memory of Alton Hempstead and other soldiers who lie buried in our soil, and the families who sent them across an ocean to liberate others from oppression. We will honor them forever." At the bottom, in smaller print, was the legend, "From the indebted Manderfield family, and a grateful Dutch nation."

"You came all this way to do this?" Delroy said, tears streaming down his cheeks, reaching out to accept the plaque.

"Yes. My family can now rest in peace also. We have acknowledged our debt, in however small a way."

On the way back to town, Therese was thinking that she had never been on a more meaningful and thoughtful mission.

♣ ♣ ♣

Back at the café, between tending to customers, Therese learned that Andreas had once carried out another very personal mission.

As Europe slowly was liberated, country by country, from Nazi occupation, the skies cleared of his nightmare bombs and rockets and were filled instead with more American B-17s, this time bringing much-needed supplies and food to beleaguered and starving countries.

Andreas remembered especially that some planes flew so low over the town square that he could see the faces of the smiling, waving pilots. The bomb-bay doors would open, and instead of deadly explosives tumbling out, cascades of candy bars spilled into the hands of cheering mobs of children waiting below. He still had some of those bars, hardened and chalky, souvenirs of a special time in his life.

"We could see them coming from aways off," he said. "They would rock the wings back and forth to let us know they carried a special cargo. I tell you, after what we went through, America always holds a special place in our hearts.

"Especially after we learned that at first the pilots and crews were providing the candy themselves, but then the big American candy companies learned what was going on and they stepped in and took over the supply issue."

Therese and a counterful of regulars nodded, chests swelling with pride at what their countrymen had done.

"We should not be surprised," Therese said wistfully. "This is what Americans do."

"Yes, and it set me off on another mission," Andreas said. "It inspired me to become a private pilot myself. In memory of those guys, I even used to buy up bushels of candy bars, and announce ahead of time where I'd be at a certain time, and then fly low over a city park or schoolyard or athletic field and drop them out to the kids waiting below.

"But times change. I had to stop when parents complained about all that sugar."

He grinned.

"So I switched to little granola bars."

♣ ♣ ♣

Andreas and Dirk stayed on for a few more days. Therese put them up in the extra bedroom in her apartment above the café. They spent their nights marveling at the offerings on American television and became daytime regulars at the café counter. Hank Lyson interviewed them for a story.

Andreas entertained everyone with more stories of World War II, the role his family played in the Resistance, complicating the lives of the Nazis, and the absolute ecstasy of residents when the first Allied tanks clanked into town.

"I will never forget the enormous cheer that went up as those first tanks rumbled through," he said, a hitch in his voice as he relived an emotional time in his life. "All the church bells were ringing. The tanks rattled the windows. Dishes spilled off of shelves. Pets hid under the beds. The heavens opened up and a golden ray of sunshine beamed down on those troops, American, Canadian, British."

He coughed and glanced around sheepishly. "Well, maybe I exaggerate a little bit."

Andreas also experienced another "welcome to America" moment, this one unfortunate. At a shopping mall, where he was loading up on souvenirs, his pocket was picked, and with his wallet went their money and the return airline tickets.

"Unfortunately, this is what some other Americans do," Therese said ruefully, apologetically. "But they're by far the minority."

While they debated what to do, their new American friends came to the rescue.

This time the regulars, with an assist from Therese, the airline and only a little anonymous nudge from the jar, replaced the tickets and raised enough in just a few days to get Andreas and Dirk back home safely.

There was a sendoff party. All the regulars were there, plus Delroy and Adelle. The mayor came. Even the mailmen, Leo and Keith.

Therese made a passable attempt at preparing the Dutch national dish, stamppot – a stew made of mashed potatoes and vegetables and served with sausage. The Leprechaun Band played.

They could not come up with an appropriate Dutch song, so they settled for "Tiptoe Through the Tulips."

Chapter 22

Dutch Treat

You know, there's something wrong with this picture," Therese said while absentmindedly wiping the counter. It was the day after the Manderfields left.

Rex and the other morning regulars looked at her expectantly.

"Something is missing. There are two sides to this story. And I have an idea."

They all leaned in to listen. When Therese had an idea it was wise to pay attention. She might not have a cure for the common cold or even a new twist on an old peach cobbler recipe, but it usually led to good things happening. And this was no exception.

Rex accompanied her on her new mission, back into the countryside, down the rutted road again. She would have called ahead, but the only way to reach Delroy was through his daughter, Adelle, and Therese did not yet have her number.

He was surprised to see her again. Adelle, a plump, 60-ish extrovert who laughed a lot, was there also. Therese liked her immediately.

"We've had more company lately than we usually get in a year," Adelle said. "Even the meter reader doesn't like to come out this far. This would be a good place for the FBI to hide somebody in the Witness Protection program."

Therese laughed and nodded, glancing out the window at the expanse of trees and fields. She turned to Delroy, speaking loudly so he could hear.

"I forgot to ask you something. Were any of your family ever able to go to The Netherlands to visit Alton's grave?"

Delroy looked out wistfully toward the little plot of graves.

"No," he said, in a shaky voice tinged with regret. "My father corresponded with some town official there right after the war, and of course we knew some family was tending his grave, but for several reasons none of us were able to go there. My parents wanted to, but…"

He looked up at Adelle, tears in his eyes. She put a hand on his shoulder.

"And now it's too late."

"No, it's not," Therese said. "No, it's not. Would you like to go?"

It all fell so effortlessly into place that even Therese was surprised at the response. Once again the note on the jar asked for assistance, this time for someone few of the regulars even knew, but Therese's word was good enough for them.

She grinned at the newest proof of her mantra: "This is what Americans do."

Once again the jar filled with bills and even a few checks, made out to the Rainbow Café. And once again an anonymous note said any difference would be provided.

So one warm day in July, a small delegation boarded a plane for Brussels, Belgium. Therese had not intended to go along, until Rex and the others persuaded her.

"When's the last time you had a vacation?" Rex said. "You never leave this place."

So Therese left the café in the capable hands of Jean-Paul Stoquet, Adeline Enders and Harriet Harterer, quite familiar themselves with running a small business. They agreed on the condition that Therese bake enough peach pies in advance to tide them through her absence.

At the last minute, Rex decided that he wanted to come along.

"I've always wanted to see this cemetery," he said, looking at Therese. "I've been to the American military cemeteries in Florence, Luxembourg, Normandy... As ex-military, it's always been a special interest and mission of mine."

Therese had to admit Rex was right; she couldn't remember the last time she was away from the café for more than a few hours. Looking back later, she was glad she went.

The original contingent of Delroy, Adelle, Therese and Rex was joined at the last minute by a surprise companion.

Vernon Budleigh read about the mission in the *Herald,* and stopped by one day to talk to Therese. He lived several miles away, and the article had stirred in him an old and similar memory.

"My father was one of those B-17 pilots that Andreas remembers," he said. "He was shot down over The

Netherlands in 1943 and hidden in a barn for several weeks by a farm family before he could be repatriated back to the Allies. If it wasn't for them, I would not be here today."

He asked if he could join the little group on their pilgrimage, at his own expense, because he had his own respects to pay.

Therese could not refuse, especially after she learned that Vernon's dad died in an auto accident not long after the war and never got his own chance to return and thank his saviors. Vernon was 78 now, still very spry, and even though he had few memories of his dad, was on a mission of his own.

Andreas and Dirk met them at the airport for a whirlwind week. Andreas hosted them at the spacious Manderfield family home in the Dutch countryside for two days, where Alton's familiar face stared back at them from the family's soldier shrine, still preserved.

The highlight of the trip, their reason for being there, was the cemetery, near Andreas' home. Small American flags rippled at every one of the thousands of American graves. With Andreas' help they looked up Alton's final resting place, and spent several hours there.

Other visitors noticed their presence, and several came over to talk, fawning over Delroy in his wheelchair after hearing his story.

At one point it became too much for Delroy. The photo shrine, the cemetery, the memories, overwhelmed him, and he broke into sobs. Adelle and the others left him alone at the grave so he could have some private time with his brother.

When they returned, after strolling among the other graves, they found him covering up with dirt a small hole he had dug atop the grave.

"I thought he would like to have with him something from home, so I brought a piece of the siding from the barn. He loved it out there, with the horses."

Therese nodded, wishing she had thought of something so perfectly appropriate when her father died.

Andreas arranged with town fathers a simple welcoming ceremony on the town square. They were used to this, since Delroy was hardly the first family member to make a pilgrimage to their kin's final resting site. But perhaps he was the oldest. There were not many left among his generation anymore.

Andreas, too, was honored by the city fathers as "an outstanding ambassador to one of our special American families, and to all of our American friends."

Delroy was presented with a traditional key to the city, a rubbing of the inscription on Alton's marker, photos of the grave and cemetery, a Dutch national flag bearing familiar red, white and blue colors, and another flag of vibrant orange, the official Dutch national color. And a packet of tulip bulbs for the family plot back home.

"I will fly these flags proudly at our family graves," he said. "And the tulips will be a happy reminder of our Dutch friends."

A small crowd assembled after word spread that another American had returned to pay homage to their war dead. They applauded enthusiastically, and many came by to shake Delroy's hand.

"God bless America," said an elderly woman, pressing a bouquet of tulips into his lap.

♣ ♣ ♣

At Therese's request, and from sketchy details provided by Vernon Budleigh, Andreas had looked into the downed flier story and discovered that the name of the farm family that had sheltered him was a very familiar one in the area.

"This name is revered here, because several of its members were active leaders in the Dutch resistance during the war," Andreas said. "They hid and protected many American and British pilots, helped move them through resistance contacts back to safety. Some of them paid with their lives for their actions."

Andreas told them that a son from the family, Hendrik, almost 90, was still alive and that his children still farmed the property.

"And you'll like this," he told Vernon. "The old barn is still there."

After the two met in the barn, the rest of them stepped outside. Therese shivered as she tried to imagine what Vernon's thoughts were as he stood in the very barn that sheltered his father so long ago.

Hendrik, too, was a little boy at the time, and retained only a vague memory of the excitement surrounding the mysterious guests in the barn. They sat there and talked for a long time, in the building with so much meaning for both of their families.

With Andreas' help, Vernon arranged and paid for two commemorative gifts for the family. One was a beautiful set of wind chimes that Vernon suggested could be hung near the barn as a remembrance and reminder of those dangerous yet inspiring days.

The other was a color photo of a B-17 bomber, accompanied by a card reading, "To the family who saved and sheltered American pilot Laverne Budleigh here in the dark days of 1943." It was signed "From the Budleigh family." Andress placed it next to the Alton shrine on the fireplace mantel.

"I can still hear them overhead," Andreas said, smiling broadly and looking up. "Such a sweet sound. The sound of liberation."

Then Andreas was their tour guide to the nation.

Windmills, canals, medieval castles and tulip fields flowed past the windows of their car.

In Amsterdam there were visits to dikes and famous museums and the Anne Frank house. As they passed by the notorious Red Light district, Therese sniffed and looked away.

Andreas and Dirk saw them off at the airport.

"Thank you for all of this," Delroy said, squeezing Andreas' arm. "I cannot tell you how much this means to me. I, too, have now fulfilled a family mission and obligation."

Vernon Budleigh added his own thanks.

"I can never repay what they did for my father," he said, "but if he's watching from somewhere, and I'm sure he is, I think he is smiling."

Therese recalled her earlier memory that she had never been on a more meaningful or thoughtful mission than that visit to Delroy's home back in the states.

She was reconsidering. This was even better.

♣ ♣ ♣

Back home, Therese began to wonder if there was any program stateside for providing markers for cemetery or family plots attesting that one of their loved ones, a military casualty, never returned and was buried overseas.

She was told by a government agency that they were not aware of any such organized program.

So she started one.

It began with a new label on the jar, soon boosted by an anonymous push.

She advertised in veterans' publications, religion magazines, on senior-citizen and genealogy websites.

A Hank Lyson story in the *Herald* was picked up by the newswire services and brought it more attention.

A small trickle of initial orders gradually grew into something substantial. Therese was not sure at first how much interest there would be in honoring soldiers buried overseas so long ago, unless a grandson or granddaughter or other relative with a deep sense of history and family pride picked up the reins to commemorate a family hero.

She needn't have worried.

She recalled from her own youth one of her dad's stories, about a hometown sailor who perished on the USS Oklahoma at Pearl Harbor.

He was buried in Hawaii, and many years later, when the remains were finally identified, he was returned to the U.S.

"The remains were flown into an airport 50 miles away," she remembered him saying. "Then a military motorcade to his hometown.

"All along the route, through little towns and at country crossroads, people lined the way, waving American flags, as the hearse passed by. A Navy admiral came to give a eulogy at the reinternment rites.

"People do not forget the sacrifices our military people make. That's just another one of the things that we do."

Therese found a local monument company willing to make the bronze plaques, which would state simply, "In memory of John Smith, 1922-1944, buried in the American Military Cemetery in Normandy, France."

She was fearful at first that the cost of such a plaque would be prohibitive for a lot of people, but the owner of the company, a veteran himself, reassured her that he would make them for a little over his cost.

"These are my guys," he told her. "God bless you."

As time went on and the orders for the plaques grew, Therese had to enlist Jean-Paul's help. Then they had to ask for volunteers for the project – taking orders, shipping, bookkeeping. Many local veterans stepped in to help.

But it all eventually became too much, and she found herself saying once again, "I have a business to run, after all."

Several national veterans' organizations agreed to take over the project.

Chapter 23

Joanie and Ruby

Therese met Ruby, a fourth-grade teacher at the nearby elementary school, through the Doting on Daughters group, where she was one of the volunteer moms. It was another instance where two strangers become instant friends when Ruby began to stop in at the Rainbow Café on her way to and from school.

She was 28, a bubbly redhead, a single mom with a little girl of her own. Joanie, 8, a bright, inquisitive child, was in day care most weekdays in the summer when Ruby was at work at her part-time proofreader job at a magazine.

Ruby had joined the moms group as much to find playmates and friends for Joanie as she did out of any altruistic motive. Joanie's dad had long ago disappeared, along with any sense of his responsibility.

On this bright summer day, Therese could tell by Ruby's long face that all was not well. She knew Ruby's widowed dad was in the hospital.

"My dad is so sick," she said. "I have to spend so much time with him, there's no one to watch Joanie. And she can't come to the hospital to see her grandpa, either."

Ruby's regular day care center, run out of a neighbor's home, was closing, and her only other option was too far away to be practicable. She was covered during the school year, when her work schedule coincided with Joanie's school hours, but now she had no one to watch Joanie when school was not in session.

That night, with Ruby and Joanie on her mind, Therese slept restlessly, tossing and turning, until by 6 a.m. she concluded she might as well get up and face the day. She was used to absorbing her customers' problems and taking them home with her, and sometimes posting a new "cause" on the mysterious donation jar. But the jar could not help Ruby's immediate situation.

It came to her while she was in the shower.

"Of course!" she shouted in the stall echo chamber.

She couldn't wait to get to the cafe to try out her idea.

Rex Warnevar was the first one through the door, so she leaned on him first. He grinned when he heard her idea and agreed to help start it off.

So Ruby was stunned into tears when the schedule was presented to her.

On Mondays, Joanie was to hang out at the ice cream shop. Ruby expected no resistance from the grinning eight-year-old. Rex even put her to work occasionally, helping him monitor the ice cream manufacturing process in the back room.

"I am naming you our official taster," he told her solemnly, pinning a name tag and a badge on her blouse. "The ice cream shop reputation rests on your abilities."

But the precocious new employee set some parameters on her first day.

"I don't want to be called a soda jerk" she said earnestly. "That's such a terrible, demeaning name."

"Hmmm," Rex said, stroking his chin thoughtfully. "Well, what should we call you?"

"Soda princess would be nice."

And so it was. Dressed in a white shirt and cap and bow tie, she got to scoop ice cream for customers who were her same size. Sometimes she helped deliver orders to tables.

Rex was not quite sure how child labor laws applied in this situation, so he was very religious about her "hours" – ten minutes on and two hours off, which she spent reading and playing in a back room. Nonetheless, customers who were in on the day-care plot warned him whenever an official-looking stranger who might be a state inspector approached the shop.

On Tuesdays, Joanie was to spend the day with Molly Malone, where it was Christmas every day. Molly set her up for an hour or so in her garage, where Joanie tested the strings of Christmas lights and the animated lawn figures, replacing bulbs where necessary. Meals were provided to Molly's new "employee," so Joanie also was developing into an accomplished chef under Molly's tutelage.

The two were becoming such close friends, and Molly fussed over her so much, that Ruby had to turn away for a moment when Joanie posed a question to her one night.

"Could Molly become my grammy?" she asked. "I don't have one anymore, you know."

Ruby nodded and hugged her fiercely. "Yes, I know," she said, with a hitch in her voice. "We will ask her. I think she'll say yes."

On Wednesdays, customers along Joshua Clarver's trash route became accustomed to seeing little Joanie perched up high in the passenger seat of his enormous truck. She usually stayed there, reading or playing video games on her device.

But occasionally she would jump down to share in Joshua's excitement over a "find." Joshua began to set aside discarded but repairable toys, took them home to refurbish, and then gave them to her. One of her favorites was a talking doll she named Chantelle, after Joshua's wife.

Joanie had a promising undeveloped voice herself, and after Joshua taught her the words to a few spirituals, sometimes joined him in a favorite, "Joshua Fought the Battle of Jericho," or "Lonesome Valley."

Wednesdays with Joshua were not always harmonious. Sometimes a disdainful dowager would turn up her nose at the sight of a child riding in a garbage truck. In return, she might be serenaded good-naturedly with a verse from an old country-western song – "How Can I Miss You if You Won't Go Away?"

But more often than not the sight, and especially the sound of the two, singing duets in close harmony, brought broad smiles.

Thursdays were a special treat for Joanie. She got to spend the day with Hank Lyson at the *Herald*, where he turned her creative mind loose to make her own front pages on an antique letterpress in the back room.

She amused herself for hours assembling stories and headlines from individual block-type letters, then helped Hank run them off on the press. She also became quite expert at reading type upside down and backwards, a skill not much in demand unless you were a letterpress typesetter.

Joanie's bedroom walls at home were soon festooned with newspaper front pages blaring headlines like JOANIE GETS ALL A'S AGAIN!" and "JOANIE NAMED GIRL OF THE YEAR!"

She also created special front pages for friends. One of them, hanging on the wall at the Rainbow Café, said, "GEORGE WASHINGTON ATE HERE." The imaginative story below elaborated on the day George Abner Washington, a traveling salesman from Gumpert Corners, Iowa, stopped in for lunch.

For her friend Hank, she created a headline reading, "*HERALD* TURNS DOWN PULITZER PRIZE" with a subhead saying, "Publisher Lyson Says He Has Too Many Already."

Fridays were spent at Adeline's Annex, where Adeline put her in charge of maintaining the elaborate Christmas display in a front window, a panorama of miniature collectible houses, churches, stores and barns, a skating rink, a playground, people, animals, trees, carriages, carolers, streetlights, even a city hall, with an O-scale model railroad running through and around the whole layout.

The vintage locomotive, puffing smoke, pulled 10 cars ranging from boxcars to tankers and even a Pullman. They proceeded over bridges and along a river, up a snow-covered mountain. A brakeman, swinging a lighted lantern, brought up the rear in the caboose.

Joanie showed signs of becoming a promising artist. She drew a series of miniature billboards for the layout, touting the Rainbow Café, Adeline's Annex, Harriet's Cupcake X and Rex's Sundae Pew ice cream shop, among other familiar establishments such as car dealers and insurance agencies.

The Christmas layout was popular all-year round, so Joanie tinkered with it constantly, but especially in late summer and fall as the holidays grew closer. In between, Adeline kept her busy finding room for new shipments of stuffed animals, and dusting and organizing display cases holding collectibles ranging from inexpensive figurines to costly crystal.

She also was learning how to maintain and keep track of inventory on the store's computer system. And she managed to sneak in a few rounds on a video game here and there.

Joanie was so good at her "chores" that Adeline kidded her about it.

"I might open a branch store and put you in charge of it."

Therese and others filled in some days when necessary. Molly sometimes ran out of things for her to do because she was so efficient with the Christmas lights, and Hank occasionally was out of town.

On those days, Juval Platt let her run the coin-wrapping machine at the bank or Therese kept her busy at the café with simple tasks like counting supplies, washing and slicing peaches, or even trying her hand at a dessert.

After her first attempt, Rex told her, "You make the second-best peach cobbler in the whole town."

Harriet Harterton borrowed her some days to help decorate and frost cupcakes. They got along so well that Harriet began to dread the return of the school year.

"She has become the frosting on my life," she told Ruby.

"We're not going anywhere," Ruby replied, laughing. "I'm sure you haven't seen the last of her."

Ruby sometimes choked up when thanking Therese for her intervention, and for orchestrating Joanie's multi-faceted "training," especially after Ruby's dad died.

She showed Therese a picture Joanie had drawn. It was a remarkably convincing cartoon-like portrait of the Rainbow Café regulars, all perched at the counter before plates of peach pie, with Therese hovering in the background.

"Joanie looks on all of you as her family," she said. "And she's right. Her grandpa's gone now, and she has nobody else except me. I mean us."

The Rainbow Café donation jar soon sported a new sign asking for assistance in finding someone willing to open a new day care center in the neighborhood.

Word passed from a friend to a friend, and from a friend to a friend of a friend, and there was an ad in the *Herald*.

Some of the moms in Therese's Moms and Dads program were a great source of potential names also, so it wasn't long before there was a new day-care center, helped along by donations from the regulars and underwritten by a note in the jar.

Chapter 24

Hands Across the Sea

Therese and Ruby talked and laughed often about the time Ruby's thoughtful fourth-graders caught them both up in an international story.

Usually, Ruby stopped by to unwind after a day of herding elementary school students.

But this particular day she had burst through the door more excited than Therese had ever seen her.

"Therese, the sweetest thing happened! You will love this story! I'm so proud these kids came up with this themselves! Any teacher will tell you that this is the kind of special reward you can get, far better than any money, any salary, could ever provide."

It all began because the newspapers and television channels were preoccupied with stories about a tragedy unfolding in Italy. The little town of San Estella had been badly damaged by a massive flood of the Arno River.

Especially vivid were video and photos of an elementary school, where desks and chairs were floating in classrooms and hallways. Children were trapped inside for a time, had to flee to an upper floor and be rescued through the windows by boats.

"We were talking about this in class, and one of the kids mentioned that his grandfather had come from that town and his family was concerned if their relatives there were OK," Ruby said. "Then they all started talking, and wondering if there wasn't something they could do to help."

"All of their books are probably ruined," one of them said.

"Another added, 'If the school is damaged, their houses probably are, too.'

"Pretty soon the whole class was involved."

It started small enough, with nickels and dimes and quarters. The kids put up signs all over the school asking teachers and students to contribute to a collection to help the little town. Then it became a topic at a PTA meeting. Horizon Heights parents, not to be outdone, contributed generously to help the damaged school and town.

"We can't let our kids show us up,' one proud mom said. "They're setting an example for _us!_"

Soon they had enough to warrant sending.

"Dear Mr. Mayor," began Ruby's letter on behalf of the kids. "We are fourth-grade students at the Horizon Heights Elementary School in the USA and we have been watching with alarm the stories about what has been happening to your town, and especially your elementary school.

"One of us is Lorenzo Salsini, whose grandfather came to America from your village many years ago. We, and our

216

parents and teachers, would like to help in some way, so although it's not much, we hope this money will assist you and your town, and especially the school, in getting back to normal one day soon. *Ciao,* your American friends."

It was signed by all 25 students in the class and contained an international money order for almost a thousand dollars. Lorenzo's name was at the top.

It was several weeks before they heard back.

"Dear precious children," said the mayor's letter. "Thank you for your concern about our little town, and for your generosity. We are slowly starting to clean up the mess and repair the damage.

"Your contribution will help immensely. In return, we are sending you some small tokens of our appreciation. *"Grazie mille per la tua gentilezza."*

Ruby helped them translate: "Thank you so much for your kindness."

Hank Lyson at the *Herald* got wind of the episode and wrote a story. It was picked up by the newswire services and appeared all over the country. "Fourth-graders come to aid of stricken Italian town," said one headline.

Reporters and TV crews descended on Horizon Heights Elementary.

Little Sarah Slocum was interviewed and her quote went national: "This is what Americans do."

At the cafe, watching this on TV, Therese beamed so proudly you might have thought Sarah was her own child.

Inspired by the story, teachers and schoolchildren across the country began sending their own contributions. What began as a small stream was now a river of real money. Juval Platt at the bank took over managing the flow and readied it to send to the mayor.

But first, Therese had another of her ideas, and dropped a note into the Rainbow jar.

"My God, this is so silly," she told herself. "It's getting ridiculous. Just look at you, a grown woman, negotiating with a glass jar. This is nuts."

Whatever it was she proposed, the jar came through, and provided the means to bring a delegation of San Estella students to Horizon Heights, along with their "token of appreciation," and to treat them to a taste of America.

Therese sent a wire to the mayor, and when the "token" arrived in a few weeks it was accompanied by an official San Estella delegation of five honorary student escorts, their teacher, and the mayor. One of the students was Felicia Salsini, a distant cousin of Lorenzo.

Everyone had been waiting anxiously to see what the "token of appreciation" might be.

"Olive oil," guessed one student.

"Pasta!" said another.

"Pottery!"

"Chocolate!"

"Well, one thing we can be sure of," concluded one parent. "I don't think they'll be sending wine to elementary school students."

The tokens were trees – a dozen Italian maple saplings – with all the necessary permits and paperwork required by Italian and US customs regulations.

A note was tied to one of the trees – "From your Italian friends. Let us grow together in friendship."

Mr. Zimmer, the science teacher, researched the trees. Since they would grow fast and become tall and slender, he proposed planting them along the north side of the athletic field to help screen it from harsh winds, and perhaps some day it could become a small picnic glade.

Photographers and TV cameras were there to record the moment.

Ten students, five from each school, plus a teacher from each, lined up with shovels and spades to plant the saplings. Ruby was the teacher chosen for the Americans.

The visiting delegation was treated to a picnic by Lorenzo's family. There were sister-city pledges, a parade, and a tour of nearby parks, cities, farms and attractions. The local lodge of the Sons and Daughters of Italy in America honored them at a reception, where Juval Platt turned over to them the mushroomed fund.

The mayor's eyes widened in disbelief when he saw the numbers.

The jar's response to Therese's note also provided enough to send the delegation to Washington, D.C. to see its monuments, with a side trip to Fairfield, New Jersey, said to be "the most Italian town in America," where more than half of its residents were of Italian descent.

"We were lucky to get out of there," one of the teachers said. "They wanted us to stay."

Everywhere they were treated with respect and admiration, and calls of *"Viva l'Italia!"*

Back in Heritage Hills, as the Italians prepared for departure, the two delegations pledged to stay in touch, and even made plans for a 10-year reunion picnic in their grove of towering-trees-to-be.

Each member of the departing delegation received a gift bag, containing a cowboy hat, barbecue sauce, and a Native American dream catcher, among other American souvenirs.

An awe-struck Italian student, boarding a car for the airport, exclaimed in wonder:

"Everything we have heard about America is true!"

Speculation about the force behind the donation jar ramped up again after the delegation left.

Jean-Paul Stoquet was appointed to keep a constant watch on the jar during the day, since he was always there. But he wasn't always out front.

Molly Malone volunteered to give up a night's sleep and hide in a booth for an all-night snooping vigil. Nothing, except a lost night's sleep, although she admitted that she did doze off once or twice.

Ruby and little Joanie were asked to take one of the notes to Ruby's school, where a widely-known handwriting expert was on the faculty.

Even little Joanie could see the problem with that.

"All the notes are from a computer printer," she pointed out.

"And anyway," Ruby added, "we would need handwriting samples from an awful lot of 'suspects.'"

Therese continued to deny any personal involvement, and insisted again that she was simply the custodian of the jar. The regulars agreed that she didn't seem to know any more than Juval Platt, the banker who acted as the conduit for jar bequests.

There were some interesting theories, ranging from romantically sublime to patently ridiculous. One morning when most of them were at the café, the regulars aired a few of their theories.

Adeline Enders wondered if a long-ago resident made good somewhere and now wanted to share his blessings with his beloved hometown.

Samantha Broadland, the 911 operator, speculated that an evil, unscrupulous billionaire who made a fortune by bilking others was now trying to appease his guilt and buy his way into the Hereafter.

Harriet Harterton, the cupcake lady, imagined that an eccentric recluse had attempted to leave her vast fortune to her cat, but her lawyer persuaded her that the residents of Horizon Heights, her hometown, were more deserving and a better investment risk.

Ruby said her little Joanie, currently enmeshed in third-grade history lessons about local legends, was reading about long-ago river pirates who were said to have buried their ill-gotten loot near the town but were slain by rivals before they could come back for it.

"Maybe they left a treasure map, hidden in a book in the library, or maybe behind an antique mirror, or maybe even taped to the back of someone's framed reproduction of *The Last Supper* or the *Mona Lisa,*" Ruby said excitedly, caught up in the drama of the moment.

Her friends all looked at her as if she were deranged, until Rex reminded them that her flight of fancy was no more preposterous than some of theirs.

Cyrus Steelfarb, the novelist and scholarship maestro, was convinced that maybe Ezra Prufong was wrong, and somebody indeed found the immense treasure that a tombstone poem said was hidden under a stair somewhere in the town.

But the ultimate fantasy, advanced by editor Hank Lyson, was that those two Revolutionary War soldiers, whose graves were found in the St. Sebastian Cemetery, carried with them an original copy of the Declaration of Independence.

It was buried with them, Hank's theory went, and sometime in the past, grave robbers sold it to an auction house for millions. Now their descendants, tortured by guilt over the shady source of their family's fortune, were trying to make it right.

After listening to all of this, smiling at the imaginative plots proposed, Therese spoke up.

"You know," she said, looking up and down the counter, "nobody really knows. It obviously has to be someone with money, someone quite familiar with or at least on the fringes of the Rainbow Cafe.

"And maybe Ruby and Cyrus have something here, with their theories about the river pirates and the tombstone poem. Think about it.

"Did one of you find the pirate gold, or the mystery stairway? Just saying…"

The crew of eccentric café regulars became very quiet and looked at each other suspiciously.

Chapter 25

The Teacher

Therese was concerned when her friend Seth Pinderton became quiet and withdrawn. He stared morosely into his coffee cup that gray November day while other regulars at the counter traded their usual barbs and jibes.

She learned the reason after the others left.

"They're pushing me to retire when the year is over," he confided across the counter. His mood was as bleak as the weather. "I guess it's time. I don't seem to belong there anymore."

Therese believed that if ever there was a person perfectly suited for teaching, it was Seth, a view also held by legions of his admiring students, both past and present. Many of them told her that he was always prepared, he was a good listener, he was patient, respectful, sensitive and creative. And he aimed to inspire them to great achievements.

"I want to send them off into the world as prepared as they can be," he liked to say.

Seth commanded respect both at the school and in the community, not only because of his imposing 6-7 stature, but also for his gift for explaining and teaching what for some students could be a difficult subject – mathematics. He also was admired because of his reputation and coaching record.

At Horizon Heights High, just a few blocks away, Seth taught basic algebra and geometry, plus calculus and trigonometry to the higher grades. It was a small school, so in between he was a chaperone on bus trips, taught physical education classes, and was the varsity basketball coach.

Seth was 64, his hair thinning and losing the battle to grayness, and was a graduate himself of the same high school, an earlier version, 47 years previous, and his name was a familiar one in the trophy case.

He was the center on the Hawks' legendary teams that won three consecutive state championships long ago, a feat never duplicated by any other high school in the state, before or since.

But times were changing.

"I'm tired of it all anyway," he told Therese, warming his hands around another cup of coffee. "Some of these kids just have no appreciation for their good luck in being born in this country. Honestly, to quote an old saying, some of them were born on third base and think they hit a triple.

"Some of them have no sense of pride in America. No sense of its remarkable history, its accomplishments, its international standing, no inkling of the many times it came to the world's rescue or what the world would be like if there was no America.

"They take so much for granted. They are buying into socialism and other woke nonsense. They are so unaware of the evil and the dangers that are out there in the rest of the world."

The patriotism issue was a particular thorn for Seth, since after high school he had served four years in the Marines before college.

"God help us if the preservation of freedom is left up to some of this crowd. I hope it's not going to take a war, and the draft, or something else, to wake them up."

His patriotic views were derided and ridiculed by some of the other teachers, and by some students and parents, too.

"I've been called Pollyannish, delusional, unrealistic for saying we need to return to the values of an earlier time. Some people just can't see past America's 'sins' to its underlying, basic decency."

Seth's wife, Priscilla, died three years earlier, and he did not seem to have any particular group of friends. Therese suspected that his daily visits to the Rainbow Café pretty much summed up his social life.

Only Therese and Juval Platt knew that Seth lived a sort of secret second life.

Like many teachers, he often bought needed school supplies out of his own pocket. He provided lunch money for needy kids when necessary. He had no children of his own, but Juval at the bank could tell everyone, but wouldn't because he was sworn to secrecy, that an anonymous scholarship fund there was financed by Seth.

Over the years, many aimless, drifting students from unstable families turned to Seth for advice and support with personal problems. Often, it was Seth who turned to them, when he suspected there might be trouble at home. At least one of them, Harry, was bailed out of jail by Seth after a serious drug possession incident.

He instilled in several generations of students a love of learning, of solving problems, of creating a better world for themselves and future generations. And a love of America and fair play.

One of the best stories about Seth came from his years as a basketball coach.

He was in the café one day with Ernie, one of his former students and players, when Therese overheard them laughing and telling other customers about the time they took the floor with only four players.

"Wait," she said, coming over. "Start again. What's that all about?"

Ernie launched into a story that soon had them all laughing again, but in admiration.

"We were playing Thomaston, a small school that usually could only come up with eight players, and that would be on a good day," Ernie said. "Even so, they had a great team, and we were having a so-so year. It was late in the season, they were undefeated, no doubt on their way to the state tournament.

"And to complicate things, everybody knew that because they were such a small school, they were scheduled to be consolidated out of existence in another year or so. So in a way, this was their last hurrah.

"Well, Billy Hansen was their best player, and his mom had been in a serious car accident the day before, so he wasn't there. Another guy's bad grades made him ineligible to play.

"Then one of their guys fouled out late in the second quarter, and they were down to five players.

"Coach told us at halftime we had to be fair, to be extra careful about putting them in fouling situations. We got what he was saying – we should give them an honest chance at their perfect season.

"But despite that, late in the third quarter, another guy fouled out. It was because of a stupid move by one of our guys."

Ernie paused and blushed.

"Well, it was me. I was fighting for a rebound with one of their guys, and he fouled me badly in the process. I should have just let him have the ball. There was a long pause before the ref called it, but he really had no choice.

"He calls a timeout, goes over to the other coach, tells him his team will have to forfeit, they can't play with only four.

"The stands are buzzing, people are confused, wondering what's going to happen.

"Well, Coach Pinderton goes over to the ref, who was about to declare the forfeit, and says, 'Wait a minute, I have an idea.'

"The ref listens and grins and calls the other coach over. 'Coach,' he says 'Coach Pinderton here has proposed that we continue with the game, and he is suggesting that he put only four men on the floor also.'

"Well, the other coach can't believe what he is hearing. 'Is that even legal?' he asks. The ref pulls out a rulebook from his back pocket, riffles through the pages so fast that he couldn't possibly have found a rule, and says, with a wink, 'There's nothing in here I can find that says we can't proceed.'

"So the game goes on.

"And I know you're wondering," Ernie said. "We played our best but got clobbered anyway. Both teams played maybe the cleanest, foul-free fourth quarter ever played. When it was over, both teams were hugging each other and dancing a jig together out on the floor like it had been a joint victory. And it was. We were happy for them. We knew all these guys. The schools were not that far from each other. Parents of both teams were all teared-up in the stands in pride for their sons, if maybe for different reasons.

"And after it was over, the ref comes up to Coach Pinderton and shakes his hand and says, 'Sir, today you have given all of these young men a priceless life lesson in good sportsmanship, fair play and setting a good example, better than they could ever get out of a book or a classroom.'"

Seth blushed.

"And that wasn't the only time Coach did something like that," Ernie added. "At least one other time he told us to let the other guys score because he knew the ref really blew a call when he missed a flagrant foul by us."

All of this gave Therese another idea.

♣ ♣ ♣

"Can you stop by tonight?" Therese asked Seth one morning several weeks later. "I need some help delivering some stuff to the school and you're the only one I know with a minivan."

So he helped her load several large boxes into the vehicle. At the school, they had a hard time finding a parking place because so many cars jammed the lot. Seth wondered what could be going on; after all, it was a weeknight.

"Did you forget? It's the senior class banquet, that's what all this stuff is for. All the parents probably are here."

With a puzzled look, he helped her unload the van at a side door of the gym. She waited while he found a place to park.

"OK," she said, opening the door. "Let's get started. We're probably not the first ones here."

As he entered, the lights came on and a huge crowd erupted into cheers, whistles and cowbells. Seth looked around, confused, until he caught sight of a huge banner: "Seth Pinderton Night."

The high school band was playing the rousing school song and cheerleaders were doing cartwheels around the center-jump circle. Every spot in the bleacher-style seats around the gym was filled.

He could see old faculty friends in the seats, as well as current administrators and teachers, townspeople. Familiar faces from generations of former students. Many of the athletes he had coached were there, some in their old varsity letter jackets.

So much for the big crowd for the senior banquet.

Tables filled with coffee urns and desserts were spread around the floor of the gym. Several teachers came over to shake Seth's hand and fetch the boxes, which were filled with Therese's peach pies and other Rainbow Café delights.

Two other restaurants had jumped at Therese's invitation and joined to help pull off her surprise dessert reception. Student wait staff were already seating people at the tables.

Several of Seth's students, former and current, escorted him to the head table.

Therese was the emcee for the program that followed. Administrators, fellow teachers and former students all told their stories about Seth Pinderton.

"He would be here until late in the evening counseling students or working with them individually," said a former principal. "The janitors complained that they couldn't go home until he went home."

A teacher colleague recalled that Seth was famous for springing pop quizzes on his classes.

"But they got even. One day nobody showed up for class, and he found them all out in the hallway, giggling. When he asked what was going on, they told him they were having a pop absence."

One former student had a special message for him.

"I was ADHD in a time when it wasn't much understood," a middle-aged woman said. "Mr. Pinderton was so patient with me and gave me so much extra attention, steered me and my parents toward help. He changed my life."

All the players from Seth's legendary four-man basketball game were there, and the crowd applauded wildly after Ernie once more told the story.

"And we have some special guests here tonight," Therese told the crowd. "Three of the players from that opposing Thomaston team, which, by the way, continued undefeated and went on to win the state championship."

The crowd stood and cheered as the three were introduced. It roared when one of them took the microphone and said, "We are sorry we could not come up with a fourth."

Therese had reached out to the school's principal for help in finding them.

"No problem," he said, "several of them are still nearby, but one is overseas with the military. I know Seth is a legend at your school, but he's a legend over here, too."

It went on, as former students and faculty told Seth Pinderton stories. His phone was pinging constantly as former students all over the country tried to reach their favorite teacher on his special day of recognition.

Harry, the student Seth bailed out of jail, gave an emotional speech about how Seth's intervention had changed many lives. Harry now was sheriff of Horizon County.

Fellow teachers stepped up to tell stories about Seth and his students, about some of their own, and about the joys, rewards and humorous moments of teaching. Especially the humorous moments.

"Seth always told the one about the time he asked a student why his paper wasn't done," one of them said.

"'It's still in my pencil,' the kid said."

"I remember a time I assigned students to draw a picture of one of Columbus' three ships," said another colleague.

"One student turned in a blank piece of paper with a single black dot in the middle.

"What's this?" I asked.

"'That's the Santa Maria, way out in the middle of the Atlantic.'

"I had to give him credit for at least knowing the name of one of the ships. And the right ocean."

An elementary school colleague told of the time a third-grade student burst into his classroom with big news: The little boy said he had heard that the librarian was leaving.

"I guess by now she's read all the books," he said.

A kindergarten teacher recalled the time she was trying to teach students proper restroom etiquette.

"Now, what's the last thing you do after you're done? I asked, meaning flush the toilet, put the seat down and wash your hands. And a little boy's voice in the back of the room said, 'Shake it!'"

It could have gone on all night as a Seth roast, so it was getting late by the time Seth himself took the podium in response to loud calls for "Speech! Speech!"

Seth made a brief attempt, but by that time he was a little wobbly from too much punch, and mostly could only mumble his thank-yous. In the time-honored tradition of students everywhere, the fruit punch had been spiked.

But he did get off one story himself. It was about a mother who went in one morning as usual to wake her son because it was time for school. He didn't want to go.

"Give me two good reasons why you can't go to school today," the mom says.

"Well, the kids all hate me, and the teachers all hate me, too."

"That's no reason not to go to school. Now get ready."

"Give me two good reasons why I should go to school."

"Well, for one you're 59 years old. And two, you're the principal."

Some of his teacher golfing partners gave him a parting gift – 12 personalized golf balls, carefully cradled in an egg carton, with a coupon for 12 more. Their spokesman reminded everyone that golf balls were like eggs – they were white, roundish, sold by the dozen, and in a week you had to buy some more.

The last business of the evening was a presentation by Juval Platt, who revealed that Seth's anonymous scholarship fund at the bank was anonymous no more, had been sweetened considerably just recently by patrons of the Rainbow Café, and by an unknown donor, and would provide full-ride college scholarships henceforth every year to five qualifying graduates.

Seth went home with some gifts from his students: a sweatshirt that said "School's Out Forever" and a new set of golf clubs with a plaque on the bag reading "Seth Pinderton: Always on the Fairway."

Seth did not stay retired for long. Some former students and teacher colleagues coaxed him into becoming principal of their new charter school, where the emphasis was on Americanism.

He also taught classes in American history and civics.

Chapter 26

Trouble

Rex Warnevar noticed him first. He was on the sidewalk opposite the café, walking up and down the block, writing in a notebook, taking photos of buildings. He certainly was not trying to be discreet. He wore orange slacks, a checkered red-and-white shirt and a green straw hat.

"Wow!" Rex said. "He's a walking Day-Glo blinking neon sign all by himself."

"He's been around here before," said Hank, hands cupped around the container of to-go coffee he was taking back to the newspaper office. "He's obviously not a fashion consultant."

"I'd wager he's not married, either," said Joshua Clarver, whose trash truck was idling out back in the alley, "or his wife almost certainly would have said, 'You're not going out looking like THAT!'

"I've seen him taking photos on other streets in the neighborhood, too," Joshua added.

"Really?" Rex said. "I don't like it. He's up to something. And probably something not good."

Therese came to the window to look, just as the man was joined by two others, a pair that Therese recognized immediately. One was Hector Gunsterfritz, the city councilman for her district; the other was the city attorney, Osgood Spiegelshank. Therese glared at them through the window. They had a history, going back to when she purchased the café and made some changes.

Gunsterfritz was a prissy, bald, effeminate little man of about 60, who walked with such tiny mincing steps that he appeared to be prancing. He needed to demonstrate to Therese that he was in charge of this block, so she underwent a grilling before her permit paperwork and change of ownership were grudgingly approved.

Their relationship did not start well. Obsessed with every detail, he had challenged the design, color and placement of Therese's attractive new sign.

She couldn't help herself.

"Apparently you were not much concerned with the buzzing, flickering, rusting old neon relic that preceded it," she snapped.

Gunsterfritz frowned, his face reddened. He was not used to being challenged in his own bailiwick. This upstart needed a lesson. He saw to it, with Spiegelshank's help, that the permits for her remodeling project were unnecessarily delayed.

Over the years they had many other disagreements, culminating in open hostility when Therese had the audacity to place a campaign poster of his election opponent in a café window.

Spiegelshank, tall and thin with the phony adulation mannerisms of a typical yes-man toady, was always at Gunsterfritz' side. Therese suspected the attorney saw the councilman as a potential mayoral candidate, and perhaps bigger things above that, and was positioning himself accordingly.

"These guys are bad news," Rex said. "I've had my own problems with them over the years. They've never been caught at it, but the word is out there on the street that they are on the take, use their positions for their own gain."

What they were up to became evident a few days later, when Therese, Rex and other merchants on the street received official letters from the city advising them that their block, one of the oldest in the city, had been targeted as part of an urban renewal project aimed at expanding the city's services, including a yard to park city vehicles, and a new homeless shelter.

"The city is quite anxious to get these unfortunate folks off the streets, out of parks and cars and RVs, and into safe shelter," the letter said. "Several alternatives have been identified as potential sites for these vitally-needed expansions of our city's services. We are prepared to purchase property, or seize it by eminent domain, if necessary."

It added that public hearings would be convened soon to explain the scope of the project, at which citizens could voice their opinions and concerns.

"I have some opinions, yes," Therese said bitterly. Her family had been down this road before.

Her father had been the victim of eminent domain, an episode that she always believed contributed to his despondency and decline after her mother died. He owned a small bookstore in a strip mall, and when the mall was condemned to make way for a road widening project, he lost the thing that might have kept him occupied and distracted during a difficult time.

He scorned the buyout offer as laughable, and his new location proved to be poorly suited for a bookstore.

"Losing my mom was bad enough," Therese told Rex over the café counter one day. "Losing his business also was just too much."

So Therese and her troops at the Rainbow Café settled in for a fight.

"Two can play this game," she said. "This is war. But I need some artillery, some ammunition."

She didn't have long to wait, or go very far to find some.

Thanks to the jar – that pot of gold at the end of the counter – Therese had long since abandoned any skepticism she had about the concepts of destiny, fate, purposeful coincidence, kismet, miracles, even divine intervention. Her own story was proof enough for her that the lightning bolt of serendipity could strike anytime. And it didn't always come out of a jar.

"Ma'am, you'd better come see this."

It was Jean-Paul Stoquet, her handyman-cook-waiter, motioning to her from the top of the stairs to the basement. He had been investigating the source of the water seepage down there, and had found it.

"Do I have to go down there? Can't you just tell me?"

"No, ma'am, this is something you have to see."

She took a deep breath and followed him down the stairs. It was as she remembered, a hard-packed dirt floor, dark, damp and cobwebby, a single light bulb hanging from a ceiling cord.

"A good place for another horror movie about teenagers hiding from a serial killer," she said to herself, shuddering.

Jean-Paul was standing near a back wall, holding a crowbar and a big flashlight.

"Look through this," he said, motioning toward a small hole he had punched through the wall. He rapped his knuckles against the surface. "It's hollow behind here." There was a thin layer of water on the floor at their feet, trailing away toward a channel dug along a side wall.

Therese peered through the hole, but even with the flashlight it was difficult to see much. But when her eyes adjusted to the gloom inside, she could make out what appeared to be a small room. Puddles of standing water on the floor were seeping into the basement itself.

"What is it?" she said, alarmed that the building could be in danger.

"I don't know," Jean-Paul said. "I waited to see if you want to open it up more."

"By all means, yes."

Jean-Paul hefted the crowbar and enlarged the hole. The basement walls were of the fieldstone and mortar common in foundations of the nineteenth century, but the space where Jean-Paul had punched a hole and was working, was about the size of a doorway. It had been covered over with wood-lath and plaster long ago, and the surface painted with mock stones in a respectable attempt to make it blend in with the surrounding stonework.

Therese peered in again. The room was perhaps five feet by five feet. The back wall was entirely of brick.

Jean-Paul peered in also.

"I'm guessing this might have been a root cellar," he said. "They were common here in the U.S. and elsewhere in the old days, before refrigeration. From the looks of it, it appears that down here it's the original foundation, and that the building above has been remodeled or maybe even rebuilt over the years. Maybe a fire?"

Therese didn't know.

"Let's open it up," she said.

He tore off some of the lath and plaster covering the opening, and they stepped in. More fieldstone walls, cool to the touch, cobwebs, mold. A mouse scurried into a crack between the stones, and Therese jumped.

Some of the wall fieldstones here were stacked and staggered, and served as crude shelves at waist level. There was enough space to store root vegetables, plus fruit and vegetable preserves, jams and jellies, salted meat and fish, to keep a family going through a long winter.

Here and there on a shelf was an ancient forgotten jar, the ingredients inside long since congealed and hardened into an unrecognizable black lump.

"No doubt," Jean-Paul said. "A root cellar. And this is very interesting," he added, eyeing the brick back wall. "Why is that there? It must be sealing off something else. Shall we have a look?"

Therese nodded. This old place had held its secrets long enough.

Jean-Paul carefully opened a small hole by knocking out several bricks. A wave of cold, musty air rushed into the room, ancient ghosts being released. Therese shivered.

Jean-Paul peered through the opening. His eyes widened as he turned to Therese and handed her the flashlight.

She had to stand on her toes to see through the opening. It appeared to be another room, but there was so much rubble tight against the brick in some places that it was hard to tell. If there had ever been a ceiling, it had long ago collapsed and was now part of the rubble.

Something attached to a shoring timber on a side wall caught her attention. Faded lettering of some kind, the print still legible.

"Look," she said, eyes wide with excitement, handing the flashlight back to Jean-Paul.

He peered through the hole, then turned to her, puzzlement obvious in his scrunched face and squint.

"What is it?"

Therese smiled mysteriously and put her finger to her lips.

"For now, this is our secret. You must not breathe a word of this to anyone. Open up the hole a little more so I can take some photos."

She reached through the hole with one hand as best she could and took several photos with her phone. She did not want to risk opening the wall any larger for fear the rubble pressing against the bricks would spill into the room and make the water problem worse.

"Okay. Now hang a blanket over this. We need to get some help."

Chapter 27

The Invisible Man

Therese was anxious to pursue her suspicions about the basement, but became distracted and enmeshed instead, as usual, in the lives of her customers and the affairs of the neighborhood.

Lorenzo Escarro was one of them. He received a regular paycheck from the Pfaltzer GPS Company, a manufacturer of devices used with the Global Positioning System. The firm operated out of a factory complex in an industrial park a mile from the Rainbow Café.

His reliability record was impressive. His punch card showed he rarely missed a shift. He was a faithful member of the union, his performance reviews were exemplary, he was admired and respected among his fellow workers.

There was only one problem. Lorenzo, a recent immigrant, was hardly ever there.

Therese learned about this phantom employee from Ira Grandling, a foreman at the company, who often stopped in after a night shift. His wife, with a daughter just recently gone off to college, had become one of Therese's Doting on Daughters surrogate moms.

This day, Lorenzo was with him, and he introduced him to Therese. Still somewhat unfamiliar with the language spoken all around him, Lorenzo looked on as Ira explained the situation.

"Don't tell anyone, but I am involved in a conspiracy, a massive coverup," he told Therese, grinning and with a finger to his lips.

"But it's with noble motives," Ira added. "We're all afraid our house of cards is going to come crashing down one of these days, and then what will Lorenzo do? We cover for him as best we can, but one of these days..."

The sentence trailed off into a question mark.

Lorenzo smiled and nodded at the mention of his name.

"He's such a good guy. He's had a run of bad luck and we're just trying to protect him until his life settles down."

"Coverup and conspiracy. Such devious, dangerous words," Therese said. "But tell me more."

She learned that Lorenzo, a recent legal immigrant from Central America, was hired as a temporary employee at the firm, and so impressed his supervisors with his ambition, ability and work ethic that there were plans to bring him on full-time as soon as there was an opening.

"The guy is impressive," Ira said. "He works harder than anybody else, he's smart, conscientious, always looking for better and more efficient ways to do things. He fills in for other guys who need help or time off, even goes to their houses to help with their repair jobs. He's just so happy to be in America, he would be a credit to any company."

In his short time at the factory he had earned the friendship and respect of everybody around him. But Lorenzo had another problem besides his temporary job status. His four-year-old daughter, Marisol, needed surgery soon for a congenital heart defect.

As a temporary employee, he was not covered by the company's health and sick leave plan. So he volunteered for all kinds of inconvenient shifts, overtime assignments that few others wanted. But still, he was urgently needed at home, too.

Lorenzo's wife had been shouldering most of the responsibility for the needs of the family, which also included two small boys.

"So he began to call in sick a day here and a day there so he could help out at home," Ira said. "Then as his daughter's condition worsened, and she was hospitalized, he needed to be gone more often.

"We were all concerned that management would begin to notice his many absences and that his job would be in jeopardy."

So despite the risks to their own jobs, they stepped in to help their new friend. Therese was astounded at their story at first, but then remembered her mantra.

The plant was a complex of three separate buildings for design, production and assembly of GPS devices. His friends were gambling that given the size of the operation, if they could cover for him now and then, nobody would notice the peculiarities of one employee's unusual schedule.

"We punched his time card for him on days when he needed to be absent, did his work for him so the slack wouldn't be noticed," Ira said.

"The plant is so big there's not much danger that his absence will even be noted, as long as the production numbers don't go down. As his foreman, I was a crucial cog in the conspiracy. At my own peril, I might add."

There were some bumps along the way.

The union steward, while not unsympathetic to their plan, threatened to blow the whistle because if it was discovered, he would be held responsible for not interceding.

He was persuaded to drop his opposition when he was reminded of all the help his own family received years earlier when one of his children was seriously ill.

Lorenzo's co-workers tried to help him buy a temporary catastrophic-coverage health insurance plan, but he was turned down because of the pre-existing condition.

Union family members helped, too. One of their wives, a nurse at the hospital, got herself assigned to Marisol's floor and stopped by regularly to check on her condition.

But despite the efforts of Lorenzo's new friends, it did not end well. Marisol died during the surgery.

"We were all afraid we would be denied permission to attend the funeral," Ira said. "So we arranged to leave a skeleton crew behind to keep the place running.

"What were they going to do? Fire all of us? They got along OK when Lorenzo wasn't there some days. They could survive with a minimum crew for a couple of hours."

At the funeral home, they were surprised when the plant manager showed up, too.

"I don't know who you guys thought you were kidding," he told Ira. "We are quite capable of accounting for all of our employees, and we are not without some genuine human traits, you know, such as sympathy and empathy.

"We were on to your game early, but decided to let it play out, look the other way. We need guys like him. His assembly-line streamlining ideas have already saved us a lot of money. We'll also help with your fund."

Employes had set up a fund to help the family through their ordeal, to pay their significant medical and funeral expenses. The regulars at the Rainbow Café also helped out. Father Dunne at St. Sebastian Church encouraged Lorenzo's fellow parishioners to get involved, and then Therese stepped in, too.

Once again she played intermediary, dropping another note in the jar.

"We are becoming quite good friends, me and the jar," she mused.

And it wasn't long before a note from the "friend" pledged to take care of any shortfall.

Therese volunteered to sponsor Lorenzo for citizenship, but learned that she had to get in line. He already had offers from the plant manager, the union president and several fellow employees, including Ira. So instead, she sent meals to the family for several weeks.

Lorenzo's absences continued for another month, and his friends continued to cover for him, while he tended to his own and his family's grief. A few weeks later, the personnel office was mystified when for the first time ever, someone declined to accept the Employee of the Month award. Lorenzo demurred, aware that it was based partly on an exemplary attendance record.

He told the plant manager to deduct installments from his paycheck until all the wages he had received during his unauthorized absences were repaid.

His offer was declined.

Chapter 28

The Storyteller

Therese was annoyed that before she could get back to the discovery in the basement, she would have to handle yet another interruption. But Archie Casperson was dying, and because she was one of his few friends, everything else would have to wait.

Archie, one of the newest of her eccentric regulars, was not everyone's favorite. Some of the others were tired of his stories.

"He's a blowhard, a braggart, a phony and a fraud," Hank Lyson complained. "We hate to see him come through the door some days."

Therese tended to agree, but felt sorry for Archie. She sensed that he made up his dubious, questionable stories to embellish what had been an unremarkable, ordinary life.

To hear him tell it, Archie was a war hero, an inventor, an internet pioneer, an Indie 500 race car driver and a movie actor, among other fabulous things.

His wife also had been a remarkable person, and his kids – doctors, lawyers, athletes, musicians – were at the top of their professions.

He always sat at the same stool at the café counter. Therese and the others were so used to his loud complaints whenever he found somebody else sitting there that they warned others away from the stool, or placed a napkin dispenser on it if Archie was expected.

Archie was 82, widowed, lived in a retirement home apartment nearby, and his only outside activity seemed to be his daily visits to the Rainbow Café. He was frail and pale, and all that was left of a once-full head of black hair were a few gray wisps. Therese could not tell by the stubble on his chin if he was trying to grow a beard or if it was just neglect.

He first showed up at the café a year earlier, after he moved into the retirement home. And by now even Therese was becoming weary of his stories. They were not boastful, just a recounting of what seemed to be a very eventful and colorful life, stories that the rest of the regulars found hard to believe.

"If he's not lying, he has a helluva imagination," Hank said.

But lately the tales were becoming incoherent and rambling. The regulars had heard them all so many times they could tell when his latest version differed from the one he had told the last time. Therese suspected that he was slipping into dementia.

Archie was a war hero.

"I'll never forget that day near Da Nang. We were under heavy fire and a lot of our guys were wounded. I had to crawl through rice paddies and machine gun fire to pull two of my buddies to safety. Even got a medal for it."

Archie was an inventor.

"I worked on a lot of stuff that would make people's lives a lot easier, and help save the planet at the same time. For example, I came up with food packaging that was itself edible. How's that for a great idea? When you're done with the spaghetti box, just eat that, too.

"One of the big food companies tried it out, but their product testing folks said no matter what flavor they used, trying to make it taste like a dessert, I guess, their focus groups complained that it still tasted like cardboard."

Archie told this story with such earnestness, as he did with all of his tales, that the others were inclined to believe him at first.

"Or maybe he's just putting us on," Hank said. "But he never ever even cracks a smile."

Archie was an internet expert.

"I was working on this artificial intelligence thing, and then found out somebody had already beaten me to it. Some bunch of robots, probably."

Archie was an Indie 500 race car driver.

"Might have placed back in '73 if I hadn't been bumped against the wall and my car flipped upside down."

Archie was a movie actor.

"Not big-time, you know, but lots of character actor stuff. Look me up in *Apocalypse Now, The Deer Hunter,* and *Jaws.*"

Archie was a pro baseball player.

"Went to spring training with the Tigers in '62, but got cut after I banged up a knee when I collided with a fence."

Archie was a Washington insider.

"Worked in Tip O'Neill's office, when he was speaker of the house, back in the Reagan days. Worked on some pretty important, top-secret stuff. Remember the Iran-Contra Affair?"

Archie had some interesting jobs.

"I worked for a paint company, was in charge of coming up with names for new shades. You know, like Morning Mist and Fairway Fog and September Sky. A perfume company hired me away and I created names for scents -- Autumn Breeze and Summer Wind, Primal Lust, Hunger, stuff like that.

"My last job was with a pharmaceutical firm, working in their lab creating catchy gibberish names for new products, you know, like Prizfamulab and Rezkirpolaz and Kipstiterstan. Won a company prize for that last one.

"Two others of mine never made it because they were already taken. 'Btfsplk' was rejected because turns out there's a character in a 'Lil Abner' comic by that name, and well, everybody but me knew I guess that there's a Mr. Mxyzptlk character who antagonizes Superman. You don't want to be sued by Superman."

Archie's kids were all geniuses, celebrities in their professions.

"Derek, he's chief of surgery at a big hospital out east. Ben, he's a partner in one of Washington's largest law firms. Kathy is the lead violinist and concertmaster with a major metropolitan orchestra. Emma, before she married, won a lot of money on the women's pro golf tour."

And most of all, Archie did not always tell the whole truth.

Everybody knew it, because some of his stories were becoming so preposterous, straining credibility to the breaking point, that their eyes glazed over whenever he started in. And today's version often contradicted an earlier one.

"If all of what he says is true, then I'm mayor of Chicago, own houses on five continents, and drive a 1929 Hupmobile," Hank scoffed.

The café regulars humored Archie, writing off his exaggerations, like Therese did, to his age, grief and loneliness, and a delusion that somehow he needed to prove he had lived a worthwhile, exciting life, even if. he mixed up and juxtaposed some of his own tales.

Therese, always concerned about the welfare of her regulars, checked with the retirement home and learned that Archie had been a meter reader for the electric company for 40 years. His children were bus drivers, computer technicians, landscapers and receptionists.

But there was one thing Archie had not lied about: his wife.

Archie met Lorraine at a public library. He was checking out some mystery novels, she was a romance novelist and was checking out the competition. They bumped into each other in the stacks, and dropped the books each was carrying,

"I wonder if there's a category called romantic mysteries," Archie said, eyeing the mixed jumble on the floor.

"They could call it 'mystantics," Lorraine said.

"Or romanteries," Archie said.

"Love in the Stacks" could have been one of the titles.

Soon they were living a love story of their own, and co-authoring several little human sequels.

"Maybe," Therese surmised, since his wife had been so successful at creating imaginary worlds, "in his strange mind he figured he would try his hand at it, too."

They had been married for 52 years when Lorraine died five years earlier. She was the author of a long series of romance novels, specialized in "meet-cute" plots like their own, and was extremely successful at it.

Archie never really recovered from her death. Therese, too, suspected the long grieving process had something to do with his gradual decline. Lorraine had been confined to a nursing home for several years before her death, and Archie spent every day there.

"He had a lot of time to concoct some fascinating stories," Therese said to herself, shaking her head sadly.

249

When the retirement home called one day, Therese was alarmed.

"It's Mr. Casperson," the administrator said. "He's suffered a stroke and has been moved to the hospice part of our facility. I've notified the family, but I know you're a friend, and I hate to add that he's probably not going to make it."

Therese rushed over to the retirement home hospice and found Archie sleeping fitfully.

"I'm so sorry, my dear friend," she said. His eyes fluttered slightly and then opened. She noticed a piece of notepaper clutched in his hand. It smelled faintly of perfume.

"What is this?" she asked.

"Read it. It's my entrance ticket to where she is." He smiled faintly.

"My love," it began. "Our love affair, its joys and riches, its rewards and subplots, has been far superior to any storyline I could ever have imagined. It will continue some day up there. I will look for you in the heavenly stacks."

It was signed "Lorraine" in a shaky hand written when she herself was at the end.

When Therese put the note back in Archie's hands, they were turning cold. He was gone.

♣ ♣ ♣

As she was leaving the building, the administrator called her aside.

"You know, I'm sure his friends at the café were tired of hearing his stories, right?"

Therese nodded knowingly.

"Well, we were, too, until we did some research into his tales and were astounded at what we learned. Not only did he do a lot of that stuff he bragged about -- well, in some cases it was a matter of 'sorta but not quite' -- and he actually left some things out.

"For example, he *was* in a whole bunch of movies -- cameos, walk-ons, crowd extras, anonymous folks walking on a sidewalk or beach, soldiers in action scenes, like that. In one, he danced with a partner in the background while the two major characters feuded in front of him.

"He was in Vietnam but spent the whole time writing stories about other guys' heroics. And get this, we found a newspaper story describing how he actually made a fortune by inventing shoes with replaceable soles – when one sole wore out, just slip another one in."

"I have an idea," Therese told Cyrus Steelfarb. "You are a writer. How about a story, maybe even a kids' story, about an old guy who claims he did all kinds of fantastic stuff in his life, and nobody believes him, makes fun of him, but when they check into it, it's all true?"

"Well, that's a little out of my line," said Cyrus, whose previous fictional success was with a blind physician who had a supernatural sense of smell," but I'll give it a shot."

With the help of the jar, they found a publisher for their little book.

"Short Tall Tales," it was called. It did only moderately well.

Chapter 29

Ammunition

Therese decided she should bring Rex Warnevar and Joshua Clarver into her confidence. After all, this was Rex's building too, since they were attached, and Joshua was a historian, an amateur archeologist of sorts, and if her suspicions about the tunnel were correct, he would have a special interest in this discovery.

Joshua peeked through the hole in the bricks, looked for a moment, and stepped back. His face was so sad and grim that Therese stepped up and slipped her arm through his.

Rex took a look and smiled grimly, shaking his head.

"Let's get on with it," Therese said.

Jean-Paul stepped up with a sledge hammer and began pounding at the bricked-up wall. Joshua whacked at the bricks with a pick-axe. Soon it was in rubble at their feet, except for four courses of brick that they left in place as a water barrier. Jean-Paul began loading the bricks into a wheelbarrow and hauled them off to a corner of the basement.

They stepped over the barrier and turned toward the wall.

It was an old faded poster. In big, black, still readable letters it read:

$200 REWARD.

Ranaway from the subscriber

in Jefferson County, Mississippi, on June 5, 1847

FIVE NEGRO SLAVES

In archaic typography, the poster gave physical descriptions of Washington Roak, 25, his wife Mary, and their three children, Malcomb, Matilda and George. It added that, "It is supposed they were accompanied by a white man, and were traveling chiefly at night."

The poster was signed by their "owner."

"Well, I think we know what this means," Therese said. "This place was a stop on the Underground Railroad before the Civil War. This right here is probably the end of a tunnel, filled with rubble now, and ran down to the river, which isn't that far. But what's that poster doing here?"

Joshua's face was somber.

"So that's what an entire black family was worth in those terrible days. Two hundred fricking dollars."

He looked away quickly, blinking, then bent to read some faded crude hand-lettering at the bottom of the poster.

"What does it say?" Rex asked.

Joshua grinned.

"It says, 'We have absquatulated!!!'"

"What does that mean?"

"Nineteenth century slang. It means Roak probably carried that poster with him as a gruesome souvenir, and posted it here as yesterday's equivalent of the finger, or 'In your face.' It means 'skedaddled.' And look at those exclamation points! They say more than any words could convey."

They all smiled sadly, in admiration of a man expressing his defiance at an obscene practice, but also for his ability to retain a sense of composure in such trying circumstances.

Therese looked toward the tunnel entrance, filled with rubble almost to where they were standing.

"Just imagine," she said, "the courage of this family. Go, Washington, go!"

Joshua reminded them of the story of the Underground Railroad, the slavery situation in the South at the time of the Civil War, and how abolitionists in both the North and South encouraged and assisted runaway slaves to escape north.

They were passed along from safe house to safe house, until they finally reached safety, sometimes in Canada.

"It wasn't really a railroad, of course. That was a term used to describe the escape network. Often, the fugitive slaves were moved along rivers."

"And that's how they got here," Therese said. "This was a station, and this building, a private residence in those days, was a safe house."

Joshua nodded. Over the years he had read and heard stories from old-timers about the history of the town, and knew that the Rainbow Café building went back at least to Civil War days. Therese had been told by the previous owner that it was built originally as a private home by a wealthy merchant who made his fortune by moving goods up and down the river.

"The 'goods' he was moving apparently included some contraband human cargo," Therese said. "Let's not forget that there were a lot of decent, moral people around in those days, too.

"Back when we first glimpsed the poster, I looked this original owner up. He was a fervent abolitionist, from an immigrant family that fled persecution and an oppressive regime somewhere in Europe.

"When constructing the house, he directed the builders to provide a hidden tunnel leading from the house to the river. At first it was for his own quick access to the river, and for the amusement of his kids, but later he supervised, through his river barge traffic, the escape of many Underground Railroad refugees.

"I admire this guy. I'm proud to be one of his successors in this building."

Therese was told the house was in the "country" back in those days, was remodeled and rebuilt several times, and eventually became a dry goods store as the town expanded and enveloped it. A succession of businesses followed in the space, including several restaurants, and then the café.

Rex's ice cream store next door, originally a harness and carriage shop, was attached to it at some point. A livery stable stood nearby somewhere.

Therese also remembered the previous owner telling her that since the building had a somewhat mysterious history, she considered exploring national historic site status for it, but feared that would mean she would be restrained from doing any remodeling.

"As for your water problem," Joshua said, stepping across a puddle, "It's probably not coming from the river; too far away and downhill besides. More likely seepage from above. What's up there, above the tunnel?"

"A lot with a garage, where some wealthy guy stores a couple of vintage cars."

"At one time it must have been an open field," Joshua said, "which no doubt sank some when the tunnel collapsed, then was filled in. Maybe the seepage can be corrected with a little re-grading up there."

They cleared away more of the rubble, in an attempt to gauge the extent of the tunnel, but it was futile. The material was too tightly packed, like concrete, had been there too long. Opening it would require more than the four of them, and some bigger equipment.

"You know," ventured Jean-Paul, "it might not have just collapsed naturally. Perhaps it was deliberately destroyed in hopes of erasing any memory of those terrible days."

Therese nodded. She took more photos of the entrance and the poster. Then they re-hung the tarp. She looked defiantly at Joshua.

"Now I have some ammunition."

Chapter 30

Showdown

It was standing room only at city hall the night they took up the proposed major changes to the Rainbow Café neighborhood. Community interest in the issue was high; it was the most significant proposed change to this old neighborhood in 100 years. Nearby residents and merchants were doubly concerned: "Who's next?"

Every one of Therese's regulars was there, some of them with enough clout in the community to hopefully make council members listen.

Editor Hank Lyson was there. Banker Juval Platt. Father Marcus Aurelius Dunne. Plus Adeline Enders, Harriet Harterton, Joshua Clarver and Brady Stollwitz, shop owners themselves. Jean-Paul Stoquet, excited to see this demonstration of democracy in action, was wishing his father was there to see it, too.

Seth Pinderton was there, along with a cadre of students from a high school civics class. Samantha Broadland and her new friend Sarah, and little Eddy, too, now a bigger Eddy. Sarah was home for a few days, on leave with her Marine husband. Molly Malone, Cyrus Steelfarb, even Delroy Hempstead, with daughter Adelle pushing his wheelchair. At the rear of the room, Ruby and little Joanie looked on excitedly.

Therese thought she spotted her ex, Junior Tourneaux, in the crowd.

"What's he doing here?" she wondered, alarmed. "I thought he left. Whatever he's up to, it can't be good."

The meeting had to be moved to an auditorium when so many people showed up that even the spacious council chambers could not hold them all. Citizens were standing along the walls. Outside, in the lobby, those still denied a seat milled around a big-screen monitor to watch the proceedings.

Therese had stewed for weeks over this threat to her business, her block, her neighborhood. She vowed to fight Councilman Gunsterfritz and Spiegelshank, his toady. She spent the time gathering and verifying her evidence and arguments, and she was ready. But she feared that the hearing might be just a show, that sinister actors were already assured of the verdict they wanted.

So many residents, business owners and other interested parties, including all of the regulars at the Rainbow Café, wanted to speak that it had become unwieldly. During a strategy session at the cafe, Rex suggested that they appoint a spokesman for their group to avoid redundancy and to speed up the process. He was chosen.

The session began with some routine city housekeeping matters, and then a last-minute attempt to add an item to the agenda.

Therese watched in disgust as Junior was handed a microphone. At his shoulder was a figure familiar to many in the crowd, a corner-cutting developer notorious in the community for substandard structures.

But before he could say anything, Mayor Destiny Byington shut him down.

"Mr. Tourneaux," she said, "You already have been told that your request to have us consider a low-rent housing project for this location will not be taken up tonight. Surely you must know that to secure a place on the agenda you must go through proper channels."

Therese breathed a sigh of relief and caught Joshua's eye across the room. He winked and dialed a number on his cell phone.

Then came a slide presentation of existing facilities, the proposed new vehicle yard and the homeless shelter, which was greeted with a loud round of boos. The mayor banged her gavel in warning. The manager of public works described the need for a new vehicle yard -- the existing space could no longer accommodate the city's growing fleet of vehicles. Officials from the city's social service agencies made an impassioned plea for a new shelter.

Then it was Rex's turn.

He took the podium and opened a folder full of papers.

"Your honor, council members, thank you for this opportunity to defend our neighborhood. I am here to tell you that this block, especially the Rainbow Café, has done more to enhance our community, support its citizens, create a sense of civic pride, belonging and involvement, and yes, provide comfort and security for residents, than any vehicle yard or homeless shelter would ever be able to do."

Byington had to bang her gavel again when a chorus of voices shouted "Hear! Hear!"

"Ms. Martin is a one-woman social services agency all by herself. Let me list for you just a few of the things that she, with the help of her customers, has accomplished or provided through their very personal, private generosity. You might find some of this hard to believe, but I assure you, every bit of it is true. Ms. Martin will support me on that, I'm sure."

He could see Therese off to one side, and nodded. They had decided not to mention the jar's mysterious anonymity. It would only set off a firestorm of guessing, and it was best not to create a distraction now and a lot of gossipy conjecture.

Rex recited a litany of good works that had flowed from the Rainbow Café's donation jar. He told about the many small businesses that had been started, and several others that had been saved. A new much-needed day care center had been created. He told the council about mother-daughter and father-son groups that had been very successful, thanks to Therese Martin.

"The Rainbow Café not only helps satisfy the basic nourishment needs of the neighborhood, both physical and mental, it also functions as a psychiatry couch, a job center, a reunion hub, communications office, refugee center, dating service and wedding consultant, even international goodwill ambassador."

He described how city playgrounds had been created, a neighborhood Christmas tradition rescued and expanded, a wedding reception salvaged, admiring overseas visitors treated to tours of the wonders of America.

Glaring directly at Gunsterfritz, he added, "All of us in the neighborhood agree that the Rainbow Café has accomplished more in the way of civic improvement and unity than any politician has ever done."

Gunsterfritz and Spiegelshank, seated at a table in front with other officials, were shifting uncomfortably in their chairs. Until now their expressions were smug, confident that their machinations had assured that the hearing was a mere formality. They had underestimated the opposition.

Rex told how veterans were honored, a cemetery endowed with a monument and a perpetual care guarantee, a beloved teacher honored with a farewell salute, how a church was saved.

"Father Dunne here can tell you, I'm sure, that the flood of Christian charity and good works emanating from the Rainbow Café might even match the output coming from his church."

Father Dunne held up his hand.

"Amen!" he shouted.

Mayor Byington, suppressing a smile, raised the gavel on the wave of laughter but then thought better of it.

"And the scholarships. I can't begin to describe how many scholarships can be traced to the Rainbow Café and the generosity of the patrons there."

Gunsterfritz and Spiegelshank were glancing nervously at each other.

"I could tell you a wonderful story about how two families on opposite sides of the Atlantic, tragically touched by World War II, were brought together to commemorate their common sorrow. But you've probably already heard it. It was in all the papers, on all the TV channels.

"And you no doubt read in the *Herald* the heart-warming story of how one of our elementary school classes raised money for an Italian town and school that had been ravaged by a flood. That campaign, which brought our town international recognition and respect, and a visit from children and officials of that beleaguered town, was instigated by Ms. Martin and the folks at the Rainbow Café.

"There is a grove of trees at the school now that is a lasting tribute to the values and kindness of our youngest generation and their wonderful gesture."

Heads were nodding in agreement. Even Therese listened in admiration.

"Wow. He's pretty good at this."

Gunsterfritz tried to interrupt Rex, but the mayor shut him off.

"Let the man finish."

"I am finished your honor. But I ask you, do we want to let this diamond, this treasure, this source of good works and good neighborliness, this fountain of hope and achievement, vanish from our town, our neighborhood? And for what? What is to take its place? Surely you can find a more suitable site for your purposes.

"And I speak not only for the Rainbow Café, but for others along this street, one of the oldest in the city and with a storied past. Some buildings go back to the Civil War. Ms. Martin will have more to say about that.

"If you remove the Rainbow Café, you have stabbed this neighborhood in its heart."

As Rex turned to take his seat, the room erupted in applause. Gunsterfritz glared at him and wiped his brow with the back of his hand.

"Ms. Martin, you are on the agenda as our other speaker," the mayor said.

Therese rose slowly from her seat and made her way to the podium, carrying a folder of maps, photos and notes.

"Thank you, your honor, and council members." Then, bowing toward Rex, "and to Mr. Warnevar."

She took a deep breath, and looked defiantly at Gunsterfritz and Spiegelshank. They avoided her stare, not quite so sure of themselves anymore after Rex's presentation.

"I have two points to make. The first is this, and I will not belabor the point: Would not we be better served, would not *they* be better served, if instead of just providing free, temporary housing for these unfortunates, we prepare them also to return to society as productive, contributing citizens by providing vocational and job training? We already have several shelters for the homeless."

She could hear the whispers of agreement behind her and sense that many heads were nodding.

"Does not establishing more of them just encourage more homelessness? It enfranchises homelessness as a permanent state, and institutionalizes what should be a temporary lifeline. And it encourages those who might choose this way of life."

The room erupted in a din of applause, whistles, shouts. Adeline Enders rang a cowbell so loudly that people on either side put fingers in their ears.

The loudest shout came from Councilman Gunsterfritz.

"Objection! Point of Order!" he bellowed, rising to his feet. "Ms. Martin is here tonight to speak only on the agenda item before us, the issue of acquiring private property for a vital public use. Her remarks are irrelevant to the main agenda item. I for one am not interested in her views on social services and civic responsibilities."

Everyone looked toward the mayor.

"Overruled," she said. "Ms. Martin, you may proceed."

Gunsterfritz, not accustomed to being dismissed so curtly, sat down abruptly as Therese continued.

"Well, it's not so irrelevant, because it seems to me, and to many, many others because I have a pretty good finger on the pulse of our community from my perch at the Rainbow Café, that there is widespread opposition to creating another entity to house these folks, many of whom are able-bodied but lack the ambition and incentive, and sometimes the training, to join the workforce. And some of them need treatment for a variety of addictions.

"But why not a facility to house them temporarily, yes, but also to retrain and treat them, instead of a facility to just get them inside, to hide them from tourists?

"Now, don't get me wrong. I – we – have empathy for those who, because of age or illness or other reasons, are in these circumstances through no fault of their own. Yes, we should take care of them. But some of these people are in dire straits of their own making.

"As for a vehicle yard. This is a business district of shops and services. I, for one, question whether you are planning to violate your own zoning ordinances.

"So I have now said all that I'm going to say on that subject," Therese continued. "But listen well to my second point."

Café regulars were surprised at Therese's strident, defiant tone. Most had never seen her like this. Rex Warnevar smiled broadly. A grinning Molly Malone clenched her fists and shook them up and down in approval. Hank Lyson was taking notes furiously. Adeline clutched her cowbell.

"As for this having nothing to do with the main agenda item here tonight, I disagree," Therese continued. "It has everything to do with it. Because my other point here is going to make this entire matter moot."

She looked directly at Gunsterfritz and Spiegelshank again, addressing them personally. They glanced sideways at each other, avoided her stare.

"And, if you have thoughts of rezoning or imposing land use restrictions on my property to achieve your ends, well, you can forget that, too."

The audience stirred, hitching forward in their seats in anticipation of what might be coming next.

"As you know, ladies and gentlemen, our town has a long history. It has even been said but never verified that the bones of some buildings here, my building included, go back to Civil War days and even before.

"I have discovered just recently that indeed it does. A knowledgeable friend of mine has conducted a preliminary inspection of my building, and we have uncovered, in the basement, concealed for years behind a sealed wall, a collapsed tunnel that no doubt led to the river, not that far away."

She stepped over to a nearby easel and pulled the covering away. The photos she had taken of the tunnel opening, including the poster of Washington Roak and his family, were mounted there, and transmitted instantly to the huge display screens on either sides of the auditorium and out into the lobby.

The audience stirred at the sight of the rubble in the tunnel entrance, and began to whisper loudly among themselves about the poster.

"In this tunnel we have discovered evidence that fugitive slaves once sought shelter in our community. We have found a wanted poster on a tunnel wall advertising for the recapture of runaway slaves, a poster no doubt brought here by the slaves themselves as a macabre souvenir of their bondage. They have scrawled across it, as you can see, a defiant protest about this abominable practice.

"There is strong evidence that these brave and unfortunate people sought solace and shelter here, and were warmly welcomed and aided by our community, before being moved on to Canada or elsewhere. There is very likely much more evidence to be found, farther along down the tunnel, once it is excavated.

"Yes, I am saying that our town, my building specifically, was a crucial stop, a safe house, on the Underground Railroad."

The room was totally silent for a moment as stunned residents took this all in. Then it erupted again in applause, many rising to their feet.

The mayor did not bother to bang for order.

When the din subsided, Therese continued, looking directly at Gunsterfritz and Spiegelshank.

"I am sure it is dawning on you that there is no way the city is going to be touching this historic building, at least until a full investigation can be made. In fact, I intend to apply immediately for national landmark status not only for the building, but for this entire historic block. I invite you to conduct your own inspection.

"If you plan to fight it, and I don't see how you can, it will be years before this is resolved, through the courts if necessary. I have been assured that there is little question it will be protected with landmark status. You should consider carefully the opinions of our black friends and neighbors if you try to erase this sad memorial, such palpable evidence of a regrettable, deplorable time in their continuing American struggle."

Mayor Byington, looking toward Gunsterfritz, her probable opponent in the next election, could not suppress a small smirk.

As Therese stepped down, the audience rose to its feet, applauding and shouting. There was little doubt where this segment of the citizenry stood. Adeline's cowbell could hardly be heard above the uproar.

The meeting ended with the mayor appointing a committee made up of two black council members, historical society officers and university archaeologists, to investigate Therese's story. Gunsterfritz and Spiegelshank were last seen sputtering unintelligibly and yelling loudly at each other as they left the building.

Later that night, in anticipation of the vote, there was a victory party at the Rainbow Café. So many people showed up to celebrate that the event spilled outside onto the sidewalk. The scene was so festive that on popular demand, Rex opened up the ice cream shop, and Harriet Harterton began handing out free cupcakes.

The Leprechaun Band hastily assembled with their instruments.

Soon, Molly Malone was dancing with Brady Stollwitz, and Jean-Paul Stoquet, revealing a lovely baritone, led the crowd in several choruses of "Happy Days Are Here Again." Later, as the festivities wound down, he brought tears to many eyes with his version of "God Bless America."

Therese chuckled knowingly a week later when Hank brought her the latest issue of the *Herald*.

"Corruption Exposed at City Hall," the headline said in type usually reserved for presidential assassinations or natural disasters. "Councilman, city attorney and others charged," said a second headline.

The story described in great detail a scheme by Gunsterfritz, assisted by Spiegelshank, to influence the site selection process for the homeless shelter and vehicle yard.

It said planning commission officials originally selected an abandoned golf practice range as the preferred location, but after some money changed hands, two of the planning officials involved had been persuaded to change their vote. The story revealed that Gunsterfritz held an option to buy a parcel of land in an adjacent block, where he intended to build a service station that would profit from fueling the city's large fleet.

The scheme also came apart because the two principal players blamed each other for not being aware of the Rainbow Café's significant history, and because the city attorney turned on his partner.

Spiegelshank said he had come to realize that Gunsterfritz cared only about his own interests, and was determined to exact revenge on Therese, his longtime nemesis.

"He was completely indifferent to the welfare of the town," he told investigating officials. "He was willing to replace a priceless artifact, a site of living history, a neighborhood institution.

"I finally realized he had targeted the Rainbow Café because he and the owner, Therese Martin, had a long history of disagreements, going back to when she first bought the property. This was a personal grudge."

Therese smiled as she cut up another fresh peach cobbler into equal portions. She wasn't sure if Spiegelshank was being truthful or just demonstrating again his talent for self-preservation, and she didn't much care.

"Ah, justice. They will look so good in stripes."

Hank left the copy of the paper with her, but not before pointing out another important story on the front page.

After confirming Therese's story with their own investigation, the council rejected the proposal in a 9-0 vote.

Chapter 31

Exposed

You were absolutely spectacular last night," Therese said, snuggling up against Rex on the living room couch in his apartment. She had just slipped through the pass-through, motel-style door separating the apartment from hers.

"Well, maybe, my dear," Rex said. "But we have a problem. What do we do now?"

"I don't know. We should all have problems like this."

Rex had been waiting for Therese as usual, with a kiss and a glass of wine and a home-cooked meal, after another of her long days at the café. Usually, she just wanted to settle down with a Jane Austen novel or watch TV.

They had been married for a year, but saw no good reason to make it public knowledge.

"It's nobody's business," Therese said, "and besides, I kind of like the aura of mystery that surrounds us."

And she also appreciated that both of them had doubled the size of their living space.

Rex had no problem with this, and continued to pretend that they were just close friends and maybe, someday, something more.

♣ ♣ ♣

Therese, working under a dim light in the kitchen late one night, thought she saw a shadowy figure moving in the dark, empty café out beyond the counter. She reached for a knife, groped for her phone to call 911, then hesitated in recognition as the figure approached the end of the counter.

After a furtive glance around, it slipped a note into the jar, which was asking for help with Therese's Moms and Pops groups.

It was Rex Warnevar.

"You!" she shouted, bursting through the kitchen doors to confront him. "It's been you! My God! Of all people! And how did you get in here?"

Backing away, he held up a set of keys as a reminder that they had exchanged keys in case of any emergencies at either building.

"I didn't think anybody was here. It looked so dark. You can put down the knife."

She made sure the door was locked. She did not want this conversation to be interrupted.

"Yes," he acknowledged sheepishly, caught in the act. "I have money I don't know what to do with. What better use than to help people realize their dreams? It is my mission, as you know. I don't want any credit for this. Please don't tell anyone."

Therese was so stunned she could barely speak. The knife dropped to the floor. A simmering thought rose in her mind and exploded there.

"You mean – you mean – it was you who made this possible for me?" She spread her hands, motioning around the room.

"Yes. You were a waitress then, and I saw how you treated customers, how involved you were in their lives, and they in yours, how sharp you were in business matters, your special touch with people. I told myself that you should be running this place, or have a place of your own. I even thought of trying to hire you away from here. But you are so much more than an ice cream shop."

"You did?" Her mouth was dry, open, her hand on her throat. The enormity of what he was saying began to overwhelm her; tears streamed down her cheeks and she was shaking and crying openly. Guilt, too: She relived in her mind their early dispute over the cooler issue, and then his reaction to Jeremy Cooperton's military lies.

"I, I, I don't know what to say," she stammered. "I don't know how to thank you."

Rex stepped close, put his hands on her cheeks, and kissed her.

She was startled, but managed quite easily to continue the kiss.

"I have been in love with you since those first days, he said. "I do have a soul, I just needed you to bring it out."

Rex bent to one knee.

"You can thank me by becoming my wife," he said. "Were I not so caught by surprise, I might have been able to arrive with a ring."

Five quiet seconds hung between them. He looked up at her expectantly. She was grinning.

"As Jane Austen said somewhere, "I had not known you a month before I felt that you were the last man in the world on whom I could ever be prevailed on to marry."

Rising, he looked crestfallen.

"So, yes!" she said, throwing her arms around his neck.

They were married during the trip to Holland to see Andreas Manderfield and the grave of Alton Hempstead. Delroy Hempstead and his sister Adelle were witnesses to the ceremony, performed by a civil registry official. They were sworn to secrecy.

Back at home again, Therese and Rex began to collaborate in managing the affairs of the jar.

♣ ♣ ♣

After dinner they relaxed at the table with another glass of wine.

"You know, I have some regrets," Therese said. "For one, I'm sorry I had to lie to my friends about not knowing the source of the jar funds. But I really didn't know back then. And we should have encouraged Father Dunne to continue his stand-up comic gig. What a sensation he might have been! Vegas! Late night TV! The Minister of Mirth! The Diocesan Bob Newhart!"

"I'm sure the bishop would have had something to say about that," Rex reminded her. "And you should think instead of all the successes, all the joy you brought to people through your great string of ideas."

She had to nod and smile as her mind went back to that momentous day in Juval Platt's office, when she learned the terms of her windfall: In the future, if she was able, she was to pass her good fortune on in some way, pay it forward in generous, humane gestures of her own.

She was pretty sure she had done that, and more. Looking back on the many humanitarian missions of the jar, the times she helped it steer people to their dreams, she could tell herself that she had been true to her pledge.

Their "problem" now, as Rex had put it, was that just as their enthusiasm for their anonymous donation jar charity was beginning to wane, their ability to fund worthy new ventures was growing.

Therese was peering intently at a calculator.

"By my reckoning, when I add what's left of my dad's life insurance to Adeline Enders' bequest, plus my own funds, we have going on two million. If I hadn't pledged to donate the café building to that historical preservation foundation, we'd have even more."

"We have four million when I add in mine," Rex said. "That anti-scammer robocall device is still amazingly popular. The royalties are still pouring in."

They looked at each other for a long moment.

"What are we going to do with all this money?" Rex said.

Therese laughed.

"Like I said, everybody should have problems like this."

Both were weary of the business pressures and the long hours, which for Therese had not yet been relieved, since the building would not be turned over to the historical foundation for another year. That would give her time to wind up her affairs there and for the foundation to explore the tunnel.

They intended to turn the building into a museum of the Underground Railroad, but there were opposing views on what to do with the tunnel. Some wanted it cleared of debris and reinforced for tours. At the end of the tunnel, overlooking the river, they wanted to erect a bronze sculpture of a fugitive family, all five raising their hands to the skies, and freedom.

Others wanted to fill it in permanently and seal it off, erase any reminder that it ever existed.

"Maybe Jean-Paul was right," Therese said, recalling that he had speculated if that might not be the very reason it had been filled in and hidden long ago.

"I think we should just start our own charitable foundation, hire some people, and turn it all over to them," Therese said. "But on the condition that they continue the anonymity, and look for the people, as you like to say, who will pay it forward, pass it on, do grand things for other people.

"If we get bored, we could always start a bakery-cafe-ice cream shop somewhere."

Rex grinned. "That's a peach of an idea."

"Or I could just stay home."

It was raining. Therese went over to a window, looked out, and smiled.

"Rex! Come and look!" she said excitedly. "There's a rainbow!"

Rex came over and put his arms around her.

"Besides, I now have other things to think about," she said, shooting a mischievous glance at Rex.

"What are you talking about?" he said, alarmed.

She patted her abdomen and sighed.

"What do you think of Rainbow as the name for a little girl?"

♣ ♣ ♣

Word leaked, as it was sure to. And the Rainbow Café regulars were not about to let it pass unheralded.

Some of them were sitting at the counter the day the news broke, and the rest appeared quickly. When Therese went next door to talk to Rex for a moment, Adeline Enders rapped a fork against a glass and got their attention.

"Listen!" she said, and repeated a phrase they had all heard many times before from a different source. "I have an idea!"

So this belated wedding reception was somewhat different from the others that had been staged at the cafe, since it was combined with a baby shower.

Therese, wary if her civil Dutch wedding certificate held any weight in the U.S., consulted with Father Dunne. They decided a repeat ceremony at St. Sebastian's certainly could not do any harm and would be insurance.

The ceremony was unusual in another respect: Juval and Adeline were the primary attendants, but in the front pews were many honorary co-attendants – the other café regulars, plus people who had been touched by the mystical pot of gold at the end of the Rainbow Café counter.

Delroy Hempstead and Adelle were there, and protested in jest that this might not be legal unless they were allowed to reprise the attendant roles they had performed in Holland.

"It's probably just doubly legal now," Therese said, laughing.

In the choir, Joshua Clarver and Joanie, accompanied by Chantelle, sang "Endless Love" and "Can't Help Falling in Love," as well as the traditional "Amazing Grace." Seth Pinderton read several Biblical verses about love and marriage, and added a maxim that he thought was fitting: "Love is friendship set to music."

And for Therese's benefit, a quote from Jane Austen: "I've come here with no expectations, only to profess, now that I am at liberty to do so, that my heart is, and always will be, yours."

At the reception, revelers partied again into the wee hours, spilling in and out of the café, into the street, toasting the re-newlyweds and parents-to-be with gifts and speeches. The Leprechaun Band played at a fever pitch.

Hank Lyson held up one of his tabloid front pages. Over a photo of the two, the headline blared: THERESE AND REX! WHO KNEW?

Harriet Harterton made cupcakes, streaked in rainbow colors, and in the shape of the jar. Ruby and Joanie circulated with a guest book. David and Adrienne and her new "mom" from the Doting on Daughters group came up from downstate for the occasion.

"Ruby told us about it," said Adrienne, now on the verge of young womanhood, hugging Therese fiercely. "We wouldn't have missed this for anything."

Two other surprise guests were Therese's old friends Viola and Tiffany, from her childhood. The three embraced in a tearful reunion.

Sam Broadland called in from her 911 shift to send her regrets, and her congratulations.

"I usually don't make calls," she laughed. "I'm usually on the other end."

Andreas Manderfield called from Holland. The mayor of San Estelle, in Italy, tipped off by Ruby and Joanie, sent a huge bouquet of flowers.

Therese spotted Ira Grandling and Lorenzo Escarro in the crowd.

"Even the invisible man is here!" she laughed.

Therese worried that her ex might show up and try to ruin things, but Joshua reassured her that he had been told Junior no longer was anywhere near these parts.

Brady and Twilla Stollwitz, two months returned from their honeymoon, had their own secret to tell, but didn't.

"We don't want to take any attention away from these two," Twilla confided to Adeline, finger to her lips, while Brady blushed. "We can wait."

Adeline gave a brief speech, then led a round of toasts.

"And we have a guest of honor tonight," she said, reaching behind her and then setting the Rainbow Café jar, decked out in colorful ribbons, on the table in front of her. "May we all continue to benefit from its many blessings!"

Jean-Paul Stoquet nodded his head appreciatively at all the merriment around him. This, too, apparently, was what Americans did a lot of.

Then he heard a commotion atop a nearby street trash container. It was a crow, flapping its wings furiously.

"Look! What's that doing there?"

Therese suppressed a smile.

"Probably looking for a piece of the wedding cake."

A passing motorist briefly considered calling the police because the partiers were blocking traffic, but then drove on when he noticed that the police chief was there, too.

Rainbow Two

The new Rainbow Two Foundation had its own causes and successes, some big, some small. The fund found ways to reimburse people for what they had spent on their altruism, or provide money to keep their ventures going, or to start new ones. Or sometimes they were rewarded by the fund just because they helped somebody who needed it:

•Pete, a corner grocer in financial trouble because of the liberal credit he extended to impoverished customers.

•Bill, a motorist in a long line stalled at a roadblock, who sprinted ahead asking others to pull to the side so the anxious father-to-be in a car behind could get through to the hospital in time.

- Larry, who often patrolled downtown sidewalks, putting coins in about-to-expire parking meters.
- Angela, a hospital nurse who always followed up on her patients once they were back home.
- Christian, who often paid for the car behind him in a fast-food line, because somebody did it for him once.
- Gregg, a walker and jogger who picked up roadway trash and organized cleanup days that attracted other walkers.
- Carson, who drove around in cold weather with his jumper cables, looking for motorists with stranded cars.
- His brother, Easton, who plowed out driveways for neighbors after a heavy snowfall.
- Lafayette, a brilliant student who set up free tutoring sessions for struggling classmates.
- Wyatt, who befriended a new immigrant and organized a party introducing his family to their new apartment building neighbors.
- Dawn, a young mother who stepped in to coach her son's soccer team because it needed one, and led them to a championship.
- Brett, a gifted writer who wrote beautiful farewells for reticent, nervous friends to use when they were asked to give a eulogy.
- Troy, a clergyman in an affluent neighborhood, continued his daily ventures into the Inner City, where he helped run soup kitchens, counsel teens about drugs, and assist unwed young mothers.
- Noa, who organized a drive to help a family with a stricken child and no insurance.
- Sierra, who long ago as a young mother received a hand-knit baby blanket from a family friend, now passed the keepsake back when she heard of a new pregnancy in that same family.

•Phyllis, a student who looked in on and brought meals to her widowed teacher whenever she was off sick.

•Heather, always the first to offer help to neighbors needing rides, emergency baby-sitting or a casserole to help feed unexpected company.

•Ann, who coordinated with mutual friends to provide a week of meals for the extended visiting family of a friend who had died.

♣ ♣ ♣

Therese, Rex and Joshua always wondered what became of the ex-slaves on that wanted poster in the tunnel.

Joshua looked into it and found a Washington Roak who became a prosperous farmer in Quebec. He sheltered many other ex-slaves and helped them find jobs or set up businesses.

His eldest son Malcomb inherited the property, and his descendants still farm there. Malcomb donated land when his town needed a new clinic and hospital.

Washington's daughter, Matilda, became a nurse, married a surgeon, and they founded a clinic on that same land, which eventually became one of the largest hospitals in the province.

Washington Roak's youngest son, George, became an officer in the Royal Canadian Mounted Police. His descendants crafted a video recreating their family's journey to freedom, including faded photos and written recollections of Washington Roak's children. It is shown frequently on Canadian and US television, but also to visitors every day at the new Underground Railroad museum in the old Rainbow Cafe building.

THE END

About the author

Dan Chabot was an editor and columnist with one of the nation's major daily newspapers, *The Milwaukee Journal* (now the *Journal-Sentinel*). He lives in Florida. His other books are:

Godspeed: A Love Story
The Last Homecoming
Emma's Army

Made in the USA
Las Vegas, NV
05 April 2025

20558747R00154